MW01131379

LADIES LEAGUE
FRONT NINE

by
Sandi Spaugh

authorHOUSE®

AuthorHouse™
1663 Liberty Drive, Suite 200
Bloomington, IN 47403
www.authorhouse.com
Phone: 1-800-839-8640

First published by AuthorHouse 12/18/2008

ISBN: 978-1-4389-3711-3 (sc)
ISBN: 978-1-4389-3710-6 (hc)

Library of Congress Control Number: 2008911126

Printed in the United States of America
Bloomington, Indiana

This book is printed on acid-free paper.

DEDICATION

This book is dedicated to: Zula Dougherty Spaulding.
Thank You, for giving Our Mother Life.

ACKNOWLEDGEMENTS

Stephen L Spaugh who encouraged me to write.

Melinda Sinzheimer, my daughter-in-law who designed the book cover, because of her dream.

Susan Chamberlain who created the artwork throughout the book.

Hugh Couch, my brother who inspired me because of his dedication to law enforcement.

HOLE ONE
Par Four

"Whiff, what's a whiff?"

"Well, if I don't hit the ball, then why do I have to count it?"

"These are the stupidest rules I have ever heard in my entire life!"

Diane is nearly yelling this at Beverly as she's trying to hit the ball to make it go somewhere, anywhere; comprehend a strange bunch of rules; and listen to this other woman in their foursome go on and on about the pace of play. "We're holding everyone up." She kept repeating this as though the power of her words would launch their entire foursome three holes ahead of where they were. Diane did have to admit to herself that a few of the women behind them were beginning to look a little perturbed. There was one rather large, robust woman that seemed to be getting a little more red in the face, getting a lot more sweaty-looking, and standing with her hands on her hips, always looking—no, *glaring*—in their direction. Well, what could she do? She hadn't made up the rules, and if she hadn't had to count all of those stupid whiffs, they would be moving right along. Any time she looked to Beverly for help, she got a blank stare, a puff of smoke, or both. Diane had never seen Beverly smoke as much as she seemed to be smoking that morning. At one point, she wasn't sure she didn't have two going at the same time. Jill wasn't saying much of anything. She was Beverly's friend that had played golf in her college days and had been talked into joining this *fun* group by Beverly. From what Diane could see, Jill wasn't having any better time with the game than she was. By the looks of Jill, college golf had been quite a few years ago, and if her shots were any indication, she had not played on the golf team. Oh, if Diane had only stuck with her first answer to Beverly when asked to join this little nine-hole league, she could have been enjoying the nice summer sunshine on the lake, in her convertible, or at a shopping mall. Once again, the persuasive side of Beverly had won over the common sense of Diane, as it had from the first day they met. In spite of the deep-down remorse she felt at that very moment for ever consenting to have put herself in this public display of ineptitude, she knew that Beverly was the kind of friend who had come into her life at the exact moment she needed her. In the days and months that lay ahead, she would come to realize just how important her need for Beverly's friendship was and what a major role she would play in her life.

"Oh, you can't stand there."

"What, I'm sorry, were you talking to me?" Diane asked Janet, who just an hour ago had been introduced to her as the lady rounding out their foursome. Well, at least she's not carping about holding everyone up, Diane thought as she waited for her reply.

"You can't stand there, she's putting," Janet said with a look of exasperation.

What kind of idiot did Janet think she was? Even she knew the difference between the fairway and a green. Lord knows, she had just spent most of the morning trying to get to these little beauties, and now this woman has to point out to her that Jill is putting?

"Yes, I believe I can see that," Diane stated with more than a little annoyance in her tone.

"Well," the putting official continued, "you are standing in her line." At this, Beverly blew out her latest puff of smoke as she said, "Oh, for Pete's sake, she's not standing in her line. Let the poor girl alone."

Oh, I can see what a fun little league this is going to be, Diane thought to herself as she looked at Beverly with a mix of gratitude, a deep sense of friendship, and faint homicidal thoughts. For just what person she felt the homicidal thoughts, she wasn't sure.

By 11:00 a.m., Diane started thinking about a cold beer, which was unusual for her since beer had never been one of her favorite drinks. Somehow the thought of having a beer kept her focused on finishing the game. Diane was as close to numb as she had been in a long time.

They finished the game, and the three friends decided they would have lunch at the Irish pub in town. They were waiting for their drinks when Jill wheezed. "I can't believe how tired I am. I know it's been a while since I played golf, but I don't remember being this exhausted."

Diane responded with a slight annoyance in her voice. "You at least knew what a whiff was."

Beverly peered over the top of her glasses and blew out another one of those damnable puffs of smoke. "You're tired because we looked like three friggin' windmills out there. Do you realize that most people who play golf have a score half of what ours was, and play eighteen holes and not nine?"

Point well taken, although Diane didn't have a clue as to what a good golf score was. As the conversation continued and she learned that 72 was par and par meant 72 strokes for eighteen holes, she did what anyone in her position would have done: she ordered another cold beer!

As she wound her way through the traffic on the interstate, she was contemplating how she would relate her first great golf experience to Steve. She knew he was concerned. He had tried to explain to her when she first told him Beverly wanted her to join this league what she could expect. He had played golf since he was ten years old and understood the amount of time, instruction, practice, and plain old experience this game required. Oh, how arrogant she had been. She remembered her first response to Steve after he had expressed concern for her joining the league. "How difficult can this game be? You know that I'm basically athletic, and Beverly assures me this group of women is only out there to have fun, and there's no cutthroat competition." This was similar to the response given to the young man who had sold her the golf clubs and taught her how to hold one. They had purchased a set of starter clubs the night before. She had noticed the odd look the young man had given her when she told him tomorrow would be her first day of league play, and no, he had not misunderstood her; she had never played golf before.

"So you've never played golf before?" he asked as he continued to give her this odd stare. Diane had assured him she picked things up rather easily, and her friend had assured her these women weren't serious golfers—they just wanted to have a good time. Those had been some of her thoughts as she had desperately tried to connect with the ball for the fifth time on hole four. Maybe she should stop at the little gourmet grocery store on her way home. Yes, that's it, she thought. Steve loved their steaks, and with a wonderful salad, a baked potato, and some of his favorite garlic bread, she would set the stage for the telling of the whole ugly truth.

The phone starting ringing just as she heard the automatic garage door open. "Hello."

"So what did you think about today?" Beverly asked without a hint of not being serious. What did she think about the day? Which part? The part when she realized she couldn't hit the stupid-looking golf ball and have women who are ten to fifteen years older than she was standing on the green with their scowling faces, waiting for her to hit her twelfth shot to get on the green? Maybe it was the short fat lady that laughed out loud when Diane tried to explain to her it shouldn't have to count as a stroke when someone said it was a "gimme." Or maybe it was any number of things that caused her to be thankful most people she knew didn't have a clue as to what an ass she had just made of herself on this fine summer day.

So what did she hear herself saying to Beverly? "I can see what you mean about these women being such a fun group, but boy, do I have a lot to learn about this game." Why did she do this? Why couldn't she just tell Beverly she felt like a complete dope for ever letting herself be talked into such a ridiculous sport? She resented the fact that Beverly hadn't listened to her the first twenty-five times she had told her she didn't play golf. And finally, why didn't Beverly listen to her about anything? None of these things were said as she listened to Beverly telling her what she thought they needed was to play on Thursday so they would have some practice before the next league day. Could she make it by 10:00 Am? "That shouldn't be a problem. Steve has board meetings that day so I should be available. See you then."

What was this insanity going on inside of her, she wondered as she heard "Hi, hon" and her next challenge of the day. "So, tell me how you got along today. I can hardly wait to hear how you liked your first day of golf." With this statement, she got a tender kiss. At this point, she was determined he would hear the positives of the day. She knew she was a good storyteller. In fact, when she was around any of her family, it was obvious to anyone listening this was a genetic given. Storytelling did have its prices to pay. Sometimes the storyteller got so caught up in the story that what needed to be said wasn't always said, and so it was to be tonight. The only thing she knew as she began to unravel the events of the day was that she wanted to make this man laugh with her, be proud of her, and love her, and so the story began.

Thursday came much sooner than she had anticipated. In fact, she would have forgotten about the practice game altogether if Steve had not mentioned it to her just before they crawled into bed Wednesday night. He would have to leave early in the morning for his board meetings, and realizing this, she was somewhat grateful for the diversion/challenge, whatever it was. So it was of little surprise when the phone rang at 8:00 Am with Beverly wanting to make sure she remembered their golf date. The word "date" was an important word in Beverly's vocabulary. She was a single parent, twice. She put her first husband through medical school, gave birth to two of his children, entertained, climbed the social ladder of the small town they were living in, and after five years he felt his practice was established and thanked her by asking for a divorce, marrying his receptionist, and having his new best buddy and only attorney in town handle the divorce. Other than those details and the few that Jana, Beverly's daughter, would part with, there were not many available. Beverly's second husband was the love of her life. She would say this without reservation. Had she known such a man existed, she would never have entertained the idea of marrying the first. Diane had heard her make this statement in front of Jana, and Jana would just nod and smile. Very little was known about Beverly's second husband other than he had been deeply loved, apparently not only by Beverly, but also by Beverly's children. When Robert had been hit and killed in a freak April snowstorm on the roads of northern Indiana, Beverly said she had stayed in bed for a year. Then, with the support of her friends and children, she moved into Old Town, opened up a women's apparel store, and became an active player in the community. It was a warm March day when Diane walked into her shop, looking for an evening bag to carry to a function she was to attend that night. At their first meeting, it felt as if they had known each other all of their lives. Each of them had said as much at different times and in different places. Now, three years later, they remained as comfortable with each other as the moment they had met. It didn't bother so much as puzzle Diane as to why she and Beverly could say so little to each other but somehow know exactly when to speak up and what to say. Beverly would often ask Diane if she had found a man for her. It was no secret to anyone that Beverly wanted to have another man in her life, and all of her friends, acquaintances, and passer-bys would be informed of this fact and instructed to give her a call when he had been found. So, not only was "date" a big word, it was also a big desire for Beverly. Yet anyone that knew anything about her knew he could be no ordinary man. It had been written of Carol Channing that life underlined her. Well, Diane had often thought that if Carol had been underlined, Beverly had bright magic marker set her apart from the rest of the world.

"Yes. I remembered today's golf date."

"Are you ready yet?"

"It's only eight o'clock, Beverly. I can be there in twenty minutes."

"I know that. I just thought if you were ready to go, we could meet at the Country Kitchen for breakfast."

"Hey, sounds like a great idea. I'll see you there."

It had been two whole days since the first lesson in humiliation, and it actually looked like a great day for playing golf. Diane could not believe she had the thought go through her head. As she was walking up to the restaurant with her head held high, a spring in her step, and a smile on her face, she heard another little voice whispering to her. "Enjoy this time, my foolish friend, for the golf course awaits."

Beverly was already seated with Jill on the other side of the table. Both had steaming cups of black coffee in front of them. Beverly had a cigarette already fired up and was using it as a wand to emphasize some statement she had just made. They were both dressed in the latest golf attire. Diane heard Beverly finishing the statement about ordering more ladies' golf hats for the shop. Jill worked part-time for Beverly, and at this moment, she had taken the role of employee.

"Golf hats? What kind of golf hats?" Diane asked as she slid in next to Jill.

"Well, I looked at the things they were selling at the pro shop, and you could tell a man was doing the buying in that place. My own grandmother wouldn't wear some of that stuff," Beverly stated while letting out a disgusted puff of smoke to punctuate the horror of it all.

"I don't even own a golf hat—do you think I need one?" Oh, how Diane wished she hadn't asked the question; she knew better than to question Beverly when it came to the style of anything, much less women's apparel. She was thrilled to see the server approach their table—not only would this distract Beverly from her latest lecture on the dress of most women, but it would also allow Diane to order some of the food that had been assaulting her senses from the moment she had walked into the place.

After the orders were placed, Beverly turned her attention once again to the subject of golf attire and continued the litany of complaints about men being given the responsibility of buying women's clothing. While the check was being placed on the table, Beverly glanced at her watch, and with a great flourish announced to the table and to the room that they must hurry because their tee time was in the next twenty-five minutes and they were going to be late.

This was another thing that Diane didn't get about this golf thing. The restaurant was less than five minutes from the golf course. They had a tee time, and yet they were going to be late? This had been a big deal on Ladies League Day; everyone was rushing around, but when you got to the first tee, there were all these ladies waiting to tee off, shushing each other as someone got up to swing their mighty swing, and then having to wait to hit until the group before them was out of the way. Now here they were, and once again, they're going to be late? Late for what? Of course, these were all the thoughts Diane carried in her head as she made her way to her car and gunned the engine, mostly for show, so she could get to the golf course on time. She could hardly wait to see what this magnificent course would hold for her today. Well, she would see—oh, would she see!

After the rush to get to the course, the meandering through the pro shop with Beverly as tour guide pointing at the disgraceful display of women's golf clothing, and deciding whether or not some type of beverage should be purchased, the three of them were on their way. It was a day when the course had no league play. There was going to be an afternoon outing, but that was a 1:30 shotgun, so they should have plenty of time to get this practice round in and have lunch afterward. Jill explained this to Diane as they rode out to the first tee box. Beverly thought it would be a good idea for Jill and Diane to ride together; she told Diane it would be good for the two them to get better acquainted. Not a problem for Diane; she enjoyed being in the company of Jill. In fact, she realized she liked just about anyone Beverly had introduced her to.

Jill was a widow. Her husband had died of a heart attack, she had no children, and she certainly seemed financially well off. She had been an only child and had been raised in an affluent area of the city. Her father had been a pharmacist and had owned and operated several drugstores. Her mother had died while she was still in college, and as Jill would relate the story, her father died only a few months later of a broken heart. Diane found out the broken heart had actually been a suicide, and that while Jill was still in college, she had to go through months of dealing with the IRS and questions surrounding the accounting practices of her father. Beverly told Diane it had been a very black time for Jill. She had told Beverly during this time she would not marry any man unless he was very well heeled. In fact, she had broken up with her current beau because he wasn't ambitious enough for her and she would not live a life of need. Beverly shared with Diane that she thought the reason Jill had no children was because she didn't want to risk having to struggle financially or emotionally. Whatever the reason for Jill being with her on that summer morning didn't matter to Diane. She liked the woman for a lot of reasons, and one at the top of the list was the fact that she couldn't hit the golf ball much better than she could hit it herself! Let the games begin!

Begin they did. The fact there weren't any ladies standing around at the first tee box was a great relief. The fact there didn't seem to be anyone behind them sweating, glaring, or manifesting any other body language was another relief. The fact she couldn't hit the ball any better today than she did on Tuesday was a fact. However, she did pick up another couple of golf rules. When she hit the ball in the lake on Tuesday, she was told to go to the drop area, which she had, and proceeded to hit it three more times before she got it on the green. Here she was today at the same tee box, the same lake, and the same golf shot, so why, for crying out loud, did she have to lose a ball in the lake and not just go directly to the drop area? Jill seemed adamant about this rule, and Beverly chimed in with her support on the matter, so there was nothing left for her to do but hit the ball in the water. Then off to the drop area she trucked, mumbling that this rule had to have been created by golf ball companies who stood to make a fortune from golf ball sales. By that time, she had finished the hole (it was only a par three) so on her sixth stroke she was finished. This gave her a tiny amount of satisfaction because it had been eight strokes two days before. Did this show that she was making progress?

As they were nearing the ninth green, Diane was absolutely certain this would be the last day she would ever try to play this ridiculous game. She would just have to sell her golf clubs. At least Steve hadn't spent a fortune on the crazy things. He had said at the time he purchased them that they would be good starter clubs for her, and if she decided she wanted to continue with the game, then he would get clubs that would be better sized for her. My, my, what a wise man he was. Maybe he knew what she was now discovering. This silly game was hard! And a person had to be nuts to continue with such an endeavor. Yes, she had made up her mind. She would simply tell Beverly she appreciated her invitation to be part of the Ladies League but she had better things to do with her life than to constantly humiliate herself in front of friends and strangers. There! She felt better already. Just one more hole and I'm out of here. This was going through her mind as she swung the club and hit the ball within one hundred feet of the green. She couldn't believe her eyes, nor her ears as Beverly and Jill were yelling, "Wow! Did you see that shot?!"

"You're a big girl now!" Beverly shouted as she let out another whoop, while Jill was giggling.

"I really don't know how I did it," Diane replied honestly. "I really, really don't know how I did it." She remained in this wonderment as she walked up to the next shot and saw it land on the green just three feet from the hole. This time there were a few moments of silence before Beverly looked at her and said in a deep, mocking tone, "Why, you sandbagger, you." Jill just kept going on about those being the best shots she had seen anyone hit. The fact that Beverly and Jill hadn't played golf in a couple hundred years before this summer league didn't phase Diane. She felt at the moment that everything she had told Steve and the young man at the golf shop was basically true. She was an athlete and she had figured this game out after all.

"Anyone for lunch?" she heard herself say in a bright, chirpy tone. Ah, what a nice day of golf this has been. So what if her score was 75 for nine holes? It had just taken her a little time to catch on, and now she had she could hardly wait for next Tuesday and the Ladies League.

It may have been the restaurant they chose for their lunch. It may have been Beverly telling exceptionally funny stories, something she did very well when she was in the right mood, or it may have been that no matter what was going on around her, Diane was still reliving those last golf shots. How vindicated she felt. She hoped she got to play with Janet, the "pace of play" lady next week—boy, would she show her pace of play.

She smiled to herself as she pulled into the driveway. I think I'll make one of Steve's favorites for dinner. Meatloaf. Give him meatloaf, a baked potato, and salad, and he thought he had died and gone to heaven. She could hardly wait for him to get home so she could give him all the details of her incredible ninth hole. A glance at the clock showed it was only 4:30 pm; maybe she had time to make some dessert.

Diane was just beginning to be concerned about Steve when the phone rang. "Hi, hon."

"You sound tired—in fact, a better word might be 'exhausted'," she said with some irritation in her voice.

"I am, and I need you to do something for me."

"You name it, sweetie."

"I need for you to fix me a scotch on the rocks with a splash of water. I'm just about ten minutes from the house, so if you would have it ready for me, I would greatly appreciate it."

"Wow. It must have been one bad day."

"Oh, it was. I'll fill in all the details when I get there."

Although she knew the answer, she couldn't help but ask the question. "It was Phil again, wasn't it?"

"Yeah, that and much more. I'll fill you in over the scotch."

As she hung up the phone, she decided she would join him with a bourbon and water. She hated these board-meeting days and was growing to hate them more each month. She didn't know how Steve did it. On more than one occasion, she had threatened to call Phil herself and ask him if he had any idea of how difficult he was to deal with and if he knew the toll this was taking on Steve. Of course Steve wouldn't consider the notion, not for one second. After all, he was a big boy. Had he known beforehand what going into business with Phil would mean, he probably would have done things differently, but he hadn't known, and they would have to make the best of it. Diane wished she had a dollar for every time he had told her this—they would have enough money so they would never have to deal with Phil again. The fact that was the most upsetting in all of this was Steve's medical condition. Phil understood the seriousness of Steve's cardiovascular disease as well as anyone did. He had been with her as the doctor announced he had at least four arterial blockages and would have to have open-heart surgery to correct the condition. Phil seemed as disturbed about this as she did. He was with her the day of the surgery and stood with her while they waited for Steve to return from the second surgery on that horrible day. Steve had started bleeding after his surgery. The only thing the surgeons could do was to re-enter the chest cavity to find the bleeder. She remembered being numb, not knowing what she said or what was being said around her. She just wanted someone to tell her that Steve was going be fine and they could take him home very soon. It was a couple of weeks before Christmas, and she wondered why anyone in the hospital thought it appropriate to play Christmas carols. Through it all, there stood Phil. She even caught him crying, something he told her she must never tell anyone, and she didn't tell for a long time, until one day Steve was so upset with Phil she decided to let him know about the tears during his surgery.

Now, she didn't understand what was happening. None of this made any sense. Steve worked as hard at the business as anyone in the partnership; he had spent countless hours finding the best health insurance he could find for the employees of the company. Their financial responsibility was exactly one-third of the operations. There had been more than a few nights that both of them were sleepless because of their concern about meeting payroll. No one expected to work hard for a living only to be told their paycheck couldn't be covered. No one!

Linda worked just as tirelessly. Her first disadvantage was her gender, at least as it related to Phil. He was most certainly a male chauvinist. One five-minute conversation with the man, and that would come screaming through. Something that few people knew—with the exception of Linda, Diane, and Phil—was that early in his working relationship with Linda, he had propositioned her. He didn't take the rebuff very well. Some time passed before he could be civil toward her. However, when the first business opportunity came along and Linda's husband was able to influence some of the city fathers, all had been forgiven. Why, though, had there been this change in attitude toward Steve and Diane? These were thoughts she was turning over in her mind when she heard the garage door.

"Here's Johnnie!" she said as she handed Steve the requested scotch.

The evening had gone about like she had expected it to. Steve began to recount the day's events, all of which centered around Phil and his inability or refusal to grasp what issues really were important and what issues really had little or no meaning to the operating of the business. There was nothing stupid about this man. He had graduated first in his class from both high school and college. He had earned his Master's degree on a full scholarship. No, there was nothing stupid about him, but what was going on? This question kept coming up in Diane's mind. There had to be an answer, but what was it? What was this all about? Steve had just one more day of the board meetings, and Phil was not going to be attending, so there should be no concern for Steve's physical—or, for that matter, mental—state at the end of the day. Ah, the weekend. Maybe she and Steve could play a little golf together so she could show him how well she was doing with this game, she suggested. My, wouldn't he be impressed!

"That sounds good to me," he said as he put his briefcase on the kitchen island. "We could play at Willow Tree. It's just minutes from here. I'll call and see if they have any openings tomorrow."

Oh, this was going to be a great weekend. Steve didn't have another board meeting for another three weeks, she could get another practice round in before the big Tuesday Ladies League day, and she could tell Beverly and Jill how well she had done at Willow Tree. She was really warming up to this game.

The local weatherman predicted a beautiful weekend, and as Diane rolled over that morning, she knew his prediction had been on target. Morning was her favorite time of day. This morning, the lake reflected gold slivers of sunlight while the birds began their serenades. There was always something going on, on the water. When they had first moved to this house, she would find herself just standing and staring for no reason other than to watch the latest movement, whether it be ducks taking off or landing, a wake that had been created by a passing boat, or a breeze that moved the leaves on the large trees surrounding their house. Normally, she could have laid there watching the light play on the water for as long as time would allow. Now she found herself anxious to get up, fix some breakfast for the two of them, and play some golf. Oh, what fun this day was going to be. The two of them out there, sharing this sport together, and Steve giving her some golf tips. After all, he had played this game for almost forty years, and she knew he was a wealth of information. She was sure she would be a quick study. After Thursday's display on the ninth hole, she felt certain that whatever Steve had to show her, she would be able to apply to her game.

"I cannot believe you would let those idiots play through—is that what you call it, playing through? They did nothing but make asses of themselves from the first glimpse we got of them on the sixth hole. Where did they come from, and how come you told them it was okay to play ahead of us? And why did you keep telling me to pick up? They won't let me pick up in the league—those women even make me count a whiff! So what's with you?"

Diane was out of control and she knew it, but there was absolutely nothing she seemed to be able to do to get any kind of control back. At the moment, she was in a whirlpool of emotions. She was angry, frustrated, hurt, and very disappointed in her beloved husband that very second. He had failed to give her any golf tips—except, of course, the same tired refrain: "We must keep up the pace of play, and you need to pick up." What had he done, had a conversation with Janet? Maybe the next time he wanted to play golf, he should give her a call! Oh, how could she have been so wrong about what she thought was going to happen today? Now, after this horrible game on the course, she was going to have to face Tuesday without any new golf tips and the same frustrations of not even being able to hit the ball, and now she had to constantly look over her shoulder to be sure she kept up with the damnable pace of play!

They ate their dinner quietly. After the dishes had been cleared, Steve told her he wanted to talk with her.

"Honey," he began, "I know you really want to play this game, but you just started playing it two weeks ago. There are people who have played for years and still are not very good at the sport. I think you're expecting too much of yourself. I also think you should take lessons—and that they should never be from me."

She had to admit he had made some good points. Oh, how nerve-racking it was for her to live with a man that was so sensible. She knew that he was one of the best things that had ever happened to her. It certainly wasn't love at first sight, not for her, and she didn't think it had been for him. The one thing she had not needed in her life at that moment was a man—and certainly not her boss. Besides, she thought he was stupid, arrogant, and, because of all the interested ladies he was dating, she thought he was just another male on the hunt for fresh game. She wasn't sure when it happened, but he became a friend of hers. The more she worked with him, the more she understood that not only was he not stupid, but he was quite intelligent.

Three years after their first meeting, they were married in a chapel with family and friends. In Diane's thinking, there would be no reason to change anything about the way they had been doing things. She would continue to work. For a couple of years, that was exactly how it happened. Then came the opportunity for Steve and Linda to become business partners with Phil. What a wonderful opportunity this should be. In many ways, it was just that. Initially, both of their paychecks were necessary. Diane had absolutely no problem with this arrangement. In fact, for someone that had not pursued a career, she found the responsibilities of a demanding job very gratifying. She enjoyed the challenges she faced every day, and the excitement of the risks they were taking to join Phil in this business venture. Then things changed. The business was doing nicely, and Steve wanted her to leave her job and become a full-time wife. Diane thought she wanted this as well, but she soon discovered the adjustment to this new way of living overwhelmed her. Try as she might to explain this to Steve—or anyone, for that matter—it was beyond her. She felt useless, alone, and very confused. For the first time in her life, she had the luxury of doing what she wanted to do, when she wanted to do it, and here she was, feeling immobile. Moving from the older home to a new house on the lake certainly gave her a time to be busy. For a few months, she was very busy and loved every moment of it. Steve was in the midst of trying to keep their new business growing. That's when her dear old friend depression returned. She had understood its first visit. She had clung to her first marriage with as much tenacity as she had within her being; when it failed, the depression was a daily visitor. Yet, this visit of the ailment had been a surprise and a curiosity. Was there something basically wrong with her? Reflecting on this made her realize that just perhaps this was why golf was becoming so important. One thing was for certain: this game was either going to help, or it was going to turn her into a stark-raving maniac! Right at this very moment, she wasn't sure what the outcome would be.

"So, where do you suggest I get these lessons?" she asked, looking him squarely in the eye to let him know she was still upset about the day's events.

"I'm not sure. Maybe there's someone at Twin Oaks that offers lessons. Or what about the young man at the Pro shop? You seemed to get along with him, and he did help with your stance and grip, and before you left the place, you were hitting the ball." The tone of his voice was beginning to sound a little weaker, and the look in his eyes was close to pleading. Everything in her wanted to pin all that had gone wrong with her golf on this man. She knew deep within her heart he had absolutely nothing to do with the fiasco, except having agreed to play a round of golf with her.

"Okay, I'll call the store where you bought the clubs and ask if Bill gives golf lessons. I'm sure that was his name." A smile formed on his lips as he said, "Would you like to go to a movie?" Thus ended the day, the conflict between the two of them, but not her fascination with this strange game. What was this attraction, the reason, the purpose of attaching so much importance to this sport? Years and years later, she would discover no one she had encountered while playing this game had a better answer to any of those questions than she did at that very moment.

When Monday morning arrived, she was full of new determination to figure out this game, and the first step would be getting in touch with Bill at the golf shop. When she called, someone answering to the named James told her he would be in around eleven o'clock, and if she would leave her number, he would have Bill call. Sure enough, at 11:10 Am, the phone rang, and as soon as she picked up the receiver, she knew it would be Bill. "Hello," Diane said.

"Yes, is this Mrs. Stoner?"

"Yes, this is she."

"James said you had called about a golf lesson."

"Yes, that is correct," she responded.

"Well, uh, when would you like to take one?"

"Is today too soon?" she asked, wanting to get a lesson in before the next league day.

"Would you be able to make it about two o'clock?"

"Sure. Where do you want me to be?"

"I'll meet you at the Simms Public Course on One-Hundred-Sixteenth Street. Do you know where it is?"

"Oh, yes, I've been there. Where on the course should I meet you?"

"Meet me at the driving range. I'll be looking for you. You know I charge fifteen dollars a half hour." This was more of a statement than a question, but somehow she felt it might be negotiable.

"No problem," she heard herself say. She wondered if this was a going rate for golf lessons or a rate he had just tried out on his first client.

She didn't know what other people got out of golf lessons, but by the time he was putting a blindfold on to demonstrate how far he could hit the ball, she was wondering if she hadn't just wasted her time and thirty dollars. Who cared if blind people can play golf? She couldn't, and that's why she had wanted to take this lesson!

"Now, when you're using your three wood, and that's what I suggest you use as a driver, keep your head down, your eye on the ball, and swing through the ball. Now those are your swing thoughts, and remember, no one can have more than two swing thoughts in their head while they hit the ball."

At that point, Diane was wondering if this young man—who smelled like a mixture of Zest, Clearasil, and Scope—had really lived long enough to give golf lessons to anyone. Swing thoughts. Now she could impress the ladies in the golf league with her swing thoughts. Even she was not counting on showing everyone all she had accomplished since they last played.

That evening, the conversation centered around her golf lesson. She knew she was pushing it with Steve when she told him what she thought of her new instructor.

"Diane," he began. "I don't think you understand how difficult this game really is." He sighed, lifted his glass, and took a long swallow. "Look, hon, you are simply going to have to give yourself more time. You're only in your sixth week of playing this game. I have been at this for years, and I still don't hit the shots I think I should."

She eyed him with a little more than skepticism when she replied. "You don't understand. You know you can go out on a golf course and not have people pointing and laughing or snarling because you can't hit the frigging ball more than two feet, and then walk up to the same ball and hit it another two feet. You don't understand!"

"Honey, I really don't know what to tell you. You're going to have to decide what it is you want to do. You're either going to continue to play and take lessons, or give it up. It's that simple."

She didn't respond to his statement, but two things were for certain: he didn't understand how important this had become to her, and he sure as hell didn't understand the Ladies League!

As usual, there were women of various types swarming around the pro shop to check in for league play. She listened in on some of the conversations as she waited in line. It was obvious to her that some of these women had known each other for years. They were catching up on what had happened during the winter months—marriages, births, and, unfortunately, funerals were all being discussed with the punctuated oohs, aahs, and "I am so sorry to hear that" from the listener. Something occurred to Diane as she was eavesdropping. This sport was more than a sport, or a league, or whatever it was; it was networking, a support group, interaction between ladies that wanted— no, needed—this sorority. Could this be what this was all about, and not the game itself? Maybe. By the time she had finished the first hole, she knew there were other woman in this group that wanted nothing but competition. It brought out the worst in the best of them and the best in the worst of them. Oh, my, my, what had she gone and done to herself?

"What do you mean, that was a two-stroke penalty? For what? Do you want to show me that in the rule book?" The tall redhead was asking the older, rounder lady in the foursome Diane had found herself as a member of when she checked in.

"Well, if you have hit the wrong golf ball, it is a two-stroke penalty," the round lady huffed.

"So what is your penalty? If I hit yours and you hit mine, then shouldn't you have the same two-stroke penalty?"

"I don't think I will have a penalty because you didn't identify the ball you hit."

The redhead wasn't about to give up on this. It was obvious that she didn't believe for one minute that the round lady was correctly interpreting the rules. She may have hit the wrong ball—that she seemed to concede—but to let the round lady off the hook was apparently not going to happen. Diane wasn't sure what this was all about, and since she didn't have a clue about golf rules other than the rulebook they had handed out at the first league meeting—and since she wasn't sure she would play this game from one day to the next, she really hadn't bothered to read any of it. Now, she found it rather fascinating that these two women knew enough about rules to argue.

"Well," the redhead responded, "we will just add up our scores and take this to Jim for a ruling." This statement seemed to quiet the round lady. Diane was on the side of the redhead, and she didn't exactly know why. She wondered how Beverly and Jill were making out with their game this morning. She had been a little surprised and disappointed when she checked in and discovered they were all in separate foursomes. The league president requested all players be paired with members they had never played with. She wanted to give everyone an opportunity to get to know one another. From what little Diane had witnessed about some of the ladies, it may very well have had something to do with those in the league that were difficult to get along with. So everyone had to take their turn in dealing with them. Case in point: short, round lady.

"This can't be," moaned round lady. "We've had to wait to take every shot. Something should be done about this or we'll be out here for four hours!" Now she was starting to wail. Diane thought it best to hold back any comments she might have, because she wasn't sure the first round she played in this league hadn't taken four hours. As though round lady had read her mind, she continued, "Four weeks ago we were behind this foursome, and I was so upset I nearly dropped out of the game. I called Mildred that evening and told her that if something wasn't done about the pace of play, I would not remain in this league." To put emphasis on her statement, she jabbed at a droplet of sweat on her forehead. Now it was all coming into focus for Diane. This was the large, robust woman that kept getting redder and glaring at them on the first day of league play. My, my, Diane said to herself. I wonder if she is sending me a message or if she really doesn't recognize me as one of those disgusting women that held her up for four hours? She decided to say nothing and see where this might take her.

It was the redhead who next spoke. "You know, I have always felt that this game is supposed to be fun. It's a nine-hole group, and some of the women in this group have my utmost respect. They're out here trying their best to continue to be active. They're not sitting home feeling sorry for themselves because of their physical ailments or the loss of a loved one. So, if it takes them a little longer to play, then so be it."

Round lady was quiet other than a mumbled reply about being fair to all concerned—whatever that meant. Diane looked at the redhead with newfound respect. She didn't want to undermine her statement by letting her know she had been one of the women in the foursome round lady was referring to, and she didn't suffer from any physical ailments, had not lost a loved one, and in fact was probably ten to fifteen years younger than most of the women in this league. No. These facts would not be revealed by her. She just hoped at that very moment, round lady was feeling somewhat guilty for calling Mildred, the league president, and complaining about the pace of play. Diane's next tee shot was a beauty. Her swing thought: Short Round Lady gets hers!

The round did not take four hours—it only took three and a half. In Diane's mind this was great improvement. Maybe she wasn't playing much better, but apparently she was playing faster! The first order of business, once they finished the game, was to seek out Jim and get clarification on the "hit the wrong ball" rule. Yes, there was a two-stroke penalty for both of the players. This was something Round Lady found most distasteful, and let Jim and Redhead—and anyone else within hearing range—know about it. As the redhead was turning to leave, Diane stopped her to let her know how much she had enjoyed playing the round of golf with her. She also had to admit she had not caught her name earlier in the day. Just as she was about to respond, Diane heard Beverly's voice behind her. "Joanna, it is so good to see you. I was just told that you were here, and I had to come over and say hello."

Diane realized she was being totally ignored by Beverly in favor of Joanna (that she had only known as the redhead until now), and by Jill who had walked over to join the group. It was apparent Beverly and Joanna had mutual respect for each other. Jill seemed as happy to see Joanna as Beverly had been. Diane was really beginning to wonder who this woman was and how she knew Beverly and Jill. Then it hit her: this had to be the Joanna that helped both of them with their conflicts with the city and the state. After a few moments of small talk, Joanna turned to Diane and let her know she had very much enjoyed playing the round with her, apologizing for the rule incident and her lecture to Round Lady, whose name turned out to be Evelyn Howard.

"Oh no," Beverly said as she rolled her eyes and gave out a long, low whistle.

"What? What?" Diane's voice grew a little louder. "What do you know that I don't know?" she asked Beverly.

"All of you got time for something to drink?" This time it was Joanna asking the question. Sure, all three thought they could manage to stop in the snack shop for a quick Coke.

After they made themselves comfortable at one of the tables in the corner of the little snack bar, Beverly began the dialogue. Her voice was abnormally low, and her eyes were moving around the room, searching for just what, Diane didn't know.

"What's the matter?" Again, it was Diane asking the questions. The other three women were staring at their drinks, as Beverly without looking up from hers began to speak.

"Evelyn Howard, the sweet little lady you just finished playing golf with, is the biggest troublemaker in this town—not just this league, but this town."

Jill continued to stare at her drink, while Beverly reached for a cigarette, and Joanna lifted her eyes to meet Diane's and give a solemn nod of her head. What in the world had this woman done? Beverly was not one to make careless comments about anyone. For the two of them she knew to be acting like they were at the moment was extremely unusual, and Joanna certainly did not seem to be an individual that was given to overreacting. What in heaven's name had this Evelyn person done other than behave like the rude, insensitive woman she had just shown herself to be on the golf course?

"Will someone please tell me what's going on?" As Diane spoke the words, someone came up behind her, and she felt a hand on her shoulder.

"How did things go today?" she heard Mildred asking with a forced lilt in her tone.

"Oh, it was great. My golf was horrible, but I had a great time and played with some lovely ladies." This was Beverly in her best Chamber of Commerce personality. Diane had seen her use it many times and on many people, and it never failed to amaze her how easily Beverly fell into it.

"Oh, great. Great." Mildred continued with additional information about the next league meeting. It was to be held the next Tuesday, and she hoped all of them could make it—and how good it was to see Joanna again and she hoped she would get to see more of her. It had been a long time, and on and on she seemed to drone, until Diane felt like she was going to scream. She wanted to know what was going on with this Evelyn, and Mildred seemed determined to outstay her welcome. After a few more exchanges from all of them, Mildred appeared to be satisfied that her mission had been accomplished, and moved to the other side of the room, stopping at another table of ladies to check on how their day had been on the links.

"Diane," Beverly said as she set her glass back on the table, "just stay away from Evelyn if at all possible. She is not a nice person."

"Okay. Is that all? Aren't you going to give me a hint as to why you're saying this?" Diane could hear the pleading in her own voice.

"Let's just say, sometimes there are things that are best left unsaid."

At this, Jill began talking about the inventory she needed to do at the shop. Joanna looked at her watch and announced that if she didn't leave, she would be late for her two o'clock appointment. Diane knew the conversation was at an end. "Well, I guess I need to get a move on as well. We're having some people over for dinner, and I need to stop by the grocery," she said as she swooped her golf purse up from the table. "See all of you next Tuesday." And she was out of the door.

She felt like she had just been stung, and she had just lied to these women—they were not having anyone over for dinner, and she did not have to go to the grocery store. Beverly had never acted as though she couldn't be trusted; for that matter, neither had Jill. Yet here she was, feeling as though she were an outsider who needed to prove herself worthy of their company. What was going on? Why had all three of them behaved in the manner they had? Why did she feel so hurt? Was she justified in her feelings or was this part of … of … what?

On the drive home, Diane was trying to digest what had just happened and her reaction to all of it. There were two things she was certain of. In the three years since she had known Beverly, there had never been a time she had not been candid with her about everything. Jill had seemed almost frightened, and up until today, she hadn't seemed to be afraid of anyone or anything. She lived alone; she had taken on the city and eventually the state when they were trying to annex property that had been left to her by her husband. Fought and won a battle with the government that had made the local and national news. Diane vaguely remembered the news stories and the young female attorney that had defended Jill—this had been Joanna. Joanna had also been instrumental in helping Beverly start her boutique. The town planning commission had done a very good job in setting up standards for anyone wanting to go into business within the city limits. In Beverly's—and a good number of other merchants'—opinion, the planning commission did not seem to deal with applications fairly. After Beverly's first application had been denied, she decided to find someone that would help walk her through the process. Jill was more than happy to get Joanna involved. Upon passing the bar, Joanna worked for the county prosecutor. A few years into this, she became disgusted with the ongoing politics. She left the county and opened her own law firm. Two of her first clients were Jill and Beverly. As Joanna and Beverly began to deal with the application denial, it was discovered that a daughter of one of the committee members was wanting to open her own little shop in the same quaint section of town that Beverly had cited in her application. Once Joanna pointed out to the committee that Beverly had taken all required steps—including the paying of a heavy application fee, while the darling daughter of the committee member had not been required to pay this same fee—the response from the six other committee members was immediate, especially since a reporter for the local newspaper had been invited to the meeting by Joanna. Diane had heard all about Joanna long before today's meeting. In fact, if there was anyone that would toot Joanna's horn the loudest, it would be Beverly, unless Jill was around, and then it became a contest between the two women on who could tell the more fascinating story about this fearless, crime-fighting superwoman.

Diane was thinking about all of this as she pulled into the driveway and noticed Steve was home. This was very unusual, since it was Tuesday, and he wasn't usually home for at least another three to four hours. When she opened the door, she was greeted by his voice.

He was speaking rather loudly, and she heard him say in a rather agitated tone, "I don't care what he told you about this legislation. I have absolutely no reason to want this bill to go through for any reason."

She walked over to him and gave him a kiss on the cheek, and then placed her things quietly on the counter.

"Well, we'll talk about this further at the next board meeting—and I want Sam there. There will be no excuse for his absence, and you let him know that is what I have told you." With a rather terse good-bye, he hung up and looked in Diane's direction. There was really no need for words. They had been married long enough, had been through enough problems to develop the silent communication that close couples do.

"I know it's only three o'clock, but is it scotch time?"

"No. I'll meet you and Johnnie a little later, but right now I have some calls I need to make. Will you keep the invitation open?" he asked as he crossed the room and gave her a bear hug.

"You got it, big boy."

With that, he made his way downstairs to his home office to continue dealing with the problem at hand. Experience had taught her to stay out of his way until he was ready to talk it out. In the meantime, she was going to get a glass of wine, sit out by the lake, and reflect on the day's events. Maybe it had been the wine, or the breeze, or just the movement of the lake, but as she awoke to his voice, she realized how peaceful and silent it had been, until it flashed through her mind what she had been dreaming. There was this round lady with a red face laughing at her and her friends. Steve was standing nearby with a look of total defeat written on his face.

"You okay, hon? I didn't mean to startle you. Dreaming, were you?"

"Oh, hi, sweetie. I guess I was. Are you ready for your scotch?" she said as she tried to acclimate herself to where she was at the moment and where she had been.

"I beat you to it. Before I came out here, I stopped by the Old Johnnie and picked this up." He held high the glass with amber-looking fluid and gave her a huge smile.

"Oh, where is …" before she could finish the sentence, he held up her glass.

"Looking for this?" he said with a smirk on his face. "Last of the big drinkers, are you?"

"That would be me." They both knew what a joke this was. She certainly had her moments of party time, but she would fall asleep faster than anyone he had ever known once she had consumed a glass of wine. "So, how are you doing? Everything okay?" As she watched his reaction, she knew everything was not okay, and was worried as to what the problem might be.

"I wish I could tell you that it was, but there are plenty of issues that need to be dealt with."

"You're the only one that can handle them?" Her voice revealed her irritation.

"Now, hon, let's not go down that path. Let's just enjoy a few minutes with each other sitting beside the lake during cocktail hour."

He had a good point. She wasn't sure she was fully awake, and she needed to digest the day's events.

As usual, Steve was presenting the problem with a great deal of understanding. He would deal with problems as they arose and hopefully would make the right decisions for their business. She had heard him say all of this before, but knew that he wanted to remind her why he was dealing with the stress of the moment. There was one thing that was constant about Steve. He gave everyone the benefit of the doubt. He would listen, deduce, and weigh each problem he found himself dealing with. Not so with her. She had learned many years ago that she had incredible instincts. Following her gut feeling was something that had given her an advantage over many difficult events in her life. Maybe there really was something to the yin and yang of life, and maybe that was what their marriage was; she didn't know and at this moment she didn't care. She just knew that her instincts were setting off a three-alarm fire, and he wasn't listening!

They did sit there for an hour or more, simply enjoying each other's company, their lake, and their drinks. She wasn't sure that he hadn't taken a nap himself. She hoped that he had. Right at this moment, her feelings of being slighted meant little in view of the facts that her husband was struggling with what appeared to be much larger issues. Their livelihood depended on decisions he made, and she knew she would support him with all she had in her.

"What do you want to do for dinner?" his lazy voice asked.

"Oh, my, we are awake?" she mockingly responded.

"Yes, Ms. Smartass, I am awake and want to know what you want for dinner."

"I think it would be great to take the pontoon to Rick's."

For a Tuesday night, Rick's was a busy place. It was the new "in" thing to do on the lake. Those who wanted to impress and those who wanted to be impressed were there. The food was very good, the service was fair, but the ambience was the real draw. There was always live music, usually someone at the piano trying to emulate Sam from Casablanca. "Just remember this, a kiss is still a kiss," the latest entertainer was crooning as they walked in the room.

"Is the booth okay? It looks over the lake," the hostess was asking as she was directing them to their seat.

"This is fine. Is this all right with you?" he directed the question to Diane.

"This is great. I love looking out over the lake."

Moments later, a young man was at the table, offering water for the two of them and telling them that someone would be with them soon to take their drink order. After looking over the menus, hearing about the specials, and ordering the wine, their conversation turned to the day's events.

"So what is going on?" Diane asked as she took a sip of the wine.

"Oh, it's Sam again. I really don't know why he wants to create controversy within our own ranks. It doesn't make any sense. What really set me off today was the fact that he either deliberately or inadvertently gave misleading information to our controller. I'm calling for an emergency board meeting this Friday. So far, it looks like everyone will be able to make it with the exception of Phil, and he's out of the country."

She studied his face as he talked and could see that his color was not what it should be. Ever since his surgery, she had watched him like a hawk. In fact, it had become a problem for them because he felt he couldn't do anything without her smothering him. It was an adjustment for them both, but they seemed to have found a common ground. She would work hard at not smothering, and he would promise to take care of himself. At the moment, she wasn't sure he was keeping up his end of the bargain. "Are you feeling all right?"

He could see the frown and the concern on her face. He knew the first thing she worried about any time there was a problem. Immediately, she would decide he was going to have a heart attack. "I'm fine." His voice was gruff, and as soon as the words were out of his mouth, he began to regret his response.

"I just worry about you," she began almost apologetically. "There is one thing diet, exercise, or medication cannot help you overcome, and that is this stress." Her voice was getting stronger with each word she spoke. This was a road they had been down before, and she knew it could be very bumpy.

He reached for her hand and began to rub her fingers. "Look at me. I know all you are saying is true. I also know you and I have invested a lot of time and effort—not to mention risk—to go into this business. We agreed it would be in our best interest for me to take the lead in managing the business. I only have one year left, and Linda will be on point. In the meantime, I must do what is necessary to protect, guard, whatever you want to call it, our business so we can do the things we want to do together, but if this business doesn't stay solvent, we won't have the opportunity to do anything but survive."

Most all of this had been said before in different ways and at different times. She knew what he was saying was all true. She also knew if he didn't live to see those carefree days with her, she wouldn't care if she survived. She did not want to become a widow. All the money in the world wouldn't matter if he weren't by her side.

The look on her face must have told him everything. "Honey, I promise I will not let all of this get the best of me. I promise." Now his voice had turned to a soft baritone, and he squeezed her hand as he spoke. The beginning of a smile started on her face, though the tears still formed in her eyes. How could a person keep falling in love with the same person over and over, she wondered as she gave his hand a squeeze in response.

The night sky was breathtaking. The hum of the pontoon motor and the noise of the water they were moving through were the only sounds. Seawall lights surrounded them as the stars above them appeared to grow in number and intensity. Could anything in this world be so bad, she wondered, with all of this being so beautiful? One thing was for certain. She was with the man she loved in the middle of a beautiful summer night, and she could not be bothered with any problems. That included her interaction with Beverly, Jill, and Joanna—and it most certainly included golf!

The next morning was another beautiful day. Diane was thrilled to hear the weather was going to continue to be dry and unseasonably cool. She loved having the temperatures in the high seventies instead of the humid eighties that it normally was this time of year. Steve was up early getting some things done ahead of time for the next day's meeting. They were just getting ready to walk out the door when the phone rang. As soon as Steve picked it up, she saw the expression on his face and heard the tone of his voice, and she knew it was Phil. He was calling all the way from Cancun. Anger flashed through her entire being. How did this man know when to step in and ruin the best of days? His timing was perfect when it came to doing that. The conversation was short. Yes, he would call him this evening. If it got to be too late, he would call early in the morning. "Oh no, don't do that," Phil had responded. "No matter what time it is, just call this evening, you know me," he had said, "I'm the night owl, not the early bird." Ha, ha. Steve was relaying all of this to Diane as they were pulling out of the driveway. She wondered when it had started. This feeling of … of … she wasn't sure she could have described the feeling to anyone, even to herself. She had grown to think of Phil as disgusting—yes! Maybe that was what she felt: plain, old, ordinary disgust!

"Now, don't let him ruin this day for us," Steve was saying as he moved onto the interstate. "We're on our way to a 'date day.' Besides, I'll give Phil a call when I'm ready and not when he tells me to." This was something Diane saw happening more frequently. Phil would tell Steve he had to do something, and Steve would refuse to meet his demands. They had both been employees of Phil's before they took the plunge and became his partners. He never accepted the fact that all of that had changed once the business began to grow. Well, frankly, that was Phil's problem, not theirs. This statement was often made by Steve when Phil attempted to make ridiculous demands. Steve was right about one thing: neither of them should give this man any control over this special day.

"I know exactly what you're saying. However, I think this approach is our best option."

For several moments, Beverly stared at her coffee cup. When she spoke, her voice was strong as her eyes rested on Joanna's. "I will ask Diane if she wants to go to golf school with us. If she agrees, I want you to understand I will not allow her to be hurt in any way. Do you understand what I'm saying?"

Joanna gave Beverly a solemn nod as she repeated, "I know exactly what you're saying."

She was busy working her way through a mound of dirty laundry when she heard the phone.

"What's you doing, sunshine?" Beverly's voice brought a smile to Diane as she began her conversation.

When she hung up, she realized what a comfort it was for her to have a friend like Beverly. Had she been jealous the other day after golf? Whatever it had been, a warm sense of friendship engulfed her as she sorted through dirty underwear.

She was getting familiar with the check-in routine. She even recognized some of the women she had seen the last couple of times she had played in the league, and a few greeted her with a smile and a quick hello. Mildred was standing near the check-in desk, making sure they all remembered the league meeting would be held after their play. A buffet lunch was going to be served, and the meeting would be conducted as they ate so that those who needed to get to their early afternoon appointments could do so.

"I'll see you after golf," Mildred said to Diane as she smiled and then asked, "How are you liking the league?" There wasn't a smile as she asked this question. Mildred's expression reminded her of a nurse that was attending a recent accident victim.

What's this all about? Diane thought as she smiled and said, "Oh, yes. I have met many nice ladies—just wish my golf was as nice." It sounded lame, even to her, but she didn't want to cause any problems for this woman, or for herself.

Again, she found herself with three other women she had never met. Her cart partner was a delightfully sweet lady named Ruth. She had been playing golf for the last twenty years. She had played in the eighteen-hole group but had to come back to the nine-hole league because of her worsening arthritis. They fell into easy conversation the minute they were introduced. The other two women had just started or returned to the game of golf this year. Sue had just retired from an executive position in a large utility company. It was obvious she was trying to adjust to retirement. Diane understood how she felt, and found herself asking questions that not only had Sue reflecting on her feelings about this recent change, but somehow helped Diane reflect on her own. Sherri was the youngest of the foursome. On the surface, she seemed very friendly and open. Diane thought she was a phony. Her husband was a dentist. She wasn't sure, but she thought the woman had introduced herself by saying, "Hi, I'm Sherri, and I am married to Dr. Miller, the dentist." Of course, she hadn't heard that. It never ceased to amaze her how many women she had met in life that seemed to think their only worth was tied up in a title, or an address, or social circle. Sherri was tied up in one or all of those, and Diane felt a sadness for her. Now that all the preliminary introductions were out of the way, they all hit their first tee shots and rushed to find all the errant golf balls because they needed to keep up the pace of play! As far as she could tell, the only thing she was starting to get good at was this pace of play. She hated to admit it, but try as she might, she doubted she would ever walk away from this game.

"No, no. I'm sure that is a rule. You must not pick up the flag stick until everyone has putted out." Sherri was saying this with great authority. Diane didn't think that made sense, but then again, as far as she could tell, a lot of these rules didn't make sense.

It was Ruth who spoke up next. "I don't think that is a rule. If it bothers a player, then their request to leave the flag on the ground should be honored, but I really don't believe it is a rule. If it is a rule, do you know the penalty?"

Sherri looked a little less confident than she had just a few moments ago, and had to admit she didn't know what the penalty was.

Watch out, Jim, we're coming in for another ruling! Diane thought as she wound up for another mighty hit, which of course turned out to be a lousy swish. What am I doing? She made the mistake of asking that question out loud, and there were no less than six tips given to her from the three ladies. Yeah, right, she thought to herself. If all these women are such great golfers, why are they playing in this league? Hole number nine loomed before them, and the promise of a lunch and a tall glass of iced tea. Please let me finish this hole and just know I have put another terrible game of golf behind me.

There were already many women in the room. They were diving into the salad buffet like they had never seen food before. It seemed all of them were talking at the same time. She was about to scan the room for Beverly or Jill when she heard her name being called. "Diane. Diane. Over here. We need to talk to you, and we've saved you a seat." Beverly was beckoning her over to the other side of the room with typical Beverly flourish. "We want to know if you'd be interested in going to golf school with us."

"Golf school? What golf school?"

"Jill has all the information. It is really a good deal. The cost includes meals, lessons, and room rate. Jill is going, I'm going, and we think Joanna is going to be able to make it. What do you say, want to go?"

"Yeah, this sounds great, and Lord knows I need lessons. When are you planning on going?"

"The week after next. Oh, it will be so much fun. Patty went last year and said she dropped five strokes off her handicap."

"Wow," was all Diane could say as she wondered what a handicap was.

Without turning around, Diane felt someone approach the table. "Hello." She heard a saccharine-sounding voice coming from behind her. The look on the faces of the women in front of her revealed the identity of the woman. When she turned to face Evelyn Howard, she was not the least bit surprised. "How did everybody do today?" she said while giving the biggest, cheesiest smile Diane had ever seen. Beverly took charge by giving her best performance. Letting Evelyn know how much fun all of them had playing this great sport, how this was such a wonderful day to be out in the beautiful weather, and had she gone through the buffet line because the salads were absolutely marvelous? She dragged the word "marvelous" out for so long, Diane was she sure she was going to lose it.

Evelyn continued to smile her ridiculous smile all the while Beverly was talking. Her only response to all of them was simply, "Oh, it looks like Mildred is getting ready to start the meeting. I guess I had better take my seat."

"Did everyone else feel that?" Joanna asked as Diane was taking her seat next to Jill.

"Feel what?" Beverly asked. "The pall that just lifted from the table?"

As Diane began preparing dinner, she was turning the day's events over inside her head. This game was mystifying. One minute. the player was feeling their abilities to play the game; the next minute, that same player was convinced the only thing left to do was to give the game up. Hitting a small ball in the direction of some tiny hole yards and yards away in itself seemed ludicrous. To play the game with strangers who had nothing else in common but to hit this small ball seemed even more absurd. Yet here she was, falling into the same obsession that hundreds—no, she suspected, hundreds of thousands—had fallen into before her.

As they sat down to eat, she announced she would like to go to golf school. Steve was thrilled to hear she wanted to take this step, and as he flashed a wide grin, he said, "It will be like a grown-up slumber party."

"I hope it will be more than a slumber party; I really want to get better at this game."

She really, really did want to get better.

HOLE TWO
Par Three

After many phone calls and discussions on when everyone would leave, who would drive, and how they would room, Diane decided that Steve had been correct about this being a slumber party. She couldn't imagine what was going to await her. Try as she might to act like this was no big deal, she realized that she had the same excitement she had felt the first day of league play. As usual, Beverly was in charge. It seemed she and her daughter were going to drive up by themselves. There were relatives that lived near the school, and when Beverly finished her session, she and Jana were going to stay up there for a few days to visit. This disappointed Diane because she knew how much fun it would have been to travel with Beverly. She found humor in everything. It was determined that Jill, Joanna, Patty, and Diane would all go together. They were to leave right after league play. The check-in at the school was 3:00 pm, and their first day of lessons would begin the next morning at 8:00 am. The first evening, there would be a short program immediately after dinner, and then early retirement. Then a 6:00 Am breakfast and lessons until noon with open play for the afternoon. Maybe this didn't sound so much like a slumber party after all.

Patty was a bubbly person. In other words, she talked a blue streak. By the time they had made it to the county line, Diane already knew about her childhood, education, marriage, and golf game. Diane was extremely fearful Patty would start talking about her sex life. This was going to be a long three-hour trip. Jill and Joanna didn't seem to be bothered by the constant chatter coming from Patty. Of course not! They were having a two-way conversation of their own. Joanna was driving, and Jill was riding shotgun. There had been a plot against her; of this Diane was certain. She had been the novice of the group, and all of them had taken advantage of her ignorance. For shame! She knew Jill well enough to tell that something was wrong when they were loading all their gear in the van and Jill couldn't look her in the eye. Joanna seemed just a little busier than required, and now, after thirty minutes of being held captive in the backseat, it was all coming together.

You ladies will pay for this, Diane was thinking as Patty said, "Don't you agree?" Agree? Agree to what? Diane was trying to bring herself back to any connecting word she had heard Patty utter. Try as she might, she simply couldn't come up with anything Patty had recently said.

"I'm sorry. I'm just a little nervous about this school, and my mind wandered. Agree to what?"

Without missing a beat, Patty repeated her question, which had something to do with the way Mildred was running the league. She was off on another tangent. Diane knew the only responses she would need to give for the next few hours would be, "Oh, yes," and an occasional "I see."

There was a little confusion on whether they should have turned right or left at that last road. Patty was becoming increasingly adamant that they should have turned left instead of right. They would be late for check-in. They wouldn't make it for dinner. Before she had worked herself up into a complete frenzy, they saw the sign: Green Meadows Golf School. There it was. A large, dark green sign with bold white letters, sitting in the middle of a meadow. It had been a cow pasture not more than three years ago, and from the smell of things, a lot of the cows had stayed around. The headlights of the van picked up the parking lot and Beverly leaning against the porch railing while puffing on a cigarette. "We were getting worried about you." She was standing across from where they parked with a halo of smoke above her head.

This was the only comment Patty needed to hear and she was off and running. "I knew we hadn't given ourselves enough time, and I know how tight the schedule is here. I tried to tell you that; didn't I, Joanna? Are we too late for dinner?"

"No, you're not too late for dinner," Beverly said as she rolled her eyes in Diane's direction. Golf bags and luggage were unloaded, all at the direction of Beverly. They were holding the sign-in desk open for them. As soon as they got their things in their rooms, they needed to get down to the dining room. Most of the students were already there, so they needed to get a move on. This sent Patty into the outer stratosphere. Between the noise coming out of Patty, the directions coming from Beverly, and the giggling coming from Joanna and Jill, Diane wasn't sure if she was supposed to be checking in at a golf school or performing on America's Funniest Home Videos.

The pleasant-looking lady at the sign-in desk handed her a form that stopped her cold. Beverly walked up next to her when she saw her face go white. Diane grabbed her arm and said, "This thing is asking for my handicap, and I honestly don't know what it is."

"Put down thirty-eight. If you say you are a beginner, they're going to give you a terrible coach. We're all putting down thirty-eight so we'll be together." Having no clue about any of what this meant, "thirty-eight" went into the space. That evening, she would be told who her golf instructor was going to be. As Beverly had predicted, all of them would be together. Their golf coach's name was Will. He had just recently retired from his position as golf coach at the local high school. He seemed like a pleasant-enough-looking gentleman, Diane thought. She wondered just how long it would take him to figure out they were all beginners. It turned out it took him a nanosecond.

The first day of golf school was a day Diane would rank right up there with having her first baby or recent root canal. They had both been painful, she didn't know what she was doing, she was taking instructions from people she didn't know, and she had done a lot of sweating! Even Beverly, with all her bravado, didn't fool Will. No sirree, Bob. Old Will had their number, and he was going to show no mercy. That became clear to Diane when she watched him put Beverly through her paces. As usual, Beverly had turned on her charm. Will had responded with an equal amount of charm, and then told her to pick up her seven iron and proceeded to show her exactly what he wanted her do until he came back. The four of them had been lined up along the driving range with three other students that had been given the dubious honor of having to join them. Diane was next to a guy from Chicago who was a professional bass player. His wife had sent him to golf school as a birthday gift. She could tell he would have preferred a tie, a baseball bat, a Chia Pet—anything except what he was enduring at the moment. When she was sure Will wasn't watching, she looked down the line of these students. They were all swinging away. If someone connected with the ball, there was a moment of wonder by the participant and any one of the students that happened to witness this phenomenon. What in the world had she gotten herself into? Will reached her just as she was seriously doubting her sanity.

"How long have you been playing golf?" was the first question that came out of his mouth. The next question was why did she want to play golf. Now he was getting down to the hard questions. Why did she want to play golf? Because Beverly had told her to? Because she was trying to find something she could share with her husband? Because after years of being challenged in her job, she now wanted a challenge on the golf course? Because she was a masochist and had not had enough pain in her life, so she thought she'd go for golf? Even she couldn't believe the answer that came out of her mouth.

"Golf is one of things in life I've always wanted to do, and now it looks like I'm going to have time to pursue it." What a load of crap! She had been trying to keep her head above water when she met Steve. After they married, she thought they would work until the time came for them to enjoy retirement with their Social Security checks. Not once had she thought about taking up golf until Beverly had told her what a fun group this was and how much she would like the game. Will studied her for a few more seconds, and then began to give her some basic instructions. He had informed the entire group before anyone was allowed to pick up a club that his goal for the week was to give them the basics of their swing. He had highly recommended that after lunch they should play at least nine holes, eighteen if their endurance would allow. They should work on the things he had talked about during the morning lesson. After this, he outlined what the remaining days' agendas would be. Tomorrow they would all be videotaped, and on the last day of school, these tapes would be viewed and critiqued as part of their classroom instruction. It seemed like days had gone by before she heard her master's voice announce that it was time for them to break for lunch. He hoped he saw all of them out on the golf course. Diane wanted a tall cold drink, food of any kind, and a nap. As she saw Beverly walking toward her, she knew the nap was not going to happen. Ready or not, here we come.

Diane's cart partner was Patty. Try as she might to block much of what this woman said, she couldn't. The chatter didn't bother her as much as the instructions. In Patty's mind, she was the experienced golfer in this group, and therefore she vocalized "expert opinions" on how they were doing with their swing, their stance, the rules—you name it, she knew it. If Diane had found herself in any position of strength, she would have challenged her on a couple of the statements, but the truth is the truth. Diane didn't have a clue on how to refute anything that came out of Patty's mouth. One thing was certain in her mind: tomorrow someone else was going to ride with Patty. That was the only thing she was sure of.

She had just gotten to her room when she heard someone knocking on the door. Oh, please, she prayed, don't let it be Patty. Then she heard Beverly's voice. "Open up. I know you're in there; don't try to hide." She saw a very tall bottle of wine, two glasses, and Beverly smiling from ear to ear. "Jill and Joanna are going to be here in a few minutes; they're bringing the snacks."

As announced, Jill and Joanna showed up with another bottle of wine; salty, fatty snacks; and two more glasses.

"Is Patty coming over?" Diane asked cautiously.

"Are you kidding? Do you think we're out of our frigging minds?" With that, Diane laughed harder than she had in days. To answer Beverly's question, she did think they were all out of their frigging minds.

"Patty has a sister that is on her way to pick her up and take her out to dinner," Jill said as she gave Beverly a sideways glance. "Her schedule brought her to this part of the country, so she worked it out to spend some time with Patty." She finished the sentence with a long sip of wine as she stared at the stem of the glass.

"Whatever," Beverly said as she busied herself looking for an ashtray.

"Oh, come on, you two, you're going to terrify Diane. Patty is just, well, Patty," Joanna announced as she flopped down on the end of the bed.

"What the hell does that mean?" Beverly countered.

"Simply," Joanna went on to explain, "she was probably born talking. She doesn't know that she talks so much; it's just her way of, well, her way of feeling like she belongs."

"She keeps it up, and she isn't going to belong! If we had told Diane what she was in for, do you think she would have agreed to come up here?" Beverly asked as she blew out a large puff of smoke.

As fascinating as all of this was, Diane felt a little offended. "Wait just a minute. Was I asked to join this group at the golf school because someone needed to entertain Patty?" As she spoke the words, she felt the emotion being released in her tone.

"Oh, no," she heard three different voices in chorus.

"Please. Don't misunderstand," came Jill's plaintive tone. "We really, really wanted you to come to the school with us."

"I cannot believe that you would think that I would just want you here to entertain, baby-sit, whatever you were thinking," Beverly chimed in with her eyes growing wide. "I'm the one that talked you into joining this group, and that was for one reason only. I wanted you to be a part of this group!"

It was now Joanna's turn. "Diane. I know we haven't known each other for very long, but Beverly has told me a great deal about you. After being around you, I understand why Beverly thinks so much of you. Please don't think for a moment that we just wanted you to entertain Patty. To show you how serious I am about what I've just said, I'm volunteering to ride with Patty tomorrow."

"Oh, thank the good Lord. We don't have to draw straws," Jill said, laughing as she took another long sip of her wine. With that, all four women began laughing so hard, tears were running down their cheeks. Maybe it was the strain of the last few days, the trip, the stress that accompanies any new learning experience, the adjusting to new friends. Whatever it was, at this moment there was a release in their laughter that each of them felt deep within themselves.

As Diane surveyed this group of women, she realized there had been a bond formed. It wasn't because of Patty—she was a good person—it wasn't even about the golf school they found themselves experiencing. It was something that felt comfortable and natural. Instinctively, she knew it was more than that. She had felt it before, and she was feeling it now. Try as she might to shake it, there continued to be this strange feeling about these three women sitting in her room sharing wine and laughter. She was certain that somehow her destiny was intertwined with theirs. She had no idea what these feelings were all about, but she knew at the moment the events of a turbulent future had already begun.

Diane awoke early the next morning. She hadn't slept well, and she would have given anything to pack up her bags, get in the car, and get home to her husband. They talked for almost an hour on the phone. As soon as she heard his voice, she knew something was wrong. At first, he tried to assure her that he was fine, everything was fine, and she should just enjoy golf school.

"I can hardly wait for you to get back so you can teach me all you know," he had said jokingly, which was an attempt to throw her off her line of questioning. How long would they have to be married before he understood this didn't work?

"Okay. So everything is just hunky dory?" she asked in a sarcastic tone.

With that, he grew serious. "Honey. You have been looking forward to this for a few weeks. You're with people you enjoy being with, and everything else just needs to take a backseat right now. We'll talk when you get home. Until then, there is nothing you can do, so stop your worrying."

"It's about Phil, isn't it? He's causing problems for you again?" she asked, ignoring his last statement.

"All right, I can see you're not going to drop it. Yes, part of what's going on is about Phil."

"What else is happening? Is there a problem at the association?"

"Some of that as well. Look, honey, nothing will be served if you and I try to hash this out over the phone. You get all this off your mind. Concentrate on your golf, and I promise, when you get back, we'll have a long talk."

"You know," she began, "if you don't at least tell me something about what is bothering you, I won't have a good time, be able to think about golf, or care who I am with. So how about a bone being thrown to this dog?"

Sensing his defeat, he began to give her an outline of what had happened. She felt the anger build as she listened to some of the demands Phil was trying to impose on Steve. She didn't know much about this State Senator Howard other than he was from their district and Phil liked to brag about the fact that they were fraternity brothers from the University. They had been invited to one of his fund-raising parties Phil and Karen hosted, and Steve had made a donation to his campaign with some arm-twisting by Phil. However, she had not met the Senator, nor had she met Evelyn Howard until she played golf with her a few weeks ago. She vaguely remembered some of their colleagues talking about a senate bill that was coming up for a vote in the fall. Now, all of this seemed to be coming to a head, and her beloved husband looked like he was going to be in the middle of it. After she hung up the phone, she felt sick to her stomach. She didn't know what all of this meant, but she knew none of it was good. She turned out the light and tried to go to sleep. When she finally got to sleep, she dreamed about a short, robust, red-faced lady glaring at her as she was trying to hit her golf ball off of the top floor of the State Capitol Building.

Diane made her way to the dining room, ambled through the buffet line, and started looking for their group, when she heard the voice of her shy and retiring friend. "Hey, sleepyhead! We're over here. What'd you do, finish the wine we left in the room?"

Beverly was in a sunny mood, donning her latest golf attire topped with a hat the size of a lampshade.

Diane answered the question as she threaded her way to their table. "No. I didn't sleep very well."

"Well! You need to keep those men out of your room." This time it was Patty, who giggled at her own joke. She really is a nice person, Diane kept saying to herself as she tried to get into the swing of things.

"Believe me, there were no men in the room, no additional consumption of wine, no nothing except a phone call to my husband."

The "uh-oh" came from Beverly, who quickly and effectively changed subjects as only Beverly could. "Okay, ladies. Are we ready to show Will just how wonderful our short game is today? All those ready, say aye!"

A chorus of ayes were heard around the dining room. Some of the nearest diners glanced in their direction. Diane looked at Beverly and wondered how this woman had developed the sensitivity she had. Maybe a person couldn't develop a sense of anything. It was there or it wasn't. She pondered this as she pushed her spoon through a bowl of oatmeal.

"Are you okay?" Joanna asked as she gave her a look of concern.

"I'll be fine. It's just that my husband is so tolerant. Sometimes he shouldn't be as tolerant with some of the people he deals with." As she spoke, she could see Joanna's look grow into a frown. As an afterthought, Diane asked, "Do you know anything about Senator Howard?"

At this question, Joanna blanched. Diane could see the color drain from the woman's face. What had she said? Why did the name Howard bring such reactions? Oh, no! The dream. The League Lady. Evelyn Howard. The dots were starting to connect. Connect to what? How were these women connected to what was going on in her life? No answers, just more questions.

"Diane," Beverly called to her as they were walking to the dining room for lunch. "After we get off the course, we would like to come to your room and have a little wine before we go to dinner."

"Sure. Sounds great to me. Do you think Joanna will have recovered from an afternoon with Patty?" She was trying to be funny, but even she didn't believe any humor was coming through.

"Patty has another engagement, so it will just be Jill, Joanna, and yours truly." This was an unusual tone for Beverly, and apparently she sensed Diane's reaction and threw in, "You know Patty, the party animal, you just can't keep the girl down on the farm."

"Well, you know where I live, and I would love to have company tonight. "

She looked at her watch and knew she had plenty of time to shower. It was too early to try to get in touch with Steve, so she would call him after they had eaten dinner. As she turned on the water, she began to grin; by the time she stepped from her shower, she was laughing out loud. Poor Will. She had no idea how much the man got paid, but whatever it was, he hadn't received nearly enough money for today's work. Today, they were going through the basics of the short game, and the short game was the part of the game that Patty and Beverly believed themselves to be experts. She could still see the look on his face as Beverly demonstrated to him how she held her putter and why she held it that way. His face reflected a mixture of emotions. She wasn't sure he was going to laugh (which he did a couple of times), throw a temper tantrum (which she expected), or break down and cry. Neither of those two women showed any mercy. To say that the two of them had very unorthodox mechanics to their short game was an understatement.

Beverly looked like she was playing water polo with her putter, while Patty's arms and upper body movements gave the appearance that she suffered from some dreaded deformity. Unfortunately for Will, he was going to correct these problems for the both of them, or so he thought.

"Why do you insist on holding the shaft of the putter so far down?"

It seemed like a fair enough question to anyone but Beverly. "Do you see how I am built?" she replied as the wind lifted the rim of her lampshade hat. "I have arms like a gorilla, and if I held it the way you just did, my elbows would look the wings of the stealth bomber!"

"Well," Patty chirped. "I like to have my elbows point out; it helps my follow-through." She wasn't sure, but she swore Patty had just batted her eyes at Will.

"Oh, please!" Coming from Beverly. "The only reason you hold your elbows out is because your boobs are so huge, they can't go anywhere but out."

At this, all eyes were trained on Will. Will's eyes were trained on the ground directly beneath him. No one seemed to move for a few seconds as Beverly and Patty were staring at each other. Finally, Patty recovered enough to state that she couldn't help it if she had been well-endowed.

Beverly's response to that statement was a long glaring stare. "Yeah, Patty. The rest of us are just little boys."

"Uh-oh," Jill murmured.

Joanna looked at the two of them and said, "None of us look like little boys; although some of us seem to be behaving like little girls." Having this statement made by Joanna seemed to quiet both of the women and visibly relax Will.

With newfound determination, Will announced in his most teacher-like tone, "I want everyone over by the bunkers. We're going to work on sand shots." As they were making their way to the bunkers, Joanna fell in step with Diane. "We need to talk."

"Okay," was all she could say before Will was giving them more instructions. Years later, Diane realized that her hate for sand bunkers had taken root on that day. Never had she felt so dirty, been so hot, and been so frustrated as she had been with her sand wedge in her hand and Beverly at her side.

The eighteen holes of golf had actually been pleasant. Joanna had been Patty's golf partner. Beverly was having some great shots. Jill had been paired with the bass player from Chicago, and from the animated conversation, it looked like she was having a good day. Diane and Beverly had ridden in carts by themselves. Diane had enjoyed the opportunity to be alone, not having to worry about keeping up a conversation and actually taking in the beauty of day. Yes, Diane thought to herself, I think I really will like this game. She was reflecting on the day's events as she was getting ready for her company. A glance at her watch indicated her guests would soon be arriving. By the time she had dried her hair, applied her makeup, and put on a fresh shorts outfit, there was a knock at the door.

"Hello. Hello. We know you're in there, we can smell your perfume." Of course, Beverly's voice was in its finest tenor, and Diane was comforted by the sound of it. When she opened the door, she was greeted by the smell of pizza, three ladies with loads of food, snacks, anything that wasn't healthy. "What? I thought we were going to have a little wine before dinner. What's all this?" Her words were being drowned out by—

"Where should we put this?"

"How about pulling out the desk chair?"

"Who's getting the ice?

"Diane, where did you put the ashtray?"

"Ladies," Diane began. "I thought we were just going to have a little wine before dinner; what is all of this?"

"This, my dear," Beverly spoke with her best stage voice and a wide sweep of her hand, "is a pizza party."

The only thing that came form Diane was, "Oh."

Once they had poured the drinks, dived into the pizza, and devoured breadsticks with cheese and marinara sauce, the room became quiet, except for the "Oh, this is so good," and "Are there any more breadsticks left?"

As Diane surveyed their little group, she realized for the first time since she had been in school that she had never felt so comfortable with a group of women. Whatever elements needed to be present for relationships to flourish were present in this group.

Just as she was about to get all warm and fuzzy, Beverly piped up with, "What the hell did you do with your hair?"

"I washed it!" was all that Diane could spit out along with a fleck of pizza.

"It's all frizzy. Your hair hasn't looked frizzy before."

"Maybe it's the company I've been keeping that's making it that way."

With that, Jill began to snicker, and Joanna laughed out loud. Beverly looked at her for a few moments and then said, "I've been meaning to talk to you about that."

At this, the other two laughed harder, and Diane and Beverly joined in. As Diane was laughing, she realized for the second time that day how much she enjoyed the friendship of these women. As the party began to wind down, Diane sensed something between the three other women that had not been there earlier. Beverly was nearly chain-smoking; this was always an indication she was troubled. Jill, never the big talker, was even quieter than usual. Joanna seemed to be watching her closely. Why? Was this her imagination? Not long after she had these thoughts, the pizza party came to an abrupt end, as did the gaiety that had surrounded it.

"Diane," Joanna began, "all of us need to talk to you."

"All right," was all she could say as she felt a tightness in her throat.

Joanna was the one that headed the discussion. "We think you need to be included in something that the three of us have been dealing with for the last few months," Joanna continued. "It seems that we have something in common with the Howards."

"The Howards? The Howards?" Diane asked with a look of exasperation. "A month ago I didn't even know who Evelyn Howard was. Even after I played nine holes of golf with the woman a few weeks ago, I only knew her then as an obnoxious, overbearing woman, but—what the hay—this little league seems to be full of them! As for her husband, other than seeing him on television, and having our business partner brag about being a fraternity brother of his—and oh yes, last night my husband tells me that he is being a pain in his ass—I don't know anything about the man, and frankly, I am getting sick and tired of hearing about the Howards, and now you're going to tell me that all of us have something in common with the Howards?! I really don't know them, and I sure as hell don't know what all of us have in common with them!"

The room fell silent for a few moments until she heard Joanna's voice. "I'm afraid we may have a great deal in common. None of what I am about to tell you is going to be easy for you to hear, but the three of us have agreed that you must know."

Beverly was the one that walked over, took hold of her hand, and spoke to her in a soft tone. "Diane. All three of us know this; we also know that you need to be included in our discussions surrounding the Howards. So will you let Joanna continue?"

For as long as Diane had known Beverly, she had never seen this side of her. Her tenderness and concern showed on her face, this comforted and frightened Diane as she responded to Beverly's question. "I'm sorry. Of course, Joanna, I want you to continue."

At this, Joanna began to tell the story of the involvement with the Howards. It wasn't difficult for Diane to follow, as it related to Jill and Beverly. There were many ironies to their connection—the fact that they had gone to school together, lost contact, and then discovered each other in the process of fighting their separate battles. The attempt to annex Jill's property, and the rejection of Beverly's application for her shop. Joanna had discovered in fighting these diverse issues that they had something and someone in common: the Howards. In Jill's case, she discovered that the Howards stood to make a healthy return on an investment they would make if her property had been annexed. In Beverly's case, it had been a matter of Evelyn Howard telling the fine city councilman how to handle applications so his daughter would get hers approved, while other applicants would not. None of the three women understood how inexplicably they had been bound together until Joanna began to receive threatening phone calls. She first thought of them as silly pranks being played by some of the teenagers she had helped convict and were having to go through their probation. She mentioned this in passing to one of her former colleagues, who didn't think the calls should be taken so lightly. With the help of the local police and a county judge, her phone lines were bugged. After several weeks of being led to various payphones they were about to give up on trying to trace the threats. Then, late one evening, Joanna received a call that had not only become more threatening in its nature, but the caller told her what she was wearing at that very moment, and that she should change the page on her desk calendar because it was the eleventh and not the twelfth of the month.

"I don't frighten very easily, but I can tell you, at that moment I had never been so scared in my life." Diane's eyes were growing wide as Joanna continued. "As luck would have it, that was the same night the police were able to trace the call to a place other than a payphone. At first, I was thrilled to get this information, until they told me where it had been traced from. It had been the State House."

"The State House!? Like the Government State House?" Diane wondered if her voice was sounding as shocked as she felt.

"That would be the one." It was Beverly who had spoken as she blew out a long stream of smoke. Jill was sitting with her head in her hands and staring at the floor. This was a position Diane had seen Jill take when her stress level reached its maximum.

Joanna continued. "Unfortunately, there are a lot of phones in the State House, and many of them are right outside the Senate and House Chambers. You know, during session, they're used constantly by lobbyists, journalists—in fact, anyone that happens by and wants to a make a call can do so."

"But at eleven o'clock at night?" Diane interjected.

"The use of these phones at that time of night isn't as unusual as you might think," Joanna continued. "During the legislative session, there are often committees that have to meet after a regular full Senate or House meeting."

"Really. I wasn't aware of that." As Diane was saying this, she was thinking about how little she was aware of anything that related to the working of her state government.

"I could bore you with a lot of details as it relates to the investigation. The bottom line is that although it was a new twist to my phone calls, it wasn't any more conclusive than if that call had been made from another payphone."

"But how in the world did the caller know what you wearing, and that you needed to change the date on your calendar?" Now Diane knew she could hear the shock in her own voice.

"I had worked late that day and I did have on the same clothes I put on that morning. As for the date on the calendar, I'm convinced someone had been in my house the day the phone call was made. I had my locks changed the next morning and bought as good a security system as I could buy."

"Have you gotten any more of those calls?"

"Not a one," Joanna said with a look of resignation. "It seems that when that one was made, something happened to the caller, or someone just decided to back off. Of course, don't think for one second that I'm not always looking over my shoulder."

It seemed like several minutes before anyone in the room spoke. Diane was attempting to comprehend all the information she had just been given. "Okay." Diane finally spoke. "So you think it was the Howards—the Senator and Evelyn Howard—that were behind all of this? Including these phone calls? Joanna, do you really believe the Howards would make threatening phone calls to you?" The three other women watched as she stood and moved to the other side of the room. Thoughts and questions were tumbling over each other. "Evan Brookes, our illustrious city commissioner," she began, "is afraid of his own shadow, and yet you think because Evelyn was his buddy, he risked being discovered trying to get his daughter's application through? And do you really believe that because you took Beverly and Jill's cases, you were targeted?".

This time it was Joanna that spoke. "Diane. The first thing I think is that you should have become an investigator. I can tell you that I do believe there is a connection between these two cases. I'm not a paranoid type. I have friends that work in the county and state government, and frankly, if I didn't have these contacts I'm not so sure those phone threats wouldn't have already been carried out." Beverly and Jill glanced in Joanna's direction, waiting for her to include the connection with her federal government friend, but he wasn't mentioned. "As for the Howards' involvement in all of this, I can't prove a thing, not even good circumstantial evidence."

As Joanna's last word was uttered, Diane wasn't sure if she sat or fell on the end of the bed. She could feel her mouth fall open as she looked at first one and then the other. "Oh, no," was all she mumbled. The room fell silent once again. Finally she heard her own voice ask, "How does this relate to me, and having anything in common with the Howards?"

Joanna looked directly at her as she asked, "Why are your business partner Phil Matthews and his wife, Karen, going to China with Senator and Evelyn Howard?"

At that moment, Diane got a glimpse of how intimidating this woman could be in the courtroom. It took her some time to regain her equilibrium. Once it was regained, she simply said, "I have no idea. This is the first I've heard there was going to be such a trip."

Joanna studied Diane for several seconds before she revealed more facts about the Howards' and the Matthews' relationship and the connection between the Matthews/Stoner/Baker Commercial Cleaning business and government money. Joanna made it very clear to Diane that she was putting all four of them at risk if she discussed outside of this room what they had just talked about—and for the moment she would be wise not to share any of this information with Steve.

By the time everyone had left her room, it had been too late to call Steve. That had been a good thing. She wasn't sure her voice wouldn't have betrayed her. Just as she knew when he was trying to cover over problems they might be facing, the reverse was also true. She fell into a light and troubling sleep. For the first few moments upon awaking, she wasn't sure the pizza party had really happened or if it all had been a strange dream. Like the one she had about the round, robust lady watching her hit the golf ball off the top floor of the Capitol Building. Then, reality gripped her as she rolled over to see the time. It had all been real.

Dread, fear, anger? Maybe a mixture of all of these accompanied her as she made her way to the dining room. There they all were, sitting at their table chatting as though nothing had happened. Patty was talking and bobbing her head, pointing with her fork for emphasis. Jill and Joanna were concentrating on the plates in front of them. Beverly was looking at Patty with intense interest. How did she do it? Diane wondered as she turned from the group scene and tried to adjust to the fact that she was to select something, anything, from this array of food for breakfast. Walking to the table to join this group had been done by sheer will. She wanted to call Steve and tell him to come and pick her up and take her far, far away. This was always her reaction to stress, and she recognized it for what it was worth. Instead, as she approached the table, she heard herself say, "Good morning, ladies. Sleep well?" followed by the cheesiest grin she could put on her face. All eyes at the table were trained on her.

Beverly was the first to reply. "Why, yes, darling," she began in her familiar Greta Garbo voice. "It was divine slumber." Well, Diane thought, Beverly certainly hasn't lost her acting ability.

Joanna simply looked at her and smiled, nodded her head, and said, "Good morning, Diane. Are you ready for the video?"

Oh no. This is the day we're having those stupid videos made, Diane was thinking as she replied, "Oh, of course. Can't you tell by looking at me that I'm in my finest form?" Take that, Beverly, she thought as she set her plate down beside Jill. You're not the only one that can act in this group.

"It doesn't matter what kind of form you have in here that counts. It's what the camera catches as you swing your club that is going to count." Diane could have been blindfolded and hard of hearing and still known this comment was coming from Patty. Oh, Patty, Patty, she thought as she picked up her fork to jab at a piece of ham. If you only knew. If you only knew.

A few moments after taking her seat, the conversation of the others picked up. Jill leaned over to her and whispered, "Are you okay?"

After scanning the table, she responded. "Jill. I'm fine. Really, I'm fine."

Would this ever end? Diane had been on the driving range for at least twelve hours. Maybe that wasn't actual clock time but it was certainly that many hours in endurance time. She was the second to the last that would be videotaped this morning, and she didn't know there were that many angles a camera could view anyone or anything! She wasn't sure, but she thought Will was getting some kind of kick out of watching his students sweat. She really couldn't blame him. After all, she had seen up close what he had to endure with just two of those in her group. If Will was going to have a little fun these last couple of days, good for him.

"Wait! Now wait," Beverly was shouting at first the guy running the camera, and then at Will. "I wasn't ready, and my hat blew off. You can't get a picture of my swing with me chasing my hat!" she said as she slammed the lampshade on the top of her head.

"No. No. We'll take that over, and we won't show the class you're running for your hat." Will was smiling from ear to ear as he assured Beverly she would not be shown chasing her hat and only her swing would be seen.

"I don't think this is funny," she said as she glared at first Will, and then the guy using the camera. Another six hours passed and it was finally Diane's turn.

"The first thing I want you to do is a full swing," Will instructed as the cameraman squatted to the side of her. Oh, this feels really natural, Diane thought as she tried her best to pretend no one was around, especially the camera.

Her best effort proved that she could hit the ball ten feet. "Oh, boy. What a drive. Did you get that on film?" She gave a full smile to the camera.

"I'll say one thing for this group. You sure do seem to be a happy bunch." She knew Will had enjoyed his time with them, even if Beverly and Patty had put him through his paces. She also knew that three of them in this group were very good actresses, with one of them turning into a solid understudy. She personally thought Jill would eventually make a good actress; she just needed a little more experience. Once Cecil B. De Mill decided there had been enough golf swings photographed, they were all excused to go to lunch. Diane was starved, and they were serving fried chicken, mashed potatoes with gravy, and corn on the cob. She didn't care if she gained ten pounds and her cholesterol went up twenty points—she was going to enjoy this lunch. It had been prepared by a group of farm wives that the school hired each session. The money they earned was donated to the local churches or their favorite charity. There were a lot of good things that could be said about rural America, and at the top of the list was their cooking! This is the way her grandmother had cooked, and as far as she was concerned, there was no better-tasting food on this earth.

"Those blue flowers that are on your plate. You can't eat those; they're part of the decoration." Beverly had leaned over to give her a bad time about the amount of food she had just packed in.

"Gee, I was hoping I could scrape them off. I thought they might be blueberries." With this, she gave Beverly a lopsided grin.

"Who do you want to ride with this afternoon? Joanna?" Beverly asked as she raised her eyebrows.

"Yeah, that sounds good. We haven't ridden together before, so it should be fun."

"Oh, shoot. I was wanting to ride with Joanna," whined Patty.

"Sorry kid, you got me for your partner." Beverly responded.

By the look on Patty's face, this pleased her. "Oh, well. I guess it will have to do." Then she giggled at her little joke. No doubt about it, Patty was Patty, as Joanna had stated the day before.

This would be there last afternoon of golf at the Old Green Meadows golf school. Instead of returning home with a perfect swing, she would return perfectly confused. This game was going to be the challenge of her life. She had expected Joanna to discuss the previous evening while they were out on the course. Nothing was mentioned other than to inquire about how she was doing. Once Joanna seemed convinced she hadn't become mentally unbalanced by all the new information, they both did what they had come to do: play golf. At least, in her case attempt to play golf. What a strange and fascinating game, she mused. One minute she was trying to figure out how she was going to accomplish the assignment she had been given the night before, the next minute she was trying to figure out where this stupid ball was supposed be to in her stance—and what was the difference between back in your stance and forward in your stance? Just as she was about ponder some of the mysteries of life and this game, she heard Beverly yelling.

"Uh-oh. It looks like the gentlemen behind Patty and Beverly are in for it," murmured Joanna.

"What did they do?" Diane asked as she twisted around to see what was going on.

"Do you see that golf ball beside Beverly's cart? Well, it belongs to someone in the foursome behind them, and that is a serious no-no in this game."

Diane understood what Joanna was saying, but as she saw Beverly leave her cart and grab the errant golf ball up to take it to its rightful owner, she couldn't help but feel a little sorry for the guy. They both watched as she approached the cart with the two men in it. It was difficult to see if either of these individuals was getting a word in edgewise since the only sound you could hear was Beverly yelling, pointing while her lampshade hat kept bobbing. It also occurred to Diane that this was the first time she had ever seen Patty speechless. To think not very many months ago she had thought her life had been dull—and then she joined the Ladies League.

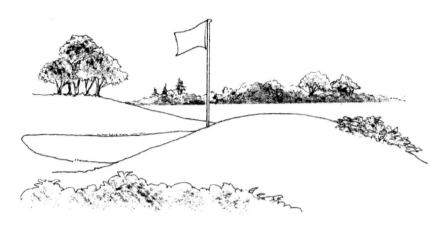

HOLE THREE
Par Five

"Karen. Karen. Kare-*un*! Oh, where is she? She knows I have to go downtown. Kare-*un*!"

"What in the world is the matter? I was on the phone with Donna until you started this yelling. I wish you wouldn't do that!"

"You're always on the phone with somebody, and I told you last night that I had this meeting at the University Club." Phil was growing redder in the face as he spoke. "I hate getting in this damn suit, but if I have to wear it, I want the tie that goes with it, and I can't find it anywhere."

"Is that what you were yelling about? You couldn't find a tie?" Now it was Karen that was starting to grow red. "Honestly, Phil, I don't understand why everything has to be a crisis with you. You have a luncheon meeting; you're not having a command performance before the queen. Honestly!"

"Well, I'm sorry that my *meetings* aren't as important as your *phone* conversations, but this a *very* important meeting, and you had better hope that it goes well."

"Oh, this sounds dire," Karen said, all the while going through Phil's ties in an attempt to locate the one he so desperately had to have. "The last time you had an important meeting with the good senator, you came home at two o'clock in the morning, three sheets to the wind, telling me how lucky I was to have a man like you to take care of me. Do you remember?"

"I don't want to hear any more about that. Today is different. I'm supposed to pick Sam up in twenty minutes so we can get to the club before the senate recesses for lunch."

"Is Steve going with you?"

"No, Steve is not going with us. He doesn't have to be included in everything. Do you think that Sam and I couldn't make a decision without Steve?"

"For heaven's sake, Phil, you're starting to yell again. I never thought for one minute that you had to have Steve with you to make a decision. I was just wondering if he was going, that's all. Here's your tie." She held it up for him as he walked over and snatched it out of her hand. "You're welcome," Karen said as she turned to leave the room. She stopped just short of the door and asked. "What's going with you?"

"What do you mean, what's going on with me? I'm busting my ass to make the kind of money that you have come to enjoy, and all I get from you are snide remarks."

"Phil, that is not true. Any time I have the nerve to ask you any questions, you treat them *and* me as though I were completely stupid, and I'm not stupid!"

"Look, Karen," he said as he struggled to get in his coat jacket. "I don't think you're stupid, and I don't have time for this." With that, he grabbed his wallet from the dresser and was down the hall. She heard him gun the engine of his new Porsche. *Yeah,* she thought to herself, *he's making the kind of money that I have come to enjoy! Oh, sure. That's what's going on here.*

Phil had met Karen while he was in graduate school. He was the one that had been smitten. She was working as a secretary in the Dean's office, and after months of unrelenting pursuit, she agreed to go out with him. He had a charm and a drive that impressed her, unlike some of the other guys she had dated. By the time he was nearing his graduation, he had asked her to marry him. She really couldn't think of a good reason why she shouldn't. So they had a small wedding with family and a few friends. While on their honeymoon, which was a weekend at a state park, he revealed to her that he was going to start his own business. A man never gets rich working for someone else, he had said. She didn't see this being anything to argue about, so she supported him in his endeavor. She continued to work in the Dean's office and made more tuna casseroles than she cared to remember. By the time she was pregnant with their first child, the money wasn't great, but they were paying their bills and had purchased a two-bedroom house in a safe part of town, and for once in her life, she didn't have to go to work. No. Phil wouldn't hear of his wife working outside the home. That had been twenty-five years ago, and she remained a stay-at-home mom. Today she had more material goods than she had ever hoped for or dreamed of. Her children had advantages she could have only imagined having in her own childhood. Phil, for the most part, had been a good father. It had been clear from the start how important having a family was to him. He had been raised by an aunt who let him know almost every day of his growing-up years how she had accepted the responsibility of raising him instead of leaving it to the state. He had tried to find out what had happened to his parents, but she would only tell him he was better off not knowing, and to leave things the way they were. Years after he and Karen were married, he decided to hire an agency to unveil his past. When the report came, he understood why his aunt had refused to discuss his heritage. As his business grew, and the monetary rewards came, the bitterness of his childhood seemed to grow in direct proportion. Karen had watched this since they had married. She kept hoping that the family they had together would heal these old wounds. After all these years, she only saw the ugliness that bitterness produces when it is given constant care.

Phil had called Charlotte on his way to pick up Sam, giving her the instructions he wanted her to pass on to him. Sam was to be standing outside their office building and was to be sure to bring any of the pricing he had been given by the vendors. "Now, are you clear on everything I just told you?" he asked Charlotte as he drove through a light that had just turned red. "It's important you have him out in front of the office in the next five minutes. I'm afraid we're not going to make it to the club before the senator gets there."

"Don't worry, Mr. Matthews. Sam is standing right here, and I will be sure and repeat to him exactly what you just told me. Now drive safely." She stared at the phone for a few seconds before she raised her head and gave Sam all the directions she had just been given. Before she had finished, Sam was making his way to the elevator with his briefcase under his arm. Charlotte watched the young man shift from one foot to the other until the elevator doors opened. What was going on? Things were definitely different around this place. She just couldn't put her finger on what it was.

As the two of them made their way to the dining room of the University Club, Phil was walking and talking faster than Sam could ever remember him doing before. Phil was not known for his speed. By his own admission, he had gained fifty pounds since he had gotten married. Most people thought seventy to eighty pounds would be closer to the truth. After checking in with the hostess and finding the senator had not yet arrived, Phil let out a long breath, loosened his tie, and ordered a vodka on the rocks. "What'll you have, Sam?"

"I think I'll just have some iced tea."

At this, Phil visibly bristled. "Iced tea? Here we are going to meet with our fine senator, and all you order is an iced tea? Young lady, bring this gentleman a Bloody Mary. You like Bloody Marys, don't you, Sam?"

"Well, yes. I like them on occasion, but this is Thursday, and I'm supposed to take my daughter to her skating lesson this evening." Sam was trying to make sure Phil understood this could not turn into one of those boys'-night-out parties. His wife had not completely forgiven him for his last night out with Phil. Not to be dissuaded, Phil assured him that he too had things that he needed to get done when this meeting was over,, and one Bloody Mary was only going to relax him for the meeting with the Senator. The Bloody Mary was ordered, and just as Phil was about to begin his questioning of Sam on the most recent figures, the senator arrived. Senator Howard was an ordinary-looking man. If it were not for the expensive clothes he wore and the differential treatment given to him, a passerby would not take notice of him.

Of course, it was Phil that started with his loudest—and in Sam's mind, overdone—greeting. "Well, well. If it isn't our illustrious senator, and I might add, old fraternity brother." This was followed by handshakes, a pat on the shoulder, and the perfunctory "You're looking great!" Phil had been right about one thing, the Bloody Mary tasted good, and it was already starting to make him feel a little more at ease. He knew the only contribution he was expected to make would be the breakdown of prices that were charged by the various vendors their company did business with. He really didn't like the position where Phil had placed him. Yet, if it hadn't been for the loan he had made to him a few years ago, he would not have been able to afford the house they bought. His daughter was going to private school and was deeply involved in her ice-skating lessons. This all cost money, and if it hadn't been for Phil, he knew none of what he was now providing for his family would have happened. It still bothered him that Phil wanted Steve and Linda to be kept in the dark about all of this. *Oh, well,* he thought as he took another sip of Bloody Mary. *I'm not one of the owners, I'm just hired help.* My, that Bloody Mary sure was good. When Phil asked if he would like to have another one, he didn't hesitate to say, "Absolutely!" So began another one of Phil's Boys' Nights Out.

Karen was in the library doing what she loved to do the most, reading. She heard the grandfather clock chime the midnight hour and the one o'clock hour. Just as she was reaching to turn out the light and go upstairs to bed, she heard the car pull into the garage. Her first thought was to rush upstairs, get in bed, and pretend she was asleep. Upon second thought, she stayed where she was with her book open, waiting to see what would transpire. There weren't many excuses she hadn't heard her husband give. Some were strange, some were funny, and some were very sad. What she heard tonight was new and frightening. It was three o'clock before they went to bed. She fell asleep as the birds were beginning to sing outside her window. For the first time since her father had died, she really didn't know what she was going to do.

"Are you okay in there? Hey. Buddy! You okay?"

"Wha ...? What? Oh. Oh, my. Yes, I'm fine, really. I guess I just went to sleep. I ... I hope I haven't caused any problems for you."

"Oh, no. No problems. I was just doing my rounds and noticed you in the car. I'm afraid I'm going to have to ask for some ID."

"Oh sure, sure," Sam said as he tried to pull his wallet out of his pants pocket. The glimpse he caught of himself in the rearview mirror told him more than he wanted to know or ever wanted to remember. After the security guard left, he started frantically searching for his keys. Then he remembered. Phil had them. A glance at his watch showed the time to be 6:00 a.m. He desperately needed to go to the bathroom. There was a McDonald's across from the office building, so he could get some coffee and use their facilities. He knew it would not be a good idea to talk to Marcia. The last phone conversation had been sometime around midnight, and he did recall her telling him she didn't care if she ever saw him again, or words to that effect. He only hoped as he shuffled across the street that the coffee was strong.

It was late morning when Diane got the phone call from Karen. They hadn't talked in quite a while, and when Karen suggested they get together for lunch, Diane was very receptive to the idea. Diane liked Karen a great deal. In the early years of the partnership, the Matthews' and the Stoners had done a lot of socializing. The two couples had made trips to Chicago and Florida and one trip to Cancun. Phil and Karen had built a house there a couple of years ago. As the business began to grow, it became apparent to Steve and Linda that Phil felt they were the employees and he was the owner. Linda's husband pointed this out one evening after a dinner party. Peter was a veterinarian with his own business accomplishments. He was opening his third animal hospital. When Phil was around Peter during business conversations, all of them noticed a decided change in Phil's demeanor. He didn't start a sentence with, "Steve, Linda, you need to find out what XYZ company is doing about charges." Sometimes it would be more than a directive to the two of them. It would be a criticism of the work they had done on any given project. Of course, he didn't see it was necessary to help with anything; after all, he was the one that had given these two their opportunities. On more than one occasion, Peter had called him on these types of statements. He had also pointed out that the financial responsibilities were equal, and so should the profits as well as the blame. None of this set very well with Phil, and he usually handled the problem with another drink order. It wasn't long before the invitations to go to Cancun, Chicago, or out to dinner met with polite refusals from both the Stoners and the Bakers. Because of the strain that had been created by Phil's behavior, all parties suffered. The first casualty had been the relationship Diane and Karen had enjoyed. When Diane had first stopped working, it was Karen who would call to check on how things were going, did she have time for lunch, would they like to come over for a cookout? Diane looked forward to each invitation until she began to see what it was doing to Steve. The last time the four of them had been together was especially troublesome. Phil's drinking was always moderate to heavy. This night, it was over the top. Fortunately, they were at the Matthews' house, and Karen wasn't going to have to worry about getting his keys away from him. No one noticed any unusual behavior until he began to argue with Steve. It had started with a comment Steve had made regarding the quality of service their customers deserved. "Are you saying that I don't feel the same way? Is that what you're saying? Is it? Is it? Is that what you're saying to me? You know, if it hadn't been for me, you wouldn't have had a snowball's chance in hell of getting into this business! Do you realize what I've done for you and Diane? For that matter, Linda and Peter? He wants to act like he's doing me a favor by allowing Linda to be a partner of mine, but he's *wrong*! I'm the one doing the favors, and what kind of thanks do I get? Nobody seems to understand the sacrifices I've had to make, and … and … Karen here, she's had no easy time of it, at least not in the beginning. Oh, how I hate to think of how we lived when we first got married, and she had to work, and she was out to here." He held his arm away for his belly to show how pregnant she had been and still had to go to work. "The tuna casseroles, oh, those tuna casseroles. Do you know I can't stand the smell or sight of tuna to this day because of those casseroles? I used to love tuna. When my aunt would give me tuna, it was a treat. It was a lot better than those damn butter and sugar sandwiches. Sometimes she used lard because she couldn't afford butter or margarine." The last part of the sentence became garbled. He was sitting on a chair beside their pool, and just as he was about to drop the glass on the tile, Steve reached over and grabbed it from his hand.

"Thank you, Steve," Karen was saying as she rose to help her husband up from his chair, leading him into the house.

"Oh, yeah. Thank you, Steve. It's always thank you, Steve. He's not the one bringing home all the money it takes to keep you in this house and in those clothes, and ..." The rest of his words were lost in the babble of the drunken. Steve followed Karen to see if she needed any help getting Phil into the bed. In a few minutes, he returned, and Karen was close behind. There wasn't anything she needed to say, but she tried to apologize for Phil's behavior, and she was sure he didn't mean half of the things he had said, and she hoped they would understand, and she was so sorry, so terribly sorry. If there had been a defining moment when the friendships of these two couples changed, it was that night. All of them, including, Phil attempted to pick up where they left off. Each of them at different times reached the same conclusion: too much damage had been done. Repair work was not possible.

Diane was thinking of that night as she was getting ready to meet Karen. They had spoken on the phone a few times in the last three months. Usually it was an invitation to a fund-raiser. Phil was always having a fund-raiser for the Party. He believed firmly that the only good politician was one that had been bought and paid for. He loved to brag to anyone who would listen how much he had contributed to this candidate and that candidate and if they had any problems with anything from the way someone's garbage pick-up was handled to the way the snow was removed, just call him and he would call so-and-so and let them know if they didn't take care of thus and so he would pull his support when it came to their next election. There were many times she wanted to ask Karen why she stayed married to the man. That was something she knew she would never do.

They had decided to meet at a small cafe in Old Town. The place was known for their quiches and salads. What both women liked about it, besides the food, was that it was a place without a lot of hustle and bustle of the business crowd. Their small talk began from the moment they sat down at the table. After the catching up was done to the satisfaction of both women, Karen asked if there was anything new going on in her life. "Well, as a matter of fact, I just got back from golf school, and I'm now a member of the Twin Oaks Ladies League." It surprised Diane at how proud she felt. It would be understandable if she had just announced she was a part of a research team that was on the brink of discovering a cure for cancer, but where and why this pride about joining a ladies' league? And a nine-hole league at that!

She was just mulling the question over, when the next words out of Karen's mouth were, "Oh. You must know Evelyn Howard; she plays in that league. In fact, we're having a cocktail party for her husband next month. You and Steve will get an invitation. I hope you'll be able to make it this time. I know you weren't able to attend the last time we hosted one for him, but maybe you'll be able to make this one." Diane recognized the role Karen had started playing. Gone was the friendly, "how-are-you-doing lunch," to "we're counting on your contribution for the senator's campaign." Diane was certain she sat motionless as she continued to listen. "In fact, I don't know if you know this or not, but Phil and Jim Howard are fraternity brothers. You did know they went to the same school and graduated in the same class?" Diane knew Karen well enough to know she wasn't looking for a response as much as she was looking for the listener to understand that her husband had gone to a very prestigious school with very prestigious people. Karen continued her script—yes, that's what this was, a script. Diane had heard her recite these same words before. "Jim went on to law school, and of course you know Phil's story. Well anyway, let me hear more about this ladies' league; sounds like you're having a good time. Are you having a good time?" Karen asked this question as she picked up her glass and hesitated for a moment as she looked directly at Diane.

Diane recognized her cue and began to respond. "Well. I, uh, I do enjoy the group. A nice bunch of ladies," she said as she took her napkin from her lap and began to fold it. Every time she performed this simple task, she always thought of the movie where Patty Duke played the role of Helen Keller and Ann Bancroft's character taught her to fold her napkin. This was the thing that convinced Helen's mother that there was hope for Helen. As she was laying her napkin beside her plate, she was wondering if there was any hope for her. She looked to Karen, who was waiting for more response. So she began. "Yes. Yes. I really do enjoy the league. I have met Evelyn Howard; in fact, I played nine holes of golf with her just a few weeks ago. She seems like a nice lady." *Liar, liar, pants on fire,* she could hear Beverly's voice saying as she continued. "When is the cocktail party fund-raiser? I'm sure we should be able to make it." Now it was Diane that picked up her coffee cup and took a slow sip.

"Well, I think it's the twenty-fourth, but I don't have my calendar right in front of me, so I'll call and let you know the exact time and date. I do hope the two of you will be able to make it. You could get to know Evelyn a little better. Have you met Jim?"

"No. I know Steve has met him and has attended a couple of those town hall meetings he has held, but I haven't had the pleasure of meeting the senator." Diane hoped this last sentence hadn't sounded as sarcastic as her thoughts had just been.

"By the way, how is Steve doing? Is he doing all right?" Karen's expression revealed true concern for her husband. After a few moments, Diane confided to Karen she was concerned for him. That there seemed to be more stress in their business than had been the norm, and she was keeping a close watch on Steve. Karen's reaction was immediate and puzzling. For a few seconds, Diane thought she was going to open up to her own concerns. Then, as Diane had seen her do many times before, she regrouped, and then came the canned reply. Something to the effect that men could handle things in the business world a lot better than we sometimes gave them credit for. Implying, of course, that we poor weak little things couldn't possibly manage the big bad things that our husbands could. *Did Phil sit her down every night and write these scripts for her?* Diane was thinking as she felt her blood pressure rise. She took in a deep breath and managed a weak "I hope you're right."

A few times during their meeting, Diane had actually felt like Karen was about to let go. It was in the tone of her voice and the way she looked at Diane that gave the impression of someone wanting direction, a lifeline, an escape. She had known Karen long enough to know that she was not misreading this woman. Then, as suddenly as it had been there, it left and was replaced by the same old crap about how wonderful everything and everyone was, especially her very own husband. Diane really, really liked Karen, but she had never seen anyone hide so effectively behind nice words. A cocktail fund-raiser. *Just what the doctor ordered,* she thought as she turned into the parking lot in front of Beverly's boutique.

"Yes. May I help you?" Beverly asked without looking up as she placed a dress back on a display rack.

"Oh, yes. You most certainly can help me," she said, and then laughed as she saw Beverly's surprised look.

"Honey. You're beyond all help. Just a minute—let me get Jana to watch the shop while we go in the back room."

Diane brought Beverly up-to-date on her lunch meeting with Karen. She was just about to tell her the way Karen reacted when the talk of their business came up when Jana came in the room and let Beverly know there was someone that wanted to talk to her and only to her. "Who is it?" Beverly barked.

"It's Evelyn Howard."

"Oh, my Lord," was all that came from Beverly as she stood to go to the front of the shop. "You stay right where you are," she instructed Diane as she closed the door. She needn't have worried, Diane thought. *Someone just riveted me to this chair, and her name is Evelyn.*

"Good afternoon, Evelyn," Beverly said with a Loretta Young turn, closing the door behind her.

"Good afternoon to you, Beverly. You don't seem very busy today; I hope your business is doing well." This was typical Evelyn, Beverly thought, pretending to be concerned about someone's welfare when the real intention was to put the individual down.

"Oh, business is great. This time of year is always a little slow—you know, family vacations, kids out of school needing Mom to take them wherever kids go these days. We use this time to catch up on doing inventory, ordering, and planning our buying trips. Thanks for your concern, but we're quite busy."

"Yes, I can see that," she said with more of a smirk than a smile.

"What can I do for you? Did you come in to buy one of these little frocks, or just a social call?" This time it was Beverly that had the smile/smirk on her face.

"Eh. Oh," she began her sentence, having been caught off guard with Beverly's question. She wasn't used to people treating her in this manner. In fact, from the time she could remember, she had always had everyone rushing to meet whatever need she had at the moment. When she started school, her father found out that a boy in her class had called her fat, and he went into a rage. He vowed to take care of the street urchin and his entire family. She still remembered him yelling at her mother about letting her go to public school in the first place. He wanted her enrolled in North Park private school in the morning. He would show this town who they were dealing with when it came to his little girl. Maybe he had dropped out of high school, but it wasn't because he wasn't smart enough; it was because of the stupid education system and the stupid teachers who worked in the system. He could buy and sell every one of them at that very moment! As young as she was, she knew the story of her father joining the Marines, coming back to town with his buddy from the corps and showing the townspeople what a man could do with brains and hard work. Why, he and his buddy had started a scrap business, and in a very short time, they were the largest scrap iron dealers in the state! Evelyn really didn't know what scrap iron was, but she had already figured out her daddy could buy her anything she wanted, when she wanted it. So every time he told the story, she listened as though this was the first time she had ever heard it. There had been rumors at the time that it wasn't just scrap iron they were dealing. None of the rumors could ever be verified, but on more than one occasion, his name had been linked to gambling and prostitution raids. However, when he ran for and won the state senate seat in the early fifties, all such rumors ceased. Evelyn had lived a privileged life up to this point; after he won the election, she believed she had achieved royal status. For this town and her position, in many ways she had. So now she was standing before a woman that truly didn't give a rip who she was or who she thought she was—she simply wanted an answer to her question.

"Well. I certainly don't want to buy a little frock," she said as coldly as she could. "I came to offer you an opportunity, one that I hope you would seriously consider."

"Okay." Beverly leaned on her elbow as she rested it on the counter, never taking her eyes off Evelyn's.

"You see, I am helping with Jim's campaign, and it was suggested we have a luncheon and fashion show at the country club. I thought you might want to get some models together, bring over whatever togs you would like to merchandise, and if there was any interest from any of the ladies attending, you would get the benefit of the sale. Of course, if you wanted to donate any of your proceeds to the campaign, they would be happily accepted, and you would get great advertising."

Wow, Beverly thought, *I would get something, but I'm not sure you would call it advertising--most people would call it the shaft!* "Evelyn." she said evenly. "I will certainly consider this opportunity. When is this fashion show planned?"

Evelyn was disturbed by Beverly's demeanor. Here she was, giving this woman an opportunity most people would jump through hoops for, and she acted as though this might be a bother. She had half a mind to turn on her heel and walk out. Yet, she knew and the committee knew that Beverly's boutique was one of the most popular shops in town, if not the county. Evelyn would have bought some dresses herself if it had not been for her size 18. She would not let Beverly or anyone else in her shop know what size she was wearing. "We have booked the Grande dining room for the sixteenth of October. We have scheduled the serving to begin at eleven-thirty, with the fashion show to begin as the dessert is being served. This will allow those women who need to be home when their children get back from school plenty of time." Beverly was a bit surprised that Evelyn would consider young mothers' problems. However, when it came to raising funds for the senator, nothing was out of the question for Evelyn. She had even allowed herself to be placed in a dunk tank at the Fourth of July picnic the town held. There she was, poured into a twenties bathing suit with a stupid bathing cap on her head. It became one of the most popular booths, and earned the senator another tidy sum for his campaign coffers.

Beverly stood and walked around the counter, all the while talking. "Evelyn. I know this is around the same time we go on the Dallas buying trip. However, this certainly sounds like a wonderful opportunity, so I will give you a definite answer by Friday. I hope you understand. I must be certain I have the staff to take care of the shop, go on the buying trip, and do justice to this fashion show. I can tell you I will give this very serious thought."

Evelyn didn't like Beverly, and for many reasons. She also knew the woman was a woman of her word, and once given would not go back on it. This she respected; this she admired.

"Very well. That certainly sounds fair. I will tell the committee you are seriously considering doing the show." As Evelyn reached for the handle of the door, she turned slightly in Beverly's direction and said, "Tell Diane I said hi." And with that, she was gone. Evelyn could have slapped her across the face and she would have been no less stunned. How had she known Diane was here? Had she known Diane was here? She didn't know Diane well enough to want to send her greetings, did she? What was she going to tell Diane?

"Okay. That's over," Beverly announced as she entered the room. Why did Diane have to look like a caged rabbit, she wondered as she glanced her way.

"What's over?" Diane asked as she looked at Beverly with fear, hope, what was it?

Beverly was thinking as she asked, "Where are my cigarettes?"

A few moments went by as Beverly looked for her cigarettes, and then Diane broke the silence. "Did she follow me?"

"Did she follow you? Why in the world do you think she would follow you? Are you going paranoid on me?" By this time, Beverly had found her cigarettes and had one fired up with smoke coming out of her nose and her mouth as she finished the last question. Beverly was nervous and Diane was scared. The two of them sat quietly for a few moments before Diane answered.

"Beverly, I don't know what's going on. Maybe I am getting paranoid, but if it's really happening, then you're not paranoid." She gave a hollow little laugh. "What do you think is happening, Beverly?"

"I wish I knew."

"So much seems to be going on all at the same time," Diane continued. "First, it's Steve. He seems more and more stressed each day he comes home. He feels, as does Linda, that they're getting the runaround from Phil and now from Sam."

"Who's Sam?"

"Oh, he's the guy that Phil insisted that the company hire a few years ago. His title is V.P. of Sales. Steve and Linda both felt at the time, and still feel, the position isn't necessary."

"So why did they give in and let Phil hire him?"

"Phil did give Steve and Diane an opportunity to get in to this business. Linda's husband didn't have the kind of cash it took to invest in the operation, and Steve and I certainly didn't have that kind of money. So, because of Phil, we were able to get loans and become partners. That was fifteen years ago, and all of us are financially solvent now. As soon as either of them disagree on any business matter, Phil never lets anyone forget where it all began and how he made it all happen."

"So he always gets his way?"

"Yup, pretty much."

"Okay," Beverly stated as she blew out another long puff. "Help me here. Phil is an equal partner, but he gets his way because he helped Steve and Linda get in the business. Right?"

"Right."

"Now he is having meetings with Evelyn's husband the senator *and* with this Sam guy, but not Steve or Linda. Right?"

"Right again," Diane confirmed as she bent over to pick up her bottled water.

"You just had lunch with Phil's wife, who I understand hasn't called you in the last three months, and out of the blue wants to know if you could meet her for lunch. Right?"

"Oh, Beverly, you're so hot! Of course that's right, and that's what I was telling you before Attila the Hun walked into your shop!" The stress, the fear, the confusion, whatever it was that Diane was feeling came out at that moment. "Beverly," she said as she looked to her friend. "I really don't know what's going on, and I'm scared."

"Hey, sweetie. Don't think you're the Lone Ranger in that department. After Joanna talked to us the other night, I'm not feeling all that brave myself. Now let's put all of that aside for a second and think about all that just happened today. Is it possible that Karen said something to Phil about having lunch with you?"

"Sure, it's more than possible. It's very likely she said something to him." "Okay. Was there anyone around your table that you can think of, that might have been listening to you and Karen's conversation?" This caused Diane to reflect on where they had been seated, and if she had recognized anyone near them. Nothing seemed to be coming into focus; nothing had seemed unusual.

"Beverly, the only thing that seemed odd to me was the way Karen acted. It was as though she wanted to tell me something and then would pull back. I'm not sure she even believed some of the crap she was feeding me about Phil. If there was anyone in that place that was listening in on our conversation, I didn't know who they were. Wait a minute. This could be true paranoia, but there was this guy that seemed really out of place. He was by himself, and I remember thinking a couple of times how uncomfortable he seemed, and when we got up to leave, he made a real effort to busy himself with picking something up from the floor. You know what? I don't think there was anything on the floor that he was trying to pick up. At the time I just thought he was plain odd."

Without missing a beat, Beverly wanted to know what he looked like, how old she thought he might have been, how he was dressed.

"All right, Beverly, are you going to ask me if he had any distinguishing birthmarks?"

"This is not the time for you to be a smartass. I don't think it was a coincidence that Mrs. Senator showed up at the shop today, and then wanted me to say hi to you. Believe me. I know this woman well enough to tell you that she wanted me to give you the message."

"Message? What message?" Diane was all but shouting at this point.

"Diane. It's all right. Everything is going to be all right." Her voice became more soothing as she continued. "Honey, she wanted to make sure that you knew that she knew you where here, that was the message. We just have a lot of things we're going to have to figure out. It's going to be all right."

This was the second time within a week that she had seen Beverly take the role of nurturer. It was comforting, but it was out of character for Beverly, and this frightened Diane more than Evelyn Howard.

Diane was trying to digest the events of the afternoon when Beverly reverted to the woman Diane knew best and proclaimed that she thought tomorrow would a great day for some golf! "Golf, what's a golf?" Diane asked as she gave Beverly her lopsided grin.

The next morning was a beautiful day. Diane was trying to remember the words to the Mr. Rogers song as she moved her car onto the interstate. "It's a beautiful day in the neighborhood" was all she could think of, and then a flashback of watching her two little towheaded boys sitting in front of the TV with a bowl of Froot Loops, watching all the marvels of Mr. Rogers' neighborhood. She wasn't sure why she started to cry. Because both of them were now young men and no longer needed their mother? Was she mourning her lost youth? Was it her fear for Steve's health? Was it all of the above? Then in the midst of her troubled thoughts, a small compact car veered over into her lane, narrowly missing her front right fender. She was waiting to hear the sound of crunching metal. Her tires made a loud screeching noise as she applied the brakes. Fortunately, the traffic behind had not been close enough for someone to rear-end her. What a jerk. Was this idiot slowing down? He was. What in the world is wrong with this man? As she began to look closer at the car, she decided it wouldn't be a bad idea to get his license plate number. She started to speed up so she could see the plate. Then the driver of the car floored it. She only got a glimpse of the plate when a large plume of exhaust came from the tailpipe. The car crossed two lanes to exit at the next off-ramp. "I hope you make it to where you wanna go, fella.!" Diane yelled at the exiting car.

After finding a parking space, she hurried to the pro shop. Beverly was a stickler for tee-time promptness. She knew her friend had already checked them in, gotten their water, and at this moment was probably checking her watch and wondering where she was. As she opened the door to the pro shop, she saw Jill at the counter. As she drew near, she could make out part of the conversation she was having with Jim. Jill took an interest in people; when she asked someone how they were doing, she really wanted to know. Apparently, she had asked Jim how the season was going, and he was telling her all about it. She admired this characteristic in Jill; there didn't seem to be one phony bone in her body. She wished that she were more like that.

"Good morning." At the sound of her voice, Jill turned in her direction and asked, "Did Beverly come with you?"

This startled Diane. "Oh no, she said that she would meet me here." Seeing the look on Diane's face, Jill was about to respond when all of them heard the ever-familiar Beverly greeting.

"Good morning, darlings!"

"Where have you been?" Jill asked in a tone that she didn't often use. Diane and Jim were looking at Beverly, awaiting her response. Jim's glance was brief, and then he busied himself with the schedule in front of him. Diane continued to stand with her mouth slightly open, trying to figure out what Jill's reaction had been all about.

"Oh, not to worry, my love. There was a last-minute phone call I had to make." Diane caught the look that Jill gave Beverly, and she knew that something was going on that they weren't telling her. *Wow*, she thought. *I sound paranoid, even to myself.* "Are we ready to hit the links?" Beverly asked Diane.

"Uh, yeah, sure," Diane responded. "Let's get out there and see what we can do today."

Well, they got out there, all right, and boy, did she see what she could do. "This game sucks!" She said out loud to no one in particular. She had just tried three times to move this stupid ball out of the sand bunker and there it was still nestled down like some proud hen had just laid the thing. She didn't know if she was going to give it another try, pick it up and throw it, or grind it into this nasty sand! *Oops! Too many swing thoughts!* she said to herself as she lifted the club, took the swing, sand flying and—surprise!—so did the ball.

"Would you look at that," came Beverly's statement, as if she had never seen a ball come out of a bunker before.

"Don't try and humor me," Diane said as she was climbing out of the bunker and brushing sand from her legs.

"Are we a little testy today?"

"No. We're *a lot* testy today." At that very moment, she was trying to figure out why on earth she continued to come out and play some game that she obviously had no aptitude for. She had gone to golf school, she had taken lessons from Jug Head—this had become her nickname for the child that had sold her the clubs and given her the first golf lesson. Try as she might, nothing seemed to be working for her. It didn't seem to matter if a person was short and fat, or tall and skinny, or any other body type. It also didn't seem to matter how they approached the ball, swung the club, or moved their body parts. One of the women in her league looked like she was about ready to chop off a chicken's head. Every time she watched her, she was sure the golf club the woman was holding would be buried a foot into the ground. Not so. She could knock that little ball a country mile. She would hear someone say about another golfer. He has a beautiful swing, or a powerful swing, or a smooth swing. So she began to watch other golfers and tried to copy the swing if that person got results from the swing. Big mistake—very big mistake. She learned very quickly that if a person she was watching had a bad habit, she could pick that up in a heartbeat, apply it to her already dreadful play, and watch her handicap get higher. As far as she knew, most of the people in the free world that had taken up this game *could* hit the ball better than she did. Right at this moment, she couldn't hit the ball if it had been the size of cantaloupe. She also had come to realize that as frustrating, humiliating, and challenging as this game was, it was doing something else for her. She was part of a special group of women that were fast becoming dear friends.

She was sitting in the cart when it happened. Jill was hitting a fairway shot, and Diane was starring off at the sky. There were huge white puffy clouds and a nice breeze blowing, and for the moment, she didn't have to try and hit her golf ball. She turned her head in the direction of where the noise was coming from and saw a goose flapping a wing and giving off the strangest sound. All this was accompanied by Jill's pitiful cry. "Oh, I hit the poor thing! I hit the poor thing." She repeated this about one hundred times. A glance at Jill and you couldn't tell if the goose had been hit or if it had been her. There didn't seem to be much color in her face, she was holding her hand up to her mouth, and she didn't look like she could move. Diane sat, torn between getting out of the cart to help Jill—to help Jill do what, she wasn't certain—and getting out to see if the goose was okay. Then she remembered the stories she had heard about geese and their ability to do bodily harm to people. She decided that unless someone came along at that very moment to give her instructions, she would just sit tight.

"It's going to be all right." Of course this was Beverly making the statement. How on God's green earth did Beverly know that goose was going to be all right? Diane was just about to ask her that very question. As though Beverly had given the goose its cue, it took a couple of steps and up it flew. "Does this mean you get a birdie?" And with that, Beverly looked at the two of them and let out a good loud laugh. Jill was some where between laughter and tears. She took her hand from her mouth, gave Beverly an incredulous look, and then started laughing until the tears were rolling down her cheeks.

For the rest of the round, Diane's golf shots seemed to do more of what she wanted them to do. At one point, she had wanted to hit the ball to the right of a tree, and surprise of all surprises, she hit the ball to the right of the tree.

As Diane was putting her clubs into the car, she knew that she could never explain to any of her non-golf-playing friends why she would spend a morning on a golf course, complain about the game, the rules, and her frustration, and then turn around and go back out and do the same thing over again. What she didn't know at the time, but would figure out over years of playing, was that she and many others like herself had simply come under the spell this game placed on those individuals that picked up a golf club and naively thought, *This looks like fun!*

She was looking forward to getting home and telling Steve the latest about her game experiences. She could hear the phone ringing as she was unloading the groceries. Grabbing her purse and a bottle of milk, she hurried to get to the phone. "Hello. Hello." There was no sound on the other end of the line. "Hello. Hello." Then there it was, the breathing, deliberate heavy breathing. She froze, just standing there listening to some sicko breathe. She was taking the receiver away from her ear when she heard it. It was a voice but not speaking into the phone. It had come from the back ground. Had it been a woman's voice? It had sounded higher-pitched than a man's, but then, it could have been a child's voice. Yes. That was what it had been. Children playing on the phone. It had just been children, maybe really young children that had no idea what they had just done. "Of course that had to be it," she said out loud to herself as she picked up the bottle of milk to put in the refrigerator. She busied herself with the dinner preparations, going through the mail, and listening for the sound of Steve's car. She surprised herself with the yelp she let out when the phone rang. She surprised herself again when she stood in the middle of the kitchen, listening to the ring, not making a move to pick it up.

Park Street had been appropriately named. The street was lined with large oak trees that were seventy-five to one hundred years old. Large, well-manicured lawns were bordered by box-wood hedges and brick-paved sidewalks. The stage was set for viewing some of the town's oldest and most expensive real estate. It had only been in the last fifteen years that this neighborhood had been resurrected from the abuse and neglect of aging. It once had been homes to the nouveau rich. As was customary during this time, each occupant attempted to showcase their success and wealth in the style and size of their home. Thanks to the Historical Society and volunteers that believed in preserving the past, many of these houses had been saved from the wrecking ball and unscrupulous developers. There was one individual that headed the charge for the revitalization of Park Street, and that was none other than Evelyn Howard. Her father had purchased one of the larger mansions after his scrap iron business became profitable. He was planning on running for public office, and he certainly didn't want to be living in an ordinary neighborhood. Evelyn remembered him making this comment to her mother on more than one occasion. It did confuse her after he began his campaign about how often he would tell his constituents that he was just a hardworking Joe that had their best interest at heart. There were a lot of things that confused Evelyn about her parents. She knew that her father adored her. He would buy her anything, take her anywhere. She simply had to tell him what she wanted and it was hers. He had a very bad temper, and more than once she had heard him berate her mother until the poor woman would flee the room in sobs. There were only a few men that she had seen stand up to one of his tirades, and the only one that didn't seemed to be phased by them was his old Marine buddy. Her father had lost his temper with her once and only once. It had been one evening that she had had trouble going to sleep. She couldn't have been more than eight or nine years of age. She heard noises coming from her father's library, so she decided to visit with him and maybe get him to tell her one of his bedtime stories. When she pushed the large mahogany door open, there was laughter, smoke, and brightly colored women, one of whom was sitting on her father's lap. He didn't see her right away, but when he caught sight of her, his eyes grew wide as his faced reddened. When he abruptly stood, the woman on his lap let out a curse as he began shouting and making exaggerated movements with his arms, shooing her back out of the room. Next were the hot stinging tears that ran down her face, and some woman in a red dress and dark red lipstick approached her and said, "Oh, she's scared. The little dumpling is scared. Come here, little dumpling. Come here."

"Get away from her! Do you hear me? Get away from her!" This was her father's voice, and at the sound of this, she turned and ran as fast as she knew how to run. She remembered crying herself to sleep. The next morning at breakfast, she did not want to see her father or talk to him. Her father acted as though that night had never happened. Years later she questioned herself on her own recollection of those events. The day her father was on his deathbed, he asked her if she had remembered that night. When she answered that she did, he told her how he wished she hadn't seen that. Evelyn had often thought how sad her father was. She had never heard him say he was sorry to anyone. For as long as she had lived, she had never heard those words, or "I love you," pass through his lips. Her mother seemed resigned to her fate. She was the daughter of one of the first mayors of the town. She had never been a beauty, but she had a wholesome look when she had been a young woman. Her parents' wedding picture captured the essence of their relationship. Her mother was plump with rosy cheeks and golden hair, staring into the camera with what could only be described as fear. Her father was standing beside his new wife with a look of triumph and defiance. Evelyn never remembered any affection between the two of them. There were times that she was convinced that they had only slept together once during their married life and she had been the result of it. When she had been very young, she remembered her papa. He seemed a kindly man with laughter that would fill the room. Her mother always looked forward to her father's visits; she seemed to come alive each time he was in the house. When he left, she would withdraw, hiding behind her needlepoint and overeating. She noticed that her father showed him respect that was reserved for few people. The two of them would talk a great deal about the political climate of the town, state, and country. It was with Papa's encouragement that her father had decided he should make a run for public office. Everyone was surprised when Evelyn's mother embraced this idea, and not only did she work tirelessly during the campaign, she was also very effective in the public appearances she made at the side of her husband. For a few months after he won his senate seat, the relationship between the two remained as energetic as it had been during the campaign. Then, slowly, her mother returned to her needlepoint and her chocolates, while her father had more frequent late nights in the city. By the time he ran for reelection, her mother had succumbed to cancer. Evelyn played the role that her mother had before her. That was when she decided that the political game was exciting and fun. Most of all it was a game, and one that she found she was a natural at playing. Now, she was approaching the same age her father had been when he died, and she knew that she had only said "I love you" once. She had never uttered "I'm sorry" to anyone, living or dead.—nor did she ever intend to.

"What in the world do you think you're doing? Who was that? You called her, didn't you?" Evelyn was standing in the upstairs room of their carriage house. Standing before her was Mac. He had worked for the senator and his wife for the last twelve years. He lived in the upstairs apartment that at one time had been the original owner's carriage house. Evelyn had taken great pains to restore the structure while adding an apartment that had been the sleeping and hay loft for stable hands. The project had just been completed when Mac showed up on her doorstep with a story that made her decide that she and the senator needed a gardener and general handyman. This had not been an easy sale for her. Jim Howard saw absolutely no reason that they should have some bum live on their property that neither of them knew. It was not only a puzzle to Jim, but to most of those that knew the Howards. As privileged as Evelyn had been, she was not known for her generosity. The old adage about squeezing a nickel until the buffalo squealed could most certainly have been coined about Evelyn. There had even been some gossip that suggested that old Mac was Evelyn's lover. Some of her more vicious enemies called her Lady Chatterley. Mac had showed up on the Howard estate right after Jim had won his first senate seat; he had served three years of a four-year term and was coming up for reelection of his fourth. Why Evelyn Howard continued to allow this man to remain on their property, much less pay him a salary for the slovenly work he did, was anyone's guess. Jim had long ago given up trying to sort any of this out, and frankly, if it kept Evelyn busy and out of his way, then Mac was earning his salary.

"Whadda you mean, what am I doing? I'm doing what her highness has asked me to do."

"You're drunk and getting drunker. Set the glass down!" Mac stared at Evelyn through his bloodshot eyes before he rested the glass on the table. He was sitting in the small living room of the carriage house apartment. Evelyn had come up to talk to him about yesterday's events, when she had walked in while he was standing with the phone in his hand, making exaggerated breathing sounds into the receiver. "I want to know, and I want to know right this minute what you were doing on that phone."

"Just entertaining one of my new lady friends." Then he laughed as though this was the funniest joke anyone had ever told.

"You're disgusting and vile. I'll talk to you in the morning before you climb into your bottle. Until then, don't talk to anyone, call anyone, see anyone, do you understand?"

His laughter left and his mouth formed into a twisted grin. "I think you might want to get a hold of yourself. I'll work with you, but I don't take no orders from you. You understand me?"

"Oh, yes, Mac. I understand you."

"I'm not so sure you do, or you wouldn't be comin' round here tellin' me I better not do this and I better not do that." He stood up and walked over to where Evelyn stood. He came within inches of her, and without saying a word, he bent down and lifted the gold diamond necklace she was wearing. "Nice piece of jewelry you got here." As he spoke the words, he snapped it off her neck. She let out a yelp and for an instant he saw the fear in her eyes; within seconds, the look of fear was replaced by a hard long stare.

"Keep it. It's yours." Before he could give her a response, she was already closing the door. He picked up his glass in one hand and held the gold necklace in the other while he was deciding how much the guy at the pawn shop would give him for this trinket.

Evelyn was shaking as she made her way to the manse. Maybe she had gone too far in trying to control this man's behavior. The first day he showed up on her doorstep, he had admitted that he liked the bottle and liked it a lot. That had been nearly twelve years ago. As strange as it seemed, she knew that they had something in common. He was driven by his drink, and she was driven by money and power. Together, they would make a good team. That is what she had believed until tonight. It may have only been his drunkenness—she had never seen him that drunk before; it may have been his greediness—he had made a few remarks recently that indicated he was no longer satisfied with the monetary arrangement that had originally been made between them. Whatever it was, she was not going to be bullied by some scumbag. These were her thoughts as she reached into her lingerie drawer and pulled out her .38 pistol, loaded it, and dropped it in her handbag. Then she walked down the stairs into the library and poured herself a tall glass of bourbon and water.

Jim Howard had just been through a particularly difficult day. He didn't like the questions that were coming out of the senate finance committee. He and Evelyn had many serious arguments about this whole plan. She let him know that if he didn't go along with her, she would publicly expose all of his infidelities and would personally start a rumor about him being interested in young boys. She was that mean and vicious, and he didn't doubt for one minute that she wouldn't do just that. As for his infidelities, there had been one. She had been only the second woman in his life that he had ever loved. Mary had been a volunteer lobbyist for an organization that wanted increased funding for shelters for abused women and children. He would remember their first meeting until the day he died. She walked into his office convinced that he was a big, greedy, grabbing state senator that wanted nothing more than to line his pockets with as much taxpayers' money as he could get by with. He was certain that she was a bleeding-heart liberal that wanted nothing more than to turn the state, and eventually the country, into some socialistic/communist state. Their conversation had been contentious and most certainly was headed toward an unresolved conflict until the moment she used her hand to emphasis her point and sent the small dish of candy that had been sitting on his desk flying across the room, with little candy hearts decorating the desk and the carpet, and one splashing in the senator's coffee, which spewed Folger's Best on the front of his shirt. Without saying a word, he reached in his cup, retrieved the candy and read it aloud. "Will you be mine?" He would forever remember the look on her face from going blank to horrorstricken to red. When their eyes met, the laughter had been loud and spontaneous. The senator's secretary came in to see if everything was okay, which caused more laughter to erupt. From that moment on, the two of them had serious discussions about programs, tax dollars, priorities, and the role of government. A mutual respect grew out of this, which led to admiration, which led to desire. Neither of them realized what was happening until it was too late. Neither of them would be considered one of the beautiful people; therefore, they never considered the fact that someone of the opposite sex would be interested in them. He finally told Evelyn that he wanted a divorce. He had felt certain that she would grant him one without hesitation, he couldn't have been more wrong. He had known for many years that his wife was a cold, calculating person, but he had never considered the fact that she could be cruel. Within days, there was a series of events that caused him to tell Evelyn that he would do whatever she wanted him to do, including retracting his request for a divorce. His last conversation with Mary had torn his heart from his chest. From that day forward, he lived life as the prisoner he was.

He was looking forward to having a glass of wine before he and Evelyn had to go to dinner. He hoped there wasn't a note from her on his desk when he got home. Actually, it was more of an instruction sheet than a note. It would tell him where they were to be, the people they were to be with that evening, and what he was to wear. Their schedule became especially frantic as the election drew near. He would give Evelyn credit for one thing she knew how to campaign, and campaigning was her life. He had often wondered how his life might have turned out if he hadn't agreed to intern that summer for her father.

He had just been accepted into law school and needed employment before classes began that fall. He was a young man whose life had taken an unexpected turn. The girl that had become the love of his life announced that she would no longer see him. He had lived days and weeks in emotional agony until his college fraternity brother convinced him he needed to get on with his life. "Why don't you apply to law school? You've always told me how much you enjoyed political science and economics, and you're great on the debate team. It seems to me that you're a natural law student."

After the pep talk from his fraternity brother and a visit with his father, he decided that he indeed needed to get on with his life. Jim admired his father more than any man he had ever known. He was a man who was known throughout their farm community for his integrity, generosity, and strength. He knew that when his father spoke, it was worth listening to what he had to say. "Son. I know that we talked about you taking over the operation of the farm. I also know that it was more of a sense of duty on your part than a desire. You're a smart young man, and you need to see what this world might have to offer you." The day his father died was the day that part of him gave up living. Up to that moment, he had continued to stand up to his wife and father-in-law; without the encouragement of his dad, he grew tired. Tired of the struggle, the arguments, the dishonesty. He didn't believe that all politicians were the same, that they all washed each other's hands and had to do deals in the back room. For a while he had rationalized that he wasn't giving up, but as the years went by, he knew he was simply lying to himself. When he and Evelyn married, he had hoped they would have a good life together. This hope was gone by the time they had returned from their honeymoon. Twenty-five years later, here he was, a shell of a man that continued to do the bidding of Evelyn Howard.

What he found as he entered the library puzzled and concerned Jim Howard. It was obvious that Evelyn had consumed more than a little alcohol. This from a woman that allowed herself two glasses of wine a day. Never in their entire time together had he seen her consume any more, not until this night.

"Well, here is the honorable senator." Evelyn lifted her glass in mocking tribute to her husband's entrance into the library.

"It's nice to see you too, my dear." *Was this day ever going to end?* he wondered as he approached the bar and poured the finest whiskey he could find into a very tall glass.

"What time did she call? How did she sound? Tell me again, why did she say they had to cancel?"

"Oh, for Pete's sake. Don't you think she might have come down with the flu?"

"Not Evelyn Howard, no self-respecting flu bug would go near that woman."

"Phil. What an absolutely horrible thing to say."

"Karen, you don't know that woman like I do."

"Really? Why don't you tell me just how well you know her?" At this, Phil did something totally out of character: he actually had tears in his eyes. "What on earth is the matter with you?" Karen asked, showing her alarm. "Does a cancellation with the Howards for dinner mean so much to you that you would have tears in your eyes? No. Oh, no. something else is going on here. Want to talk about it, Phil? It looks like we're going to have plenty of time."

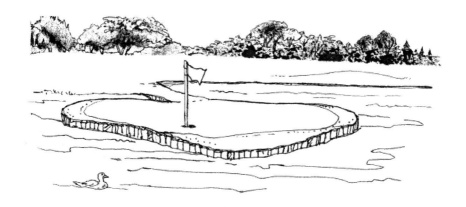

HOLE FOUR
Par Four

Jill was getting just plain old tired. She remembered her mother using that expression all during her childhood. *You know, honey, your mother is just plain old tired.* This statement was usually made after she had watched her mother spend eight to ten hours on her feet helping her dad start up another store. She never remembered her complaining, unless "I'm just plain old tired" was a complaint. Jill had always felt she had been given the best of both worlds. Her father had been raised in a family of some means. He attended the best schools, moved in the finest circles in the city, and at one time had been one of the city's most eligible and handsome bachelors. It came as a surprise, if not a shock, to his family and friends when he announced he was going to marry Jill's mother. Her grandmother had tried everything within the law to see the marriage did not take place. She had even taken Louisa aside and offered her all the money she had if she would give her back her son. The response from Louisa was a gentle and firm "no, thank you." After they were married, his mother tried another tactic to dissolve their relationship. "All right, Daniel. Since you have decided to marry this backwoods hillbilly, I am going to see that you don't get a penny from me, until you come to your senses." Her father had told his mother he was sorry to hear she felt this way and he hoped she would have a good life. There were three years of estrangement between mother and son. When Jill was born, the estrangement ended. She had been the catalyst that mended the relationship of her father and his mother. She knew her parents deeply loved each other and deeply loved her. She had no other siblings because of the damage she caused her mother to suffer while giving her birth. This fact had never been revealed to her until after the death of her mother. There were times she wished she hadn't been told; she knew it wasn't her fault but she still felt pangs of guilt. She also struggled with guilt over the death of her father. Why didn't she pick up on some of the signs that were there? Were these signs really there or had she just imagined they had been? For the most part, she felt she had handled all that followed her mother's and father's deaths relatively well. She had no idea what financial problems her father had kept from her and her mother. To say she was stunned to learn he owed a significant amount of money to the IRS would be an understatement. She was convinced she would probably never have to worry about financial security, and then discovered rather abruptly that not only would she not be financially secure, she would be lucky to keep the clothes on her back. She hired one of the city's best tax attorneys, who happened to be an old friend of her father's and was able to keep her father's name from becoming headlines in the paper. This was also the time she had first heard and indirectly had to deal with Evelyn Howard's father. He had loaned her father money, and after his death was demanding a large sum of money that he claimed was interest due him. Fortunately, the attorney she had hired was able to convince Mr. Miller it would not be wise to pursue this matter. Jill had never completely understood how her attorney had accomplished this. She didn't know or care how all of this was solved. She was a twenty-year-old college student who felt she had reached the age of forty within a very few months. She never looked back. The only decision she made that still caused her pain was the decision to let Jim know they could no longer see each other. At the time it seemed a rational decision; she didn't want him hurt if some of the facts about her father would be revealed. She also didn't want him to be ashamed of her. To her, this would have been the worst hurt of all. Looking back, she realized it had been a hasty decision and a foolish one. At twenty years of age, what did anyone really understand or know about how to deal with the affairs of the heart? How did one protect the reputation of those who could not defend themselves? She knew that she had done the best she knew how. The pain had become dull and for the most part dead. Then there would be a memory, a song, a thought, and she would feel the dull ache go through her as strongly as it had been in the very beginning.

Now this. This thing was getting her down. It had been difficult enough for her when she found herself face-to-face with the Howards as she stood firm on the battleground against the annexation of the property that she had been left by her late husband. She had stood right beside Beverly when she was going through her fight with the city commissioner and eventually the exposé that came about. It was during this time she was convinced that whatever she had felt during her collage years had long died. Had there been a flicker of flame left, it was snuffed out when she went through these last two confrontations. Now, was she willing to fight once again? For what? What did anyone really know, including Joanna? She was going to call Beverly and tell her she was just "plain old tired." Jill had decided she would talk with Beverly after today's league play. In fact, the more she thought about all of this, the more convinced she was that she was making the right decision. By the end of league play, she vowed to herself she would do whatever it took to fight the likes of Evelyn Howard.

The morning had started as usual. Everyone was checking in at the pro shop, chatting about their game, the week they had enjoyed, and the small talk which defined part of the league. Then she saw it happen. Evelyn Howard was standing at the desk, and when she was told who would be playing in her foursome, she smacked her hand down on the counter and demanded to speak with Mildred. Jim's look could best be described as someone that had just been slapped. He stammered something about having to page Mildred and would she please step to the side so he could check in the rest of the ladies who were still waiting. Evelyn moved ever so slightly to the side of the counter, glaring straight ahead and drumming her fingers. Mildred arrived and as soon as she glanced at Evelyn, her eyes became that of a startled rabbit. There was a brief conversation with Jim, a few nods of her head, a sideways glance at Evelyn, a face that began to glow from a soft pink to a loud red. It took a few more minutes before Mildred asked Evelyn to please accompany her to the ladies' lounge. As they disappeared from view, Jill decided to follow, staying safely in the restroom area but being able to hear all that was being said in the locker room. There was no question, as she reached the door of the ladies' room, who was doing the talking. Evelyn Howard was demanding—and she used that very word, "demanding"—that Diane Stoner not be allowed to play in this league. She knew nothing of the game, could not hit the ball, and was an embarrassment to this league. Mildred was trying her best to diffuse the situation. She was making some very good points about what this league had really been formed to do. She was trying to explain to Evelyn that although Diane was certainly not a great golfer, she was only a beginner, and frankly, she could hit the ball better and was now turning in lower scores than some of the older women in the league. It was clear that Evelyn was not going to have any part of it, and if Mildred did not change the lineup, she would leave this minute and resign from the league. Jill was hoping against hope Evelyn would do just that, but Mildred knew, and so did Jill, if Evelyn resigned it would be a bigger mess for all concerned. After a few more minutes of the same kind of exchange, the two left the locker room. She entered the pro shop just minutes later, and she saw Jim making adjustments with his pencil.

That is when she emotionally put on her boxing gloves. "I've had just about enough of that bitch!" were her first words to Beverly as she walked in the door.

"Well! Good morning to you, my dear chickadee," came Beverly's response with a little laughter.

"Chickadee, my ass!" Jill shot back.

At this point Beverly dropped her tone and grabbed Jill by the arm. "Jill. I don't know what's going on, but get a hold of yourself."

"Well, my dear, you're going to know what has been going on because I'm going to tell you, *and* if you aren't playing a foursome with me *and* if I'm not your cart partner, *fix it*! I'll be waiting outside." With those last words, Jill pushed open the door and was making her way to the golf cart that held her clubs.

Jim, the epitome of cool, had already heard the conversation, picked up his pencil, and made the necessary changes. By the time Beverly approached the counter, he simply nodded and said it had been taken care of. To this, Beverly responded, "Do you have a beer cart out there?"

During the round of golf, there were things Jill told her she certainly had not been aware of until this day. She knew she had suffered a great deal at the loss of her parents and the possible scandal that could have erupted when her father died. Yes, she had known about the love of her college years, but this was the first time she knew who the individual was. For Beverly to be shocked was unusual; for her to be as shocked as she was, was only second to the night the young state trooper had to inform her that her husband had died at the scene of the accident. At one point, Beverly looked at Jill as though she had never seen her before. In fact that was the truth—Beverly had never seen Jill in this light and it stupefied her. "Jill, I really don't know what to say," was all that kept coming out of her mouth. Yet Jill, dear sweet Jill, seemed to have gained the strength of some Herculean god and was ready to take on the Howards, the state, and the world. As the two of them went through the motions of playing a golf game, the serious playing of a game was in their conversation. Beverly was beginning to understand why some of her customers had made remarks about their husbands telling them that a lot of deals were closed on the golf course. The irony of the day was that Diane had called and cancelled. All of the events that had been set in motion surrounded the very individual that had no idea what had occurred. Jill really didn't care who, what, where, or when caused her to feel the way she felt. She knew Evelyn Howard had gone too far, and Jill was going to see all of this to the end, whatever the end may be. She had told Beverly not to count on her at the shop the next couple of days because she had some calls to make and some appointments to keep. Uncharacteristically, Beverly had nodded and said she understood. What Jill failed to realize at the moment was Beverly was nearly in shock. If someone had taken the woman's blood pressure, they would have phoned 911. None of this mattered to Jill—not Beverly's reaction, not Evelyn's conniption, not anything except … except … what? She was questioning herself as she was driving back to her house.

"May I please speak with Ms. Joanna Barnes?"

"I'm sorry; she is in court this afternoon. Would you like to leave her a message?" came the cool, efficient response from the voice on the other end of the phone.

"Yes. I most certainly want to leave her a message. Please tell her to call Mrs. Jill Swanson as soon as possible. No matter what time of day or night. Is that understood?"

"Yes, ma'am. She will get your message as soon as she returns to the office."

It was one-thirty in the afternoon, and it was time for a glass of wine. She had a lot of questions to ask and a lot of information to give, and she wasn't going to do all of this without a glass of wine.

The music was soft and slow. She felt the strength of his shoulder where she was resting her head. They were dancing or floating, she wasn't sure which it was. He was as handsome as she had ever seen him, and she knew she was elegantly dressed. She had never felt so lovely and could not remember being this peaceful in all of her life. She wanted this to go on forever. Then the noise, this loud harsh noise, it kept intruding and growing louder. Would it never stop? Her eyes flew open, and then the light, such bright light. It was the phone, only the phone. As she reached for the receiver, she realized how she hated this instrument and all the intrusions it had made on her life.

"Hello," she said through her fog.

"Hello. Jill?" It was Joanna.

"Yes," she managed, still trying to bring herself out of her dream state.

"I'm sorry. Kris seemed to think you sounded urgent. So you are the first one I've called since I got back from court. Are you all right?"

Am I all right? she was thinking to herself. *Have I been all right for the last thirty-five years?* "Yes. Oh, yes. I'm all right. I need to talk to you and I need to get some direction from you. For both of us, I think the sooner we have a discussion, the better it may be."

"I see. Is this about the same conversation we had while we attended golf school?"

"Yes. That would be the one."

"Do you want to stop in at the office or would you like this to be less formal? I could, eh, hang on a second." Jill listened to some canned soft-listening music for a few seconds, and then she heard Joanna's voice wanting to know if this evening around seven would be good for her to drop by.

"That will be perfect. How do shish-kabobs sound for dinner?"

"I'm looking forward to it; see you at seven."

There had been very few times in Jill's life she remembered being angry. She watched Beverly deal with anger in a constructive way. In fact, Jill had watched Beverly become irritated, agitated, even hot under the collar, and she watched her use this as a negotiating tool. Once a young, rather burly truck driver had dared to block one of Beverly's elderly customer's cars. Beverly told him how inconsiderate, rude, and even hurtful he had been simply by parking his truck in a place that would not allow her customer to leave the parking lot. She had thought this man was going to break down and cry. Real anger? Jill wondered if Beverly had ever experienced that emotion. For Jill it was different. One of the reasons Beverly depended on Jill was her ability to never seem irritated, agitated, and certainly never angry. If a vendor failed to deliver the goods when promised, or a customer was becoming especially unreasonable, Beverly would call Jill over and ask if she would please talk to this person. No matter what the circumstance, she found she could deal with the party and remain calm, asking appropriate questions, making reasonable requests, and generally taking care of the crisis with everyone involved thinking it had been a win-win situation. She knew she was a problem solver. Emotion never seemed to enter into the solving of a problem. It never occurred to her that this might be an unusual quality; it was just her personality. Now, right this minute, she knew she had entered into an emotional minefield. She had already taken the first steps, and she didn't care where the rest of the steps took her. She felt no anxiety, no fear, not anything, except maybe a sense of justice needing to be done. This was one of the first—if not the very first—times she felt like she had to stand up for what was right and she may have to fight like she had never fought before. She had stood firm during the annexation attempt, but there had been little if any emotion on her part. This time it was different, very, very, different. Too many people had been hurt, used, discarded, and, yes, abused by Evelyn Howard. In Jill's mind, it had become very clear. If you knew what was wrong and you didn't stand up to that wrong, then you became a part of the wrong! It all seemed to be such a simple truth at the moment; why couldn't others see this as well? In her heart of hearts, she knew there was something more to all of this. If she proclaimed herself to be a woman of such honesty and integrity, then she had to be honest with herself. That might be the very hardest thing she was going to have to do.

Joanna was glad to hear Jill agree to the meeting at her house. Joanna loved visiting with Jill; not only did she make her guests feel "down home" comfortable, the very atmosphere could relax the tensest of the tense. Jill's property had been a twenty-acre horse farm out in the country. The town had grown up around the property. Developers had bought farmland, subdivided it, built large single-family homes, and sold each site for five—and in some cases, ten—times what the land and the building of the home had cost. Jill and her husband turned down many offers to buy their property, some of which could have made the two of them very wealthy. They continued to run the horse farm with one of their projects being a riding academy for autistic children. Upon the death of Jill's husband and the annexation fight that soon followed, Jill determined she could not continue operating the academy. She worked with a friend who had another farm farther north of town and would offer the same opportunity Jill and her husband had given these children. The old farmhouse stood nearly at the center of the property. Jill and her late husband had renovated the house. They had brought in modern plumbing and wiring, added a swimming pool, and turned the summer kitchen into a family room with a huge fireplace and a large bank of windows that allowed for a view of the rose garden, pool, and the stone and cedar work on the outside of the horse stables. Jill had a great sense of interior design so that all of the large high-ceiling rooms kept the feel of a working farmhouse with an elegant touch of style. As she was driving up the lane, the tall river birch trees that lined the path were slightly swaying in the early-evening breeze. Joanna wondered if there could be any more beautiful place on the planet. Jill had told everyone she was not going to make any major decisions about the selling of the property until she had been widowed for at least a year. That had been five years ago. By her own admission, she couldn't bring herself to part with a property that had brought her so much joy and up until this moment had brought her so much peace. Jill had just decanted the cabernet when she heard the noise of the gravel crunching under the wheels of Joanna's car. She pulled two glasses from the cabinet, checked the temperature of the grill, and headed to the door to greet her guest. It would have been obvious to the most casual observer that Joanna had just come from her office. She was shifting a briefcase, a pocketbook, and her suit jacket from one arm to the other as she reached in the backseat of the sedan to retrieve a bagged bottle of wine. Jill watched this juggling act all the while Joanna was trying to stay steady in her three-inch heels. By the time she had reached the door, Jill had broken from a wide grin to laughter. "Having to work a little just to make it to the door—that isn't a good sign."

Joanna's response was quick and firm. "I have to get these shoes off—where can I put them?" With that, both women gave each other a quick hug, Jill thanked her for the wine, the shoes came off, the blouse was pulled from the skirt waistband, and the two were starting to sip on the newly decanted wine as they took their places at the side of the pool and enjoyed the wonderful evening. The meal was simple, and Joanna had proclaimed it to be fantastic. She had become visibly relaxed. Her bare feet were stretched out in front of her—the pantyhose had come off shortly after the shoes—her blouse was hanging lose while she held her wine glass in one hand and reached for a chocolate mint with the other. "Jill. If I lived here I wouldn't be seen anywhere except the grocery store, and then only there once a month. I don't know how you manage to leave this place."

"A few years ago, I didn't leave this place for days on end. One day Beverly came out here, looked around, and told me this may be one of the most beautiful caves she had seen anyone hide in, but it nevertheless was a cave."

"Is that when she offered you a job?"

"That's one way of putting it," Jill said as she gave Joanna a look of amusement. "She told me if I didn't get my lazy ass in town to help her with her shop, she would be sending the guys in the white jackets out to visit." At this, both of the women laughed and lifted their glasses in salute to Beverly.

"Everyone should have a friend like Beverly," Joanna said, and then took a sip from her glass. As she set her glass back on the table, she looked directly at Jill and simply asked, "Are you sure you want to do this?"

The moment Joanna asked the question, Jill had the answer. "Oh, yes. I'm ready." There would be many days ahead that the answer she had just given would haunt Jill. She was as unsure about this as she had been about anything in her entire life, yet at that very moment, she felt sure she knew what she was about to undertake. There were a lot of things that had been revealed at the golf school. Information that had stunned, frightened, and angered Jill. It had taken her weeks to sort through her emotions, her sense of ... what? Duty? Responsibility? Anger? Justice? What was she sorting out? Oh, how she wished she knew.

The first revelation was that Joanna knew exactly who had made the phone calls. It had been an employee of the Howards. Even before the phone call had been made from the state house, the police were all but certain they had their man. When the state house call came through it was conclusive, conclusive in the sense they knew who and where and of course when the call had been made. Joanna was the one that put a stop to that part of the investigation. In her own words, she wanted to go cautiously. "Don't mess things up for me, boys. I want the big fish, not some little bait." With the help of a discerning judge and a savvy police chief, everyone held off. She had no idea what she had requested until months later. Then, to the surprise of all, the call came from the FBI. It seemed they had been doing a little investigating on their own. Words were bantered about like "fraud," "criminal mischief," and the most condemning possible accusation for the senator and his wife was "kickback" for a government contract. This is when Joanna had to take Beverly and Jill into her confidence. It came as a surprise to all of them when Diane and her husband started playing a role in this drama. Neither Beverly nor Jill had a clue the partner of the Stoners would be an "individual of interest" in the FBI investigation. Beverly had already asked Diane to be a part of the nine-hole golf league, and Jill had agreed to join the group as well. When Joanna discovered this, she insisted she join and at least be a support for the two ladies, and maybe a help in finding out what role, if any, Diane and her husband played in all of this. The golf school had been a terrible experience for Jill. First, she hadn't played golf since college, had never been good at the game, and now the school had been somewhat of a ploy to get out of Diane what she knew about all of this, this ... whatever it was. The evening of the pizza party had been particularly upsetting for Jill. There was Diane looking forward to an evening with friends, and little did she know she was going to be examined, cross-examined, dissected, and lord only knew what else. She had argued with both Beverly and Joanna before that evening about how unfair all of this seemed to her, and why couldn't they just be forthright and let Diane know what was really going on? After what seemed to be many hours of endless discussion, it was decided the best course of action would be the course Joanna had outlined weeks before. As nice as Diane seemed to be, they needed to be as certain as was humanly possible that she could be trusted. Jill agreed to this after it was pointed out to her that Joanna had already suffered some emotional if not possible physical consequences for fighting the Howards. There could be no argument there, and so Jill had been a part of the night. Looking back on all of this, she was glad the other two had persuaded her to participate in this event. She did not like and would never like not being up-front with everyone about everything, but she saw at this point how important it had been that they move cautiously. It didn't take any of them very long to see Diane was at a loss as to what was going on around her, her husband, their business partner, and their business. It also didn't take very long for all of them to see Diane was as perplexed, upset, and ready to do whatever she needed to do to get this thing out in the open. There had been few times in Jill's life when she had felt such an enormous surge of relief. The night Diane had stepped forward and let them know she would do whatever it took to help them solve this investigation was one of those times. Perhaps that was one of the reasons Jill felt the way she did when she answered Joanna. *Yes. I am ready.* On an intellectual level she was ready; on an emotional level even she didn't know how unready she was. Jill had told Joanna she would call her as soon as she had made an appointment with the senator. After a few glasses of wine, Jill had felt very confident she would be able to get the appointment within the next few days. After all, the assembly was not in session, and other than some committee meetings, how busy could a state senator be? Joanna had watched Jill with growing uncertainty as their conversation continued. Again, she questioned Jill about her ability to handle this meeting. Again, Jill told her unequivocally that she would have absolutely no problem in meeting with Senator Howard.

The next morning, Jill awoke to another beautiful day. Sometimes she wondered how she could have been so blessed. The sun was shining on the sunflowers behind her house, birds were flitting about the feeder, and the sky was a clear blue with white fluffy clouds floating slightly to the east. She had just sat down with her first cup of coffee when the phone rang. Somehow, she knew it would be Beverly. Not to disappoint her, it was.

"Okay. So how did things go last night with Joanna?" came Beverly's voice, no introduction needed, never one to expect that she needed to give one. "Does she want you to find out what the senator knows? Does she think the Senator is a part of all of this? What does she think?" Jill could have laughed if it were not for the fact that all of this had become very serious. She knew Beverly had not taken any of it lightly.

"Good morning to you," Jill responded with a smile in her voice. "No. No. And I'm not sure."

"What are you talking about?" came Beverly's slightly agitated voice.

"I'm simply answering your questions in the order they were asked."

"Don't be such a smartass, I'm concerned about you. I'm not sure this is a good idea. I mean, you're going to be the damn mouse that's supposed to bell the cat! Come on, Jill, give me some credit for being worried about you."

Jill knew she would never be able to explain to her friend how much it meant to her to have her care so much. She often wished she could express her gratitude, but maybe with someone like Beverly, they would never understand how deeply they had affected another human. With those thoughts running through Jill's mind she responded, "Beverly. You will probably never understand how much your concern means to me. If it weren't for you and Joanna, I really don't know where I would be today. I sit here this morning knowing if it had not been for you, I would probably be stuck in some cookie-cutter condo in the center of town trying to figure out what happened. So please, please don't think I take any of your concern for me lightly. Frankly, Beverly, I need to do this for me. Maybe it will benefit others, but I am acting in a selfish manner. I tell you, I am doing this for me."

Nothing was said between the two women for a few seconds, and then Beverly came back in typical Beverly fashion. "Good. I'm glad to see you're finally doing something for yourself."

The next few hours, Jill spent following her daily routine. She read the morning paper, or pretended to read the morning paper. Fed Lebo, her soft-coated wheaten terrier, along with her two cats, Mr. Furls and Honey Girl, and then began her usual beauty routine. It never ceased to amaze Jill how long this routine was starting to take. She hadn't stopped to add up the hours, but she was sure for each year of her life she had added five to fifteen minutes per year to her routine. If she lived to be ninety years old, she would have to spend the entire daylight time getting ready to go to bed! "What a depressing thought," she said out loud as she exited her shower. She was reaching for her comb when the phone rang. Wrapping a towel around herself, she hurried to pick up the ringing phone. Just as she was about to pick up the receiver, she stopped. A strong feeling swept over her, a feeling of caution, dread, fear—she wasn't sure why, but she knew she was not going to answer the phone. She stared at the thing for a few more seconds, and then it stopped ringing. Why was she being so silly? It was probably Beverly wanting to tell her something else. She decided she would call her after she had finished getting dressed. She knew she was postponing the inevitable as she dressed in a soft white blouse and comfortable olive-colored linen slacks. She must phone Beverly before she did anything else. Then she would make the call to the senator's office. Jana answered the phone, and when Jill asked if Beverly had called, Jana seemed somewhat surprised and told her Beverly had been in the shop earlier but would not be back for the rest of the day. Did Jill want to get in touch with her? "Oh, no," Jill had replied. "It isn't anything that's important. I'll get in touch with her sometime tomorrow."

Resting the phone in its cradle, Jill went to the pad where Joanna had written the senator's office number down the night before. Joanna's instructions from last night kept running through her head. *Make sure his receptionist knows you're an old friend of his. Don't be the least bit hesitant; drive through the crap they'll try and throw at you. They'll want to know what part of the county you're from, are you sure this is your area senator, did you call the senate switchboard, etc., etc. Don't let anyone engage you in a conversation that takes you away from making an appointment. Stay the course.* "The course being?" Jill had asked with a raised eyebrow.

"The course is to get as much information as you know how to get out of the good man without giving him a hint of what you're up to," Joanna had explained to her for the hundredth time.

"I know, I know," Jill had said, all the while wondering if she really, really knew about anything. All of this was being replayed in Jill's mind when the phone rang. "My, my," Jill said to Mr. Furls, who was head-butting her leg. "Aren't we popular today?" As soon as she heard the voice, she knew she had frozen. She couldn't recount for Joanna what the next words had been out of her mouth, other than she had agreed to attend the fund-raiser for the senator at the Matthews' house next Wednesday evening. Evelyn Howard had wanted to call her personally, rather than have some poor volunteer bungle the invitation. She could not understand why Jill had not received something in the mail by now, and oh how sorry she was, but she knew when she hadn't received an RSVP there had to be something amiss. Oh, yes, Diane and her husband were going to be there; did she know Diane and her husband were partners with the Matthews'? And wouldn't it be fun to see some of the league ladies outside of the golf course? Ha, ha. And oh how happy she was to know that she could attend. End of conversation. Jill thought she remembered saying good-bye, but then again, she couldn't be sure. All of this had been reported to Joanna as soon as she hung up from talking to—or rather listening to—Evelyn Howard. Joanna thought this would be a better approach than calling the senator's office. After all, they were trying to raise money for his next campaign, and how difficult would it be for Jill to simply request an audience with the senator? Joanna thought the senator would be very receptive to the idea. *Indeed,* Jill thought as she hung up the phone. The senator might very well turn her request down without a bat of an eye. She didn't know, she simply didn't know. She would do what she said she would do, no matter what it was going to cost her. Maybe her mother had been a backwoods hillbilly, but those backwoods hillbillies kept their word, and she was not going to let the tradition down!

It seemed like a month or maybe a year had gone by before the cocktail party. Jill could not remember being this obsessed with what she was going to wear, how she was going to fix her hair, and what time she should arrive. Beverly had been front and center with the clothes. She had chosen for Jill a soft, flowing dress in a burnt-orange shade. The color accented the color of Jill's dark eyes and olive complexion. Jill had been blessed with a slim figure. Even as the years were added to her age, this didn't seem to change. Beverly had told her she was in about 1 percent of the female population when it came to aging and adding weight. "You don't know how frigging lucky you are to not have to worry about what you eat," Beverly had remarked to her on more than one occasion. As for the hair, again it was Beverly who had a friend who was a master at cut and color, and how glad Beverly was that Jill finally wanted to do something with her mop. That is exactly what Beverly had called her hair, a mop. Jill had never bothered with her hair; after she and her husband had started the operation of the horse farm, there really hadn't been enough time to run into town for a do. She had worn it in a ponytail or pulled back into a bun. The color was whatever color nature had determined it to be. Recently it had looked like the proverbial salt and pepper, with a little more salt than pepper. As she looked at herself, she decided it looked mousy, and she would not go to this cocktail party looking mousy. So off to the master hairdresser she would go, and hopefully he would not make her look like some old woman trying to recapture her youth, or worse yet, some woman that had just doused her hair with black shoe polish. When David whirled her around to face the mirror, she had actually gasped. She looked like she had dropped ten years from her life, and she looked like a woman that was making the most of her age—and right at the moment, her age looked damn good!

She had to stop by the shop to pick up her dress. Beverly had already been called by Mr. David and told what a stunning success she was. Of course, Beverly went overboard with "I can't believe this is you," and "why in the world have you not done something like this before," and another "I can't believe this is you," until Jill was becoming uncomfortable just listening to her friend.

"I really need to get out of here if I'm to make this grand entrance to this grand party," Jill said as she picked up the dress and made her way to the door.

"Jill," Beverly said as she dropped the shop-owner tone and picked up the friend tone. "I want you to be on your guard. Very much on your guard." With that statement, Beverly walked over and gave her a hug, stepped back, and said, "You are absolutely beautiful."

Diane had called her a few days before, wanting to know if she would like to have them pick her up for the fund-raiser. Jill quickly accepted the invitation. She had learned to go to many functions solo, but this event was different, and knowing Diane and Steve were escorting her there was a comfort. Since she had a new hair do and a new dress, she decided to go all out and have a makeup artist bring her up-to-date with cosmetics. Never being one to follow new trends, she did, however, have to admit that a little eye makeup and color to even out her complexion wouldn't hurt. As she finished the final touch to her eye shadow, she stepped back to view the final product. She stared into the mirror for a long view of a woman she had not seen in years. The color of the dress, the light auburn shade Mr. David had added to her hair, and now the shade of the eye shadow gave her an exotic Mediterranean appearance. When the doorbell rang, Lebo began dancing around with the same excitement he always displayed for visitors. Jill had often remarked to her friends that Lebo would never harm anyone breaking into the house, he would just lick them to death. She could make this remark with the full confidence he would not tolerate anyone trying to get in the house without her permission. He had proven this to her on more than one occasion. She didn't know how he knew when someone was welcome and someone was viewed with suspicion, but he knew, oh boy, did he know. A young magazine salesman discovered Lebo's defensive side. Jill was just happy to see there had been no teeth marks left after Lebo grabbed the overconfident young man by his pant leg. Tonight was different; as soon as she opened the door, he was doing his wheaten terrier dance. Try as she might to get him to stop the behavior, he simply could not restrain himself. "Hey, big guy," Steve said as he stooped to take a closer look at Lebo. "He's a handsome dude."

With that remark he jumped, flipped, licked, and finally landed on all four feet just long enough to try it all over again. "Lebo! Lebo! Stop this right now!" Jill seldom raised her voice, and when she did, it got everyone's attention. Mr. Furls and Honey Girl came around the corner to see what was going on. Lebo hung his head ever so slightly, and Steve stood awaiting further instructions. She looked at all of her four-footed friends, glanced at Steve, and wished she had a picture of the moment because she was sure they were wearing the same expression. The giggle started, and then erupted to a full deep laugh that turned into near-hysterics. Steve started laughing, and by the time they had made it to the car, Diane was beginning to wonder what had gone on in there.

She was about to ask the question when she looked at Jill, and all she could say was, "You are absolutely stunning." Jill was struck by the sincerity with which the compliment had been given. She had been very moved by it, and when she thanked Diane, both women knew each of their statements had come from their hearts. On the way to the Matthews' the entire incident involving Lebo's greeting to Steve had to be told, the reaction of Mr. Furls and Honey Girl and the look of fear on Steve's face. "Oh, I wouldn't say I was frightened; 'terrified' might be a better word." Of course, all three were laughing, but this time Jill thought the word "terrified" would better describe how she felt that very second.

When they turned down the street to the Matthews' house, it became apparent that this was not going to be some small fund-raiser for the senator. Young men in white jackets and dark slacks were standing at the front of the house to valet park all cars. There was an older gentlemen uniformed in a dark red waistcoat, white shirt, black tie, and top hat. "Oh, brother," were the first words anyone spoke, and they had come from Diane.

"Oh, brother is right." This time it came from Jill. Both women looked at Steve and watched is mouth slowly fall open. He said nothing.

"Good evening, madam," the first young man said to Diane as he reached for her hand to help her from the car. The same was happening to Jill from the backseat, and another young man was addressing Steve and handing him a claim check and reaching for the car keys. By the time the three of them had gotten by Mr. Top Hat, were handed a flute of champagne, and were led to a large open living room, it wasn't just Steve's mouth that had fallen open.

"I knew Phil wanted to have a fund-raiser for the senator, and I know he's had them before, but I never dreamed he would pop for this kind of production. Do you think the man has lost his mind?" The last remark was more of a statement than a question, and Steve had directed most of the comment to Diane.

"My dear. I don't know what's going on but this isn't the time or the place to discuss the issue. Let's just pretend we're having a good time, make some excuse on why we have to leave, and get the hell out of here as soon as good manners will allow."

"I'll drink to that," came the retort from Jill. She had not wanted to attend this function in the first place; she didn't want to deal with all the pretense of all the people in the room who only wanted to see and be seen so they could report the affair to all their less-fortunate friends and neighbors. She certainly did not want to deal with Evelyn

Howard, much less her senatorial husband. She was about to tell Diane she was going to find a small out-of-the-way corner, if there was such a thing in this spacious mausoleum, and when she and Steve were ready to leave just come and pick her up from her corner. Yes. That was what she was about to do when she heard him speak her name. As she turned to face him, she fell into a whirlpool of emotions. Maybe it wasn't just Phil Matthews that had lost his mind; maybe she would be taken away in the same Patty Wagon. "Good evening, Senator." She had a voice and she had just spoken—remarkable, absolutely remarkable, were her thoughts as she met his gaze.

"Jill," was the only thing he said as he stared at her, not moving his eyes from hers, not showing any kind of emotion, just staring at her until she began to feel uneasy. Try as she might to get her voice back, she found herself doing the same thing. How long they both stood there and looked at each other, she didn't have a clue. Then a loud, raucous voice assaulted her senses and she realized the owner of this voice was none other than Phil Matthews. His comments were being directed to her. Pulling herself from her self-imposed trance, she began to understand some of what he was saying. By his speech pattern along with a slightly disheveled look, it appeared to Jill that Phil had opened the bar up earlier in the day. He was talking about the good old days, and how come all the men he knew were getting gray but none of the women were. Ha, ha. Where had the time gone? What do think this next generation is going to do? Why they've been given everything. It didn't take Jill long to remember all the things she had never liked about Phil Matthews. She was looking for an escape route when the next nightmare walked up to their group. None other than Evelyn Howard. She was smiling from ear to ear, flashing all of her lovely jewels and moving with the grace of a wounded rhino. How this woman managed to charm half the people in this town, Jill would never understand. So as Evelyn came into their circle, she gave Jill a quick hug and an "I am so glad you were able to make it," and an "I guess you feel like it's old home week." The last comment was said with as much sarcasm as one could lend to a remark and not have the listener call foul.

"Well. I wouldn't call it old home week, I would call it a fund-raiser. That is why everyone is attending this evening, isn't it?" Jill lifted her glass as she eyed Evelyn, whose smile had suddenly frozen on her face. For a fleeting second, she saw the senator's mouth turn up in a slight grin, and then return to a straight line. Phil Matthews reassured Jill that being at the fund-raiser was a most important event, because the senator was the only man for the job, etc., etc., and we need to keep good people in office, etc., etc., and on and on he droned to the chagrin of anyone within earshot of the man. Jill thought Evelyn looked a little uneasy when Phil remarked in his dialog that the senator's reelection would do a lot of economic good for their town, and then with a wink and a weak laugh, he added he was looking forward to his personal economic growth. Jill watched Evelyn shift her stance, look at the floor, and glance in Phil's direction with a chilling glare. That same moment she watched the senator's brow furrow with a questioning expression. All of this had happened so suddenly, Jill would later question herself about the entire incident.

Evelyn began to laugh as though she had never heard a funnier joke. "Oh, Phil, what would we do without supporters like yourself? You're such a treasure." Then she put her arm through his and asked if she could see this new artwork that Karen had told her about.

"Of course. I must admit I got it for a steal. I just told the man that fifteen hundred dollars was all I would pay and he could take it or leave it. Well, when he saw the deal might fall through, he decided it might be worth getting that fifteen hundred dollars rather than sit with the piece staring him in the face on a cold winter's night." Jill could have sworn that the longer Phil talked, the more puffed-up he looked. If a person didn't know these two, they would think that Evelyn had never heard a more fascinating story.

Jill hadn't realized it, but as they both were turning to leave, she had started shaking her head. The senator looked at her, raised his glass, and just as he was about to take a sip said, "It's hard to believe, isn't it?" And with that statement, he left her side as suddenly as he had appeared. She watched him make his way through the growing crowd. Smiling, shaking hands, giving someone an extra squeeze on the shoulder. No one, love him or hate him, could deny that this man had the charisma. He was able to charm male and female, rich and poor, and do it with as much sincerity as he felt at any given moment. She couldn't help herself; she was entranced. Some Mata Hara she was going to make!

She hadn't been able to ask him if she could make an appointment to see him in the next few weeks, and she seemed to remember that had been her goal for this evening. Out of nowhere, a sadness enveloped her. She wasn't easily given to tears, but the scene she had just witnessed had moved her to tears. What in the world was the matter with her, she kept repeating to herself. She was the one that was always in control, knew what to do in any given situation, and now, now, she had never felt so out of control in her life.

"You okay?" Diane asked as she approached Jill. "What's going on? I saw the Bermuda triangle surround you. Has Evelyn done something to hurt you?" Jill knew by the expression on her face that she was concerned and would do whatever she thought she needed to do to correct the situation.

"Oh, no. No. I'll be fine, and no, Evelyn didn't do anything that isn't ordinary for Evelyn. It's just … just … oh, I don't know, Diane, maybe it's just menopause."

Diane didn't believe for one moment Jill had tears in her eyes because of some female malady. She also knew there were times it was best to let the person you were concerned about talk to you when they were ready. She was getting to know Jill, and she really liked her. She knew gaining the trust of another individual took time, and there simply hadn't been enough time for the two of them. So the two agreed to find Steve and head for the car and a nice little restaurant for some pasta. None of them wanted to stay any longer than necessary. They were making their way past the library when Diane let out an "uh-oh." Jill followed Diane's gaze and saw Steve was engaged in a rather animated conversation with a man she did not recognize. Diane looked disturbed and was making her way in to the room and up to the two men. Realizing there wasn't much else for her to do, Jill followed Diane. Steve's entire demeanor had changed from earlier in the evening. Whatever was going on was not to the liking of Steve. The other man seemed as disturbed but somehow in a different manner. As they approached, Steve began to relax his tone of voice but his body language remained tense.

Diane was the first to speak. "Good evening, Sam. So good to see you. I haven't seen your wife yet this evening, is she here?" Jill began to see Diane in a new light. It had been a polite question on the surface, but underneath there had been a probing for information. "Oh, please excuse my poor manners," Diane continued. "Sam, I would like for you to meet Jill Swanson. Jill, this is Sam Anderson."

After the how do you dos and the so glad to meet yous were exchanged, there was an uncomfortable lull in conversation until Steve brought it to an end. Looking at both of the women, he asked if they were ready to leave for their next function. "Oh, yes. I guess it is getting to be that time," replied Diane, and with that, turned toward Sam, extended her hand, and told him how nice it was to see him again. This is when Jill nodded, smiled, and wondered if she had been written into a scene from the town's Little Theater. It looked like they were going to make a clean break for it until Karen appeared. "Oh, please don't tell me you're leaving so soon; we were hoping you would be able to stay and have a cocktail with Phil, Evelyn, and Jim. I don't believe we've met," Karen said as she extended her hand to Jill. "I know you had a lovely horse farm, and *still* have a lovely place but now it has no horses." Jill could tell by the tone of her voice and the look of interest that these were not flip remarks made by the hostess of the event. She confirmed for Karen indeed she had sold her stock to another farm with the assurance they would continue the work she and her husband had started. She found herself talking about the riding academy they had begun and what wonderful results they had seen from the interaction between the children and the horses.

She couldn't recall how long she was engaged in conversation with Karen, but she became aware of the fact that Steve and Diane had accepted another glass of wine and were talking with another guest. Karen excused herself for a moment, telling all three of them to remain in the library until she returned. Like obedient children, they all three remained in the library. "Well, I guess our other obligation will have to wait," Diane said as she looked down in to her wine glass, decided there was in fact more wine inside, and took another sip.

"I know. I wanted to leave as well, but I think it might be a good idea to wait around for the senator to appear. I really have some questions I want to ask." Jill watched Diane give her husband a long, curious stare. She nodded and simply said, "Okay." Then she looked at

Jill and asked her if this would be all right, or did she need to get home? Jill assured both of them that she was fine with whatever occurred. This night had been set aside for this event, and whatever time it took, that was the time it would take. Karen returned, and after a few more minutes of small talk, was interrupted and excused herself once again and again with instructions for all of them to stay put so she could visit with them. The one question Karen had asked in passing was if Diane thought she would stick with golf. This last question was the one that lit Diane up like a Roman candle.

"Let me tell you. One minute I am never going to pick up one of those clubs again; the next, I'm ready for lessons, practice, the tour! It is the craziest game I have ever played in my life."

Karen really didn't understand this diatribe, so she smiled, and as she was leaving the room, there was another voice saying; "Golf. Golf. Did someone say golf?" The voice was unmistakably that of Patty. She burst into the library with a tad bit more flair than usual, and the usual flair was enough on any given day.

"Oh, Lord," groaned Diane. "Let the games begin."

"What? What?" Patty asked with a higher-pitched tone with each "what" followed by her infectious or annoying giggle, whatever mood you were in when she was around. Given all the odd things that seemed to be going on this evening, she actually was a breath of fresh air, for Jill and for Diane. Jill was watching Diane's reaction and remembered how put out Diane had seemed the first time they met. Now the two were bantering back and forth as though they had been bosom buddies for all of their lives. Jill saw what some of the league ladies talked about. This really was a close-knit group of women, no matter how diverse they were in any other area of their lives; this was a sorority, club, networking. Whatever it was, it was a good feeling at this moment for Patty, Diane, and Jill. "Has the queen passed by to give her your blessings?" Patty asked in a very loud, mocking tone.

"Patty," Jill began. "We are, after all, guests in the home of some people that are helping her husband raise money for his campaign. We should surely give her highness some respect." Diane could not believe the mocking tone Jill had just used. And the laughter was instant, real, and bonding. Yes. Diane thought later there was a bonding with three women that had barely known each other three months ago. Now because of a game, and because of the needs of each of them, three women in a room were knitting a relationship together that would last for their lifetimes.

"You know she's the biggest cheater in the club!"

"Patty. For shame. You shouldn't bring such things up on the night of her, uh, I mean her husband's fund-raiser," Jill countered, half-teasing, half-serious.

Patty's statement truly stunned Diane. "She cheats? She cheats at golf? You've got to be kidding. Doesn't she count her whiffs?"

"That's still a burr under your saddle, isn't it, my dear?" This time it was Patty giving Diane a barb.

"Yes. I still think that if you haven't hit the ball you shouldn't count the whiffs!" With the sheer emotion in her voice, both Jill and Patty let out hoots of laughter. "I still don't think it's funny. It's not funny." With the laughter still coming from the other two, she knew she had to give this issue up as a lost cause. "How does she cheat?" came a sincere inquiry from Diane.

"Oh, my dear," Patty began. "There are so many ways that a person can cheat at golf, and I'm relatively sure she has done it all. Let's see. There is the pencil way. You simply put down your golf club and pick up your pencil. Then there is the 'I need a better lie' way. If you don't like where your golf ball lies, you pick it up and find a better one. Then there is the 'I got a six' when you know damn good and well you got a seven. Oh, and my very favorite is the one where it is a 'gimme putt,' and the gimme is the length of a Celtics basketball player's body!"

Diane looked from Patty back to Jill and back to Patty again. "Why in the world would anyone want to cheat at golf?"

"Oh, my dear sweet child. You are an innocent after all." There was much more to this conversation Diane wanted to continue. Just as she was ready to ask Jill how they could be sure cheating really went on, all conversations in the room came to a halt. The queen and her court had just entered the room. "What a delightful evening this has been." Evelyn was addressing the room while turning slightly to Karen. "Karen. You and Phil have outdone yourselves. I know I will never attend another function that will be as eloquent or fun, and most importantly, we brought some great donations to the campaign fund." As Evelyn was beginning to bask in her own (in her mind) gracious statement, there came a loud noise from behind her. There was no doubt in anyone's mind—someone had just let out a huge belch. "Well. I guess the only thing that could top that reaction is for someone to cut a fart!" Everyone in the room laughed long and hard, with the exception of Evelyn Howard. Karen had tried to stop herself, but the more she attempted to find all of this offensive, the harder she laughed. As new information was gathered or was confessed, it turned out that Sam had cut lose with the belch and Phil had made the remark. Jill was watching Phil and could hear her own mother's voice say, "You can't make a silk purse out of a sow's ear." She looked at Karen and saw a sadness emanating from her light blue eyes; moving her eyes to the senator's face she saw the same depth of sadness reflect Karen's. The party continued for a few more hours. Diane and Patty had Karen cornered, telling her why she should take up golf. Steve and Phil were talking about something that appeared neither of them really wanted to discuss. Evelyn seemed intent on moving in tandem with the senator. Jill liked the position she held at the moment—she was an observer. An observer that had a job to do, and she had not yet completed her assignment. She was rolling the stem of her wine glass between her thumb and index finger, and without looking up from the stem she knew he was standing beside her. She stood very still, not sure she was breathing. He was so close she could smell his cologne and feel the warmth of his nearness. "Call me. We have to talk." Then as quickly as all of this had happened, it was over. The next thing she was aware of was Evelyn entering the room with another attempt at graciousness, thanking everyone for attending, their support, etc., etc. When she had finished with her speech, it was the senator's turn. He said very little, but what he said spoke volumes to Jill. She knew him well enough to know he was being tormented. In what ways? Who was tormenting him? Did she know him at all? Had the two of them become so different? She had no answers to her own questions; she knew her mission had been accomplished. She would be phoning his office the next morning and setting up an appointment.

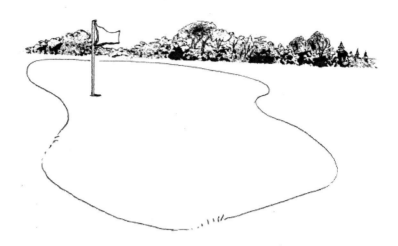

HOLE FIVE
Par Four

"Mrs. Flynn is here for her ten-thirty appointment." The sound of Joanna's receptionist startled her. She heard herself telling Vickie to make Mrs. Flynn comfortable and let the client know it would be a few more minutes.

"I will be with her as soon as possible," Joanna had all but barked into the phone.

"Yes, ma'am," came the wounded reply.

"Vickie. I'm sorry for being so sharp. I really, really, need to take this call. I hope you understand."

"Please. Think nothing of it. I'll take care of things out here."

Joanna was not someone that could be easily rattled; it had happened to her, but not often. She had to get in touch with Jacob as soon as possible, or her day would be a bust. She had already called his office and was told he would return her phone call as soon as he arrived; that had been over an hour ago. It was unusual for him not to return her call within minutes of calling, and it was unusual for him not to be in the office before the sun was up. Maybe she was overreacting. She just didn't like the way these developments were going. She had been on the phone with Jill for over an hour the night before. A lot of things weren't adding up. If she had thought for one minute that this was going to cause a hint of danger for these two women, and now possibly three, she wouldn't have involved any of them. It seemed a good idea to have Beverly and Jill get involved; they had both experienced firsthand what doing battle with the Howards could cost. Beverly was the one who discovered the connection with the Howards' and Stoners' business partner Phil Matthews. It had been a difficult decision for all three of them to invite Diane to the golf school, knowing they were going to have to reveal to her what they knew about their business partner and the Howards. Diane didn't seem at all hesitant to become involved once she knew the facts. Joanna thought in some ways she seemed relieved to know that she might be able to help. She certainly hadn't counted on this latest revelation. It was a good thing she could keep her emotions under control, because there were a few times when Jill was recounting events of the fund-raiser, she didn't know if she was going to laugh, cry, scream, or go into a catatonic state. She had convinced Jill not to make any contact with the senator, and if the senator tried to make contact with her, she was to let her know immediately. Jill had assured her she would make no contact and that absolutely she would be the first to know if an attempt were made by the senator to contact her. This promise of Jill's had calmed her for the moment, but she desperately needed to talk with Jacob. She wasn't going to wait another minute; she would call his office again, and if he still hadn't arrived, she was going to cancel her day's appointments and hunt the man down herself.

"Ms. Barnes, you have a call on line two." Joanna picked up the phone knowing she would be listening to Jacob's rich bass.

"Hey kid. Got a minute?" It was Beverly, all ready to discuss Tuesday's league play.

"Beverly. I am so sorry, but I'm up to my eyebrows in snakes and alligators right now, can I call you back?"

"Oh. I'm sorry. Not to worry. Call me when you get a chance."

"Beverly. Have you talked to Jill this morning?"

"No. In fact, she's the next one on my list to call. Why do you ask?"

"Let's just say I think the two of you need to talk about last night. I'll call you as soon as I'm able to get free. Okay?"

"Sure. Sure. Joanna? Is everything all right?"

"Beverly. At this point I really don't have an answer for you. In the meantime, if you or Jill or Diane need to get in touch with me, call. I'll make sure Vickie knows my every move, so you'll have no trouble reaching me. Okay?"

"You got it, babe. Talk to you later." Joanna knew Beverly well enough to know she would do exactly as she had told her to do. She was the most intuitive person she had ever met. She sensed things about people, surroundings, events, that others never felt or saw. This knowledge about Beverly was a comfort to Joanna. Why hadn't Jacob returned her phone call?

"I really don't have time for this, doc."

"Well, son, I don't think anyone wants to make time for something like this, but it's going to have to be taken care of or you won't have any time, period."

Jacob had spent most of the night in the emergency room, and now he was being told he was going to have to have his appendix taken out. The doctor was outlining the forthcoming procedure and how long he could expect to remain in the hospital. The good news, the doctor seemed proud to announce, was his appendix had not ruptured. "We're not going to wait around for that to happen. All the tests indicate you have one hot appendix," the doctor announced this as he was turning to leave the room. He dropped his hand from the door handle and looked at Jacob over the top of his glasses as he intently listened to what Jacob was telling him. "You don't have a lot of time. I'll send the nurse in with a phone, but make it fast. I'm going up to OR to start my scrub right now."

There was immediate surprise and concern from those in his office. One of his colleagues was going to pick up his mail, bring some personal belongings to him, and take care of any obligations that needed to be taken care of. He was told not to worry about his current assignment. If there needed to be another assigned to the case, they would be in contact with Joanna Barnes. He pushed the call cord for the nurse so he could keep his appointment with dreamland.

This day was not going well! She still had her first client of the day waiting. Her second attempt to reach Jacob had not been successful, and now she was being summoned to Judge Harrison's chambers. "Vickie. Please send Mrs. Flynn in. Has Denise gotten back from the courthouse?"

"No. I haven't heard anything from Ms. Sturgis. I'll have Mrs. Flynn come to your office. Do you want me to try and contact Ms. Sturgis?"

"No. Not right now. If she hasn't returned by the time my appointment with Mrs. Flynn is over, I may want you to do something then. Let me know as soon as she returns. Oh, yes. Would you please contact Judge Harrison's office and let them know that I'll be able to meet with him right after my appointment with Mrs. Flynn? Of course, that'll be close to noon, so just have them tell me when they want me there. Oh, yes. One more thing. I don't know what I'd do without you out there. Thanks."

She knew it wasn't Vickie's fault, or for that matter anyone's fault, for the way her day was going. She would face this day and all it had to bring. When she gave it some thought, what choice did she have? In the middle of her meeting with Mrs. Flynn, Vickie called to tell her a Mr. Wilson needed to speak with her immediately. Joanna could hear her heart hammering inside her head as she listened to Jacob's colleague tell her Jacob was in the county hospital and at that moment he was in surgery to remove a diseased appendix. She heard herself speaking with a calm, which belied everything she was feeling. Her client was fidgeting with the handle of her purse as she stared at an invisible spot on the carpet. When she hung up the phone, she was surprised to hear the next words out of her mouth. "Mrs. Flynn. This has been a very unusual morning for me. I have already kept you waiting. That is something that I rarely do to a client, especially a new client. I really would like to take your case, and I really think I would do a very good job for you. I will understand if you would like to dismiss me for what I'm about to request. I need to reschedule our appointment. A very dear friend of mine is undergoing surgery as we speak and I want to be there when he comes out of recovery." Joanna wasn't the least bit surprised to find Mrs. Flynn most accommodating; she assured Joanna she would reschedule with Vickie and she hoped her friend would recovery quickly.

Joanna didn't care if anything else in the day fell into place. She was driving across town to get to the hospital when it hit her. She knew Jacob was a special friend, they had gone to law school together, hung out with the same crowd, had stayed in contact for a short time after graduation, but because of their different pursuits and personal love interests had lost touch. As strange as it seemed, it was the Howards that caused their paths to cross each other's again. She realized she was fighting more than mere emotion as she drove through the stop-and-go traffic—she was fighting panic. "Oh Dear God. Please let him be all right," she mouthed as she pulled into a parking space in front of the hospital entrance.

Joanna hated hospitals; she hated the way they smelled, the sounds that echoed through the halls, and most of all the waiting. Any time she had to visit someone in a hospital, she had to always wait. That is exactly what she was doing this very minute. Waiting. Waiting. Waiting. She had been directed to the surgical waiting room as soon as she had arrived. That had been over two hours ago. She wanted to walk over to the volunteer at the desk and ask if Mr. White was in the recovery room. Under different circumstances, she wouldn't have hesitated, but the kind lady seemed to have a very difficult time understanding she was not the next of kin, it was unlikely he had listed her as a person to notify, and no she wasn't related to him at all, and yes that was correct she was just a close friend. All of this information had to be written down, confirmed by someone on the other end of the phone that the sweet little woman kept calling. After what seemed to be days and not minutes, she was given directions by this gentle volunteer to please take a seat. As soon as Mr. White was taken to the recovery room, she would be called. Then there was confirmation on the spelling of her name, and did she pronounce that Joann or did she want the "a" sounded? *Please sound the "a," because my name is Joanna, not Joann.* By the time she sat down she was exhausted. She was trying to concentrate on an article in *Newsweek* when she heard her name being called. She was about to get up when she realized there was a man smiling down at her.

"Are you Ms. Joanna Barnes?" he repeated.

"Yes. Yes. I'm Joanna Barnes." He held his hand out to her as he identified himself as Tim Burke, a colleague of Jacob's. She felt the tension in her spine begin to release. Knowing there was someone else that cared enough for Jacob to be here was a comfort to her. Their conversation was guarded, but she felt at ease while they exchanged information. The usual questions were asked. How long had she known Jacob? Where had they met? What did she do? After she answered the last question, she could see Mr. Burke visibly tense; he quickly recovered, yet she knew the last piece of information was something he hadn't expected. *This must be the one Jacob is working with on the case.* What Joanna didn't realize was that she visibly tensed as soon as she recognized who Mr. Burke was. Joanna discovered Tim and Jacob had known each other for over twelve years. They had met in undergraduate school, had lost contact for a few years, and then found themselves working for the same agency. "It's strange how life seems to bring us in and out of others' lives, isn't it?" Joanna was thinking out loud more than directing it as a question.

"I personally feel there is a purpose to that. I don't understand what the purpose is, but I do believe things happen for a reason."

Joanna seemed to agree with his statement by a slight nod of her head. She was about to expand on this thought process when they both heard their names being called. A woman standing beside the volunteer desk asked if they were friends of Jacob. They were taken into a small side room and told to wait until the surgeon came to give them his report. The lump in Joanna's throat was growing larger while her hands twisted the *Newsweek* she had confiscated from the waiting room.

"*Newsweek* isn't one of my favorite magazines, but it shouldn't have to die a death like that," Tim said with a wide grin spreading across his face. Joanna looked down at her hands and realized there were pieces of the magazine falling to the floor from the strength of her twisting grip. She was about to respond to Tim when the door flew open and in walked the surgeon.

"I'm so sorry. I'm so sorry," was all she seemed to able to say. Once the doctor had decided she wasn't going to become combative, hysterical, or faint, he handed her over to Tim and a nurse who just happened upon the scene. It was difficult trying to regain control of emotions you didn't suspect you had, much less lose all sense of propriety. *What was going on?* she kept asking herself as she continued to mumble "I'm so sorry." Tim had taken it upon himself to be the immediate caregiver. He had convinced her she needed something cold to drink, and by the way, when was the last meal she had eaten? Those were his words as he led her down the hall to a cafeteria where food and drink were going to be the next order of business. It had been a very long time since anyone had to tend to the likes of her. She was the one that did the tending, not the other way around. She found herself repeating, "I'm going to be all right," as much as she had been apologizing earlier.

"I don't think the doctor would have misled us about Jacob's recovery. In fact, I think our mutual friend has been damn lucky."

Joanna had to agree with the assessment. It seemed Jacob not only had a very infected appendix, which in the surgeon's words looked like a water balloon ready to pop, but a large section of his intestine had become inflamed.

"I can tell you, if he had waited another twenty-four hours, we would have been doing an autopsy and not surgery." That was the last Joanna remembered being cognizant of her surroundings. Jacob. Jacob. It had never crossed her mind that this man, this friend, this person who she had just assumed would remain a part of her life might not be there for her. What was wrong with her? What was going on here? She was a strong, confident woman who had to make her way in this world, and she knew she had done a damn good job of it. There weren't many people, much less women, that had to pull themselves up by their bootstraps and do it as well as she had done. She had grown up in a household with a functioning alcoholic for a father; her mother did everything she knew to do to keep her father from throwing one of his drunken fits. Looking back on her childhood, she wondered if this had been her mother's entire life goal, to keep her father from having fits, and protect her. She guessed she had been fortunate in the fact that her father had never been physically abusive to anyone in the family. Mental abuse was another matter. She remembered her mother cowering before him because she had forgotten to put his favorite coffee cup beside his plate. Her father had never said anything abusive to her, nor had he given her any affection. Sometimes, she thought that was the worst kind of abuse. Being ignored, tolerated, whatever it was her father had felt for her was never revealed. Now there were times she wished she had opened up a dialog with him, but by the time she would have had the courage to face all of this, he was gone. In high school she found although she was always on the honor roll, this didn't impress her classmates. In fact, in many ways this was a detriment. The popular girls ignored her, except to ask for assignments. Once she refused to share these, she was shunned by all of them. She never seemed to know what to say or how to act around any of the boys her age, so she remained quiet. It hadn't helped that she had always been one of the tallest in her class, taller than all the girls and most of the boys. These may have been a few of the reasons she had become an observer. She observed everything and everyone. She watched her parents interact with one another and began to see a pattern of behavior. She had also developed an ability to read people. She guessed this came from having to watch her father and prepare herself for whatever he was about to do. She didn't understand why her parents had stayed together. She was glad they did, because she didn't know how she and her mother would have managed without her father's financial support. As she grew older, she realized in large part that was why her mother had endured years of living the life she had lived. She watched her teachers. Some of them loved what they were doing, and it came through in every class they taught. Some seemed defeated, and that came through in every class they taught. There were a few that were in the classroom to draw a paycheck, and a couple of them were just angry people. She was never sure what they had been angry about, but they should have never made it to the classroom. Then, in her junior year, she had a teacher who turned her world inside out. Mr. Gettsinger. She had never seen such passion about a subject come from anyone. It was the United States government class, and his enthusiasm was contagious. She had remained an honor student thoughout her school years; part of the reason she did so well in school was because books brought her the escape and the company she needed. However, this class was unlike any she had ever experienced. Mr. Gettsinger brought government alive. He asked questions that made everyone, including Dale Marion, the slowest and goofiest kid in the class, think, not just a "let's see what can we talk about today think" but *think*, think. They talked about civil rights, abortion, child abuse, religion. Any subject that was having an effect on their lives or was being debated in a public forum, they discussed in his class. By the time she had finished her junior year, she had made up her mind. She was going to law school and she was going to the best one she could get into.

She had been home for fall break when she heard her mother answer the door. She was working on one of her term papers and had been vaguely aware of muffled voices coming from downstairs. A few minutes had gone by and the voices stopped. A short time later, she became aware of her mother standing in the doorway of her room. She was just staring at Joanna. "Mom. What is it? What's wrong?" It seemed as though her mother stood without saying a word for hours. When she finally spoke, it was in a monotone. Fear began to grip Joanna, a fear she hadn't felt before this time. As she listened to what her mother was saying, she didn't feel anything except her fear being replaced by concern. Concern for her mother. That was the night Joanna had become the caregiver and her mother had become the dependant. Her father had died doing what he loved to do the most. Drink. He had been visiting his favorite bar, ordered his favorite drink for the fourth time, taken a sip, sat the glass down, and slumped over. The autopsy showed he had a massive coronary. In the words of their family physician, "If his heart hadn't taken him out, his liver was going to do the job." Once it was determined he had left enough life insurance, and the company he had worked for had generous benefits for his survivors, much of the anxiety of everyday living was over for her mother. Joanna continued her education, but without having to work as many moonlight jobs. Her mother began to blossom into someone Joanna had never seen before. At first, Joanna was taken aback by the transformation. Then she became amused, and at some point, she wasn't sure she hadn't become a little jealous. This person Joanna called Mom had suddenly become aware of fashion, makeup, and, most disturbing of all, *men!* What was an intelligent, becoming-well-educated, freethinking young woman supposed to do with a mother like this? It was about this same time that she met Billy. He too was passionate. He was passionate about life, the human condition, you name it, he felt it, and would share his insightful thoughts on how to change the world. He mesmerized her with his ideas, intellect, and—she had to admit, if it were only to herself— his body. She had been aware of him the very first day of law class. He seemed so absorbed by the subject matter; more importantly to Joanna was he didn't seem to notice the superficial, over-made-up coeds. By the end of the first semester, she was convinced she had met her soul mate, whatever that meant. He was everything she had imagined a man to be. He was intelligent, passionate, sensitive, and oh yes, he did have that amazing body. It seemed only natural for her to sleep with him. He seemed to be surprised she had been a virgin; he actually began to act proud of the fact. She only knew this man was all she had ever hoped for or dreamed of. Then, as dreams have to end, so did this one. Looking back on all of it, she realized the age-old signs had been there; she was just to in love to see any of them. Months before, she had walked in on the two; he had started having to study later and later in the library. This didn't disturb her as much as puzzle her, because they had done their studying together. Then he became preoccupied; this had definitely been a warning sign she had chosen to ignore. One of the things she cherished most about her relationship with Billy was the hours they would spend talking. They were exchanging ideas on just about everything from Supreme Court decisions, the ills of society, the latest movies—you name it, they discussed it. Often these discussions would end with the two of them in each other's arms, extending their mental passions into their physical passions, leaving both of them exhausted and sated.

Then came that gorgeous fall afternoon. Her class had been cancelled, so she decided to stop at the small grocery and pick up some bread, wine, and cheese for a surprise picnic. She had splurged on a rather pricey bottle of wine and some delicious-looking grapes. She flew back to their apartment with growing anticipation of the afternoon surprise she had waiting for him. There had certainly been a surprise. Surprise was what he had waiting for her. She could live to be one hundred, and she would never be able to erase that scene from her mind. She was standing at the end of the bed, grocery bag in one arm, shoulder bag hanging from the other, mouth open, eyes wide. Someone kept saying "oh no." It wasn't her voice because she said nothing; she did nothing but stand there. She watched as the two of them hurried to get some clothing on. She stood there. He said something to her on the way out of the room. She didn't know what he had said. She didn't care. She remembered sitting in the apartment with the grocery bag at her feet, and her handbag draped loosely over the arm of the chair she was sitting in. It was dark outside. When she stood up, she knew what she was going to do, and she did it. Everything that he owned was in the apartment. Big mistake. It took her a few hours, but all of it was carted to the dumpster in the parking lot. She threw the can of charcoal starting fluid on top of his belongings, tossed the match on the pile, walked into the apartment, and called the fire department. She sat at the window and watched until it was all over. He had made one attempt to contact her about his things. A mutual friend had told him he didn't think it would be a good idea to bother Joanna about getting his "things." This friend had also told him what she had done, and if he were as smart a man as he seemed to be, he would leave her alone. That friend had been Jacob. Looking back on all of it, she realized that Jacob had been the only beacon in this tumultuous storm. As she had done all of her life, she returned to the comfort of books.

Jacob. Jacob. Please be all right. This silent mantra kept running through her mind as Tim tried to engage her in conversation. He had taken her to the hospital cafeteria, made her get a tray of food, and insisted she eat what was in front of her. She knew by the concerned look on his face that he would not leave her side until he was satisfied that she would be able to make it on her own. "So. I understand you two were in law school together." *Law school. Oh, no. What does this man know about what happened in law school?* Joanna was mentally near a full-blown panic attack. Would this day ever end? She was screaming inside.

In typical Joanna style, she heard herself give an appropriate response. "Yes. We met in law school. We even double-dated a few times."

"So. You must have known Phyllis?"

Without missing a beat she turned the question back on Tim. "So. *You* knew Phyllis?"

This woman is a sharp cookie, Tim thought as he gave Joanna a quick smile and answered her question. "Oh, yes. I most certainly knew Phyllis."

They exchanged a knowing look, and the beginning of a bond that neither of them knew at the time would become a strong lifeline for each of them and for the people they cared about.

"I knew the first time that I met her that she was no good for Jacob," Tim continued.

"Really?" Joanna responded. "Why? How did you know this?" Her question had come straight from the heart. There had been times that she had the same thoughts about these two, but she wasn't sure she had ever expressed those thoughts to anyone. Now, here was a man that she had met not more than two hours ago, and he was telling her that Phyllis had been no good for Jacob. Phyllis had been sympathetic toward her after her breakup with Billy. At the time, she felt some kinship for her. Then, either because of her own emotional state or her sensitivity to male/female relationships, she saw a dynamic between the two that was out of balance. It certainly was no surprise when the wedding invitation came in the mail. It was their senior year of law school, and although she wasn't surprised that the two of them were getting married, she was surprised that it was going to take place before they graduated. Jacob's explanation was simple. This was when Phyllis wanted to get married. She found a good deal for their wedding and honeymoon in Aruba. She didn't want to pass up the opportunity, so the date was set. Joanna bought them as nice a wedding gift as she could afford and sent regrets about attending the wedding and reception in beautiful Aruba. That all had happened over ten years ago. Now she was sitting across the table from a man she had just met, and he was telling her things about Jacob and Phyllis that she had no way of knowing. As he talked, she wished that she could have been there for Jacob as he had been there for her. Phyllis asked for the divorce. Jacob told Joanna this at one of their Friday night happy hour meetings. Joanna had not been shocked at the news but had pondered the irony of Phyllis being the one to ask for the divorce. Tim was correct; Phyllis had not been good for Jacob.

Joanna had also been correct in suspecting Tim was a partner of Jacob's in the investigation of the Howards. "Were you sent here this morning because you wanted to meet with me, or did you come here for Jacob?" Joanna had asked Tim during their conversation in the cafeteria.

"I came for both reasons." Tim candidly replied. "Joanna, I/we don't know what's going to happen now that Jacob has had this medical problem. We are certain of this much. We cannot let the investigation of the Howards come to a standstill. I am asking you to help us in any way you can help. So the first thing you're going to have to do is put the same trust in me you've had in Jacob."

"Good Lord, Tim, you make it sound like Jacob has been taken to the morgue!" Joanna said as she pushed her tray across the table in Tim's direction.

After a few seconds, Tim leaned on his arms and rested them next to the tray. Speaking in a strong voice, he simply said, "Joanna. Of course I don't think Jacob is going to be taken to the morgue. In fact, as young as he is and in the physical condition he's in, he won't be in a morgue for another eighty years, if then. I do think you will be asked by my superiors to work with me. In fact, after meeting with you today, I'm going to make that request."

"Really," Joanna said as she stared at the man sitting across from her. "Why is that? Because you've been so taken by me?"

"No. I'm making the request because of your obvious personal feelings for Jacob." With that statement made, he returned her stare.

"My what? My *what?*" Joanna's voice drew a few glances from some at nearby tables. Catching the looks, she dropped her voice to a near-whisper, leaned forward so her arms were touching the other side of the tray, and repeated the words slowly. "My personal feelings for Jacob. That is what you just said, is it not?"

Tim didn't move except to nod his head to confirm that indeed it was what he had said.

"Okay," Joanna continued. "I think it's important that I set you straight on a couple of things. First, I do have personal feelings for Jacob. He was a good friend to me when I needed a good friend in the worst way. Secondly, he remains a good friend of mine. He has helped me determine what steps to take in this mess with the Howards. I don't mind telling you there are some very good people who are helping out in this, and I worry more about them than trying to prove whatever the Howards have done or not done. I don't work for your agency, and I really don't care what you request from your superiors. I really don't care what you or any of those in your agency think about me. I do care about Jacob, and I will probably always care about Jacob, but if you're insinuating there is some big *hot* thing going on between the two of us, you couldn't be more *wrong!*"

For a few moments, she wasn't sure what was going to happen, and she didn't care. Tim didn't move, flinch, or as far as she could tell, even blink. When he spoke, it was the tenderness in his voice that threw her. "Joanna. It's really none of my business, or the business of anyone what you do. You must admit your reaction to Jacob's hospitalization has been that of someone who cares a great deal for the man. If you thought I was referring to the two of you having something *hot* going on, then you are mistaken. I see you are emotionally at risk when it comes to Jacob. Will you concede to that?"

Joanna looked at the man in front of her and as much as she wanted to remain offended, angry, whatever she wanted to be, she knew he made a very good point. She did care a great deal for Jacob, and up until this very day, she had never thought she felt any more for Jacob than she did for one of her close female friends. Yet. *Yet.* Here was another puzzle that was facing her. What did she feel for Jacob? "All right. I see where you're headed. You're also correct. I feel as close to Jacob as I could if he were my brother."

Tim's reaction to her statement was subtle but clear—he didn't believe for one second she felt like Jacob was a brother.

She had not been aware of how much time had gone by until she realized the number of people that began to surround their table. Tim was very glad to hear the report of Jill and to know Diane Stoner and possibly Karen Matthews would aid in the investigation. As though some invisible signal had been given, both of them picked up their trays and made their way back to the recovery room waiting area. As soon as they opened the door, the gentle elderly volunteer greeted them with the news that Jacob had been released from the recovery room and was now in room 608. Upon entering the room, they found a very sleepy Jacob. He smiled at the two of them and announced he had been given the most wonderful medicine.

"I don't know where it took me, but I think I want to return." Soon after those words were out of his mouth, he was asleep.

"I guess we won't get a lot of direction from him," Tim said as he looked over at Joanna. She nodded in agreement. Again, with some silent signal, they both moved away from Jacob's bedside and out into the hospital corridor. Once outside, Tim looked at Joanna and simply asked if she was all right.

She assured him she was fine. "Look," she said as she walked in stride. "I really didn't mean to make such a scene, but today has been one tough day. Oh, damn. I just remembered I didn't make it to Judge Harrison's office."

Tim could see the color drain from her face and offered to make a phone call on her behalf. "You know. Our agency seems to have some clout with many people, including some judges." She thought about this for a moment and agreed that a phone call might just help her situation. Tim assured her the call would be made before she could get back to her office. He then walked her to her car. As she was about to thank him for making the phone call and was thinking about apologizing again for her outburst in the cafeteria, he looked at her with a wide grin on his face and said, "I hope you never get mad at me enough to go for the charcoal starter fluid."

Before she could react, he had turned on his heel and was across the parking lot. Jacob had told him. *Oh! I cannot believe he told!*

When she returned to her office, she found things had been taken care of. Vickie assured her Judge Harrison had called and wanted her to know he hoped her friend was going to be all right and not to worry about getting back with him. She guessed Tim had taken care of informing the judge why she hadn't made her appointment. Judge Harrison was a nice enough guy, but he did like to throw his weight around, especially when it came to female attorneys. Appointments had been rescheduled and there was no problem with any of the clients. There were some phone calls Denise had been able to take care of, but there were a couple she would have to take care of herself. As she looked down at the messages, she saw two that riveted her. The first one had been from Jill, the second had been from Evelyn Howard.

Jill had wanted her to know she had received a call from the senator's office. The message had been left on her answering machine and it had been the senator's secretary. She was just wanting to know what Joanna wanted her to do. "I haven't responded to the message. Basically his secretary was asking for me to call the office and set up a date for a meeting with the good senator." Jill was reporting this to Joanna as she had promised her she would do.

"Jill. I don't want you to return the call until I talk with Tim." Joanna had filled Jill in on the problem with Jacob, her conversation with Tim, and the agreement she had made concerning the continuing investigation of the Howard case.

"Joanna. I'll do whatever you need me to do. I'll continue to let my answering machine pick up my calls. Don't worry about me. I'm going to be fine." Joanna appreciated the confidence Jill, Beverly, and now Diane seemed to place in her. She just wished she had the same self-confidence. The longer this thing went on, the more concerned and uneasy she felt about all of it.

"Jill, I can't tell you how much I appreciate what you've done, and continue to do. I really want your welfare to be a top priority, yours, Beverly's, and now Diane's."

"Joanna. We're all big girls here. No one has put a gun to our heads and told us we needed to get involved. Stop being such a mother hen." This was a small comfort to Joanna; she just wished Jill had not used the term "put a gun to our heads"—that was exactly what Joanna was worried about.

"Jill. I'll try my best to stop being a mother hen, I just don't know if I'll be very successful."

After catching Jill up on a few more details concerning Jacob's condition, she hung up the phone and stared at the next call she was supposed to return. It was Evelyn Howard. The only message she would leave with the office was, "Call when you get back to the office."

"Okay," Joanna said to herself as she picked up the receiver to make her next call. The conversation had been all about Tuesday Ladies League, and would Joanna consider playing in her foursome? She wasn't sure what she had said to Evelyn other than that would be fine with her.

"Oh, good," Evelyn had chirped. "I have so much I want to talk to you about. I'll see you on Tuesday."

What a day this had been. What a day. What a day.

When she arrived at the pro shop, everything and everyone was in a flurry of activity. The sound of golf clubs clanking; the chatter of the ladies checking in and making their way to the practice range or water station. Today was a big tournament day for the nine-hole group. This was their ladies' championship day. Almost everyone in the league signed up for this tournament, even though it was a forgone conclusion that one or two of the women who had the lowest handicaps, and most likely would leave the nine-hole group and join the eighteen hole group next season, would stay around for one last chance to win prizes. It had been rumored around the ladies' locker room that Sharon Barcus was a sandbagger and wouldn't turn in any scores that would lower her handicap. When this had been discussed in front of Diane Stoner, she was aghast. *Why in the world would anyone in their right mind not want to lower their handicap?* Beverly had given her some insights on reasons a person wanted a higher handicap. Should you have a handicap of thirty-six, you get two strokes on every hole. This comes off the gross score and gives you a lower net. There are prizes for lower net. If, on the other hand, you have been turning in scores that keep your handicap artificially high, when you play in a tournament and shoot what you really are able to play, you have an advantage over everyone else in the field, because you are getting strokes on holes that those who are playing to their handicap don't get.

"This is all for what?" Diane had asked. "A pair of socks from the pro shop?"

Joanna remembered this conversation as she watched some of the chief offenders of the "side game" check in. She wondered if any of them realized they weren't fooling anyone but themselves. Smiling to herself about Diane's comment, she looked down at Sharon Barcus' feet and wondered if she would be getting a new pair of socks.

"Hey, girl. How's Jacob doing?" There was no mistaking Beverly's voice. Joanna turned to see her standing behind two other women in line. She motioned for the two to go ahead of her so she could speak with Beverly.

"Guess who I'm playing with today?" Joanna asked as she waited for Beverly's reaction.

To her surprise, Beverly said, "I already know who your partner is. Diane and I will be rounding out your foursome."

As usual, Beverly had surprised, Joanna and not the other way around. "Just how did you manage that?" Joanna asked almost in a whisper.

"Oh, I have friends in high places. Besides, Mildred owed me one, and I made her pay up!"

"I see," was all Joanna was able to respond before needing to check in. It seemed to her that out of nowhere stood Evelyn Howard. Her smile looked as though it had been painted on her face; her eyes were reflecting something else. Joanna decided it was unbridled anger. Whatever it was, at that point, Joanna didn't care. She was tired. She was tired of being afraid. She was tired of playing games. Most of all, she was tired of Evelyn Howard. *Here we go again!* Joanna thought to herself as she smiled and returned the same phony greeting to Evelyn she had just been given.

"Hey, guys! Looks like this is going to be one fun day!" Diane had just arrived, and her cheerfulness was a little exaggerated, or at least it seemed to Joanna. She looked to Beverly for a sign that this was the case; there was none.

Okay, Joanna thought after she looked at the three other women that were going to make up her group. *I'm just going to watch what happens today.* She certainly found out that there would be a lot to watch during this round. There wasn't much to the first hole. In fact, Joanna was rather proud of herself because she had hit one of her better drives and had actually gotten a bogey on the first hole. *Not bad,* she was thinking to herself when Beverly walked up to her as they were leaving the green and announced in her usual stage whisper that Evelyn had already started cheating. "What?" was all Joanna seemed to be able to respond before Evelyn was approaching the cart and off they went to hole number two.

As Evelyn was standing on the tee box, Joanna looked at Beverly with a "would you please tell me what's going on" stare. Beverly simply took a long drag on her cigarette and looked at Joanna with the "I'll tell you later" glance. As Joanna was about to hit her next tee shot, she actually started to giggle. She wasn't sure why everything seemed to be so funny at the moment. Maybe she was reacting to the stress of all of the events that continued to build in her life. Maybe it was the sudden realization there was a possibility she did feel more for Jacob than she had ever imagined she could feel, and now she didn't want to feel! Maybe it was watching the three other women in her foursome who were obviously as different as four individuals could possibly be. There stood Beverly with her hair the shade of a merlot, smoking one cigarette after another while dressed in the latest golf attire. Diane still reminded her of a startled deer. It was clear to Joanna that Diane had been seduced by this game and was going to be playing it for years to come. She certainly was a quick study in human behavior and was able to match wits with any of the opponents she had met thus far. Of course there was Evelyn. It didn't take anyone very long to figure out what she was all about. The main reason she had joined the league was to find new pipe lines for her husband's campaign funds. Anyone in the community knew many of the up and coming young professional wives would join this nine-hole league. Evelyn would know the names and addresses of each one of these women before the first day of league play. If that had been all Evelyn was about, she could have been viewed as a joke. Joanna had too much information about Evelyn to know this woman was no joke. Yet, here they all stood in the bright sunshine, selecting clubs as though their very lives depended on it. Talking about where the flag was on the green, as though any of them would be up there within four, five, or six shots! Making sure that no one said a word while any one of them would be on the tee box. The fact that there were sirens blaring past the very spot they were standing still didn't allow anyone to speak! She stopped, walked away from her ball that had just been teed up, threw her head back, and laughed. When she saw the three of them staring at her, she laughed some more. Beverly and Diane started to smile, but before anyone could say anything, the golf ranger rode up to their group and announced they would have to pick up their pace of play! Beverly took charge of the ranger with her tuned-up, turned-on charm—in fact, if the ranger really did want them to pick up their pace, he should have stopped flirting with Beverly before she had to be told it was time for her to tee off. As she got in the cart with Evelyn, Joanna realized she had less challenging games in a court of law.

"All right. Listen closely and don't ask any questions." Beverly was giving instructions to Joanna as they were starting to tee off on the fourth hole. "Diane has seen Evelyn move her ball, announce she had only six strokes on the last hole—Diane is sure she counted seven for her, and Diane is certain she *whiffed*! And you know how sensitive Diane is about *whiffs*! I'm not sure, but I think she's about ready to blow!"

"Who's about ready to blow?" asked Joanna with a little more than a surprised look on her face.

Beverly couldn't believe she had asked the question. "Well, Diane, of course. I think she has about had it with Evelyn!"

"Who hasn't has had it with Evelyn?" Joanna countered. To this, Beverly had no response. At that very moment, there came a climax to the morning's event. Diane, the same Diane that had not held a golf club in her hand more than two months ago, was challenging Evelyn.

"No. That was not a six that was an eight that you just scored. Let's review." With that, Diane stood on the green facing the fairway they had just played and began to count the strokes she had seen Evelyn take. "Then you chipped onto the green and you three-putted. That makes eight strokes for you." Joanna and Beverly stood motionless, waiting for Evelyn's reaction. For a few moments the only sound that could be heard was the talking of women on the next tee box and Beverly exhaling her cigarette smoke. Joanna watched Evelyn and Diane with more than a passing interest. Diane stood there with her hand on one hip, while the other held a death grip on her putter. One glance at her face told the observer that she was not going to back down. Evelyn broke into a phony grin. The next words she spoke flabbergasted all three of them. Beverly dropped her cigarette, Joanna stared straight ahead, and the color in Diane's knuckles returned to their usual pink. In one of the best performances Joanna had seen in some time, Evelyn simply acknowledged her mistake in announcing her score and thanked Diane for bringing it to her attention.

As Beverly and Joanna made their way to their carts, Beverly expressed Joanna's very thoughts when she said to her, "Do you believe that shit?"

"Not for one minute, my dear. Not for one minute," was all Joanna was able to respond before she met Evelyn at their cart.

It was as though some invisible hand had flipped a switch and the entire round of golf took on a completely different feel. Everyone was polite to one another; Beverly even apologized to Evelyn when one of her trails of smoke drifted in Evelyn's direction. Diane seemed satisfied that she had done the right thing by calling Evelyn on her cheating—of course, no one called it that; nonetheless, all of them knew what had happened. Joanna had seen this happen in the courtroom. Both sides were fighting as hard as they knew how to fight. Insinuations would be made about the intellect, integrity, you name it, of the opposing party. If it was an insult that could get by the judge, it got thrown as hard and as fast as it could be thrown. Once the arguments were over and the jury was in their chambers, the opposing attorneys would often be pleasant to one another. Inquiring about each other's families, what would they be doing for the holidays, and so forth. She was never sure what this human behavior was all about. On the one hand, she saw it as a good and kind thing to do. On the other hand, she felt it was a hypocritical action. From what she had observed, it could be both. It depended on the individuals involved. She suspected that this was what was going on right now out here on the golf course. She was certain that one of the participants in today's game was not being kind.

Everyone had made their way to the ladies' locker room to make themselves presentable for the lunch, announcement of the winners, and a few minutes of relaxing and visiting with friends. Joanna was one of the last few women remaining in the ladies' room and was about to open the door when she thought she heard her name being called. She nearly ignored the sound, but then when she heard it the second time, she knew someone was calling her. Three other women brushed passed her on their way out as she was turning toward the voice she heard. Carefully walking into the locker area, she saw Jill's head pop up from behind one of the lockers.

"Oh. Thank goodness you heard me. I didn't want to call attention to myself so I waited until most everyone was out of here before I tried to get your attention."

"What's going on? You think you're Mata Hara?" Joanna asked, half-teasing, half-serious.

"This is no time for you to try and be funny. I desperately need to talk to you, and the sooner the better." Joanna could hear near panic coming from Jill, and panic was not common for her.

"Okay. Okay. Everything is going to be okay." How Joanna wished she believed that herself. With that, Jill let out a deep breath and told her that she would like for her to come to her house right after the awards luncheon. Did Joanna think she could manage that? "My dear. I assure you that I will be there. Now, we need to get out there before we're missed."

Mildred and the social committee had outdone themselves. One of the women on the committee had a son who owned an upscale Italian restaurant in Old Town; the women in the league were getting much more for their money than they would have otherwise. Joanna took one look at their president and decided that she had been sampling the wine that was going to be served with their lunch. She looked at the glass Mildred held and knew she could have walked over, taken the glass from their president's hand, and downed it within seconds. Oh, well. *Maybe another day and time,* Joanna thought as she made her way to the table which she had been assigned and where Evelyn Howard awaited.

"There you are. We were getting worried about you."

Joanna knew Evelyn was baiting her, and she wasn't going to take the bait. "Oh. How sweet of you to care."

Joanna sat down as Beverly was giving her best deep raspy voice. "My darling. You know how much we care, and by the way, did you see the dessert table?"

"Frankly, the only thing I've had my eye on is the wine," Joanna countered. "You had better get to it fast. I think our lady president has had half a bottle, and it hasn't been served to any of the tables." Evelyn was spouting the words with the force of someone that had just inadvertently tasted vinegar. The other three looked at Evelyn with the same curious stare. Was she upset because Mildred had been drinking wine? Or was she upset because she hadn't been served any? It was Diane that asked both of those questions while Joanna and Beverly pretended to be interested in the breadbasket.

"Well," Evelyn responded with a little more than necessary volume to her voice. "I certainly have no problem with having wine at noon, *but* I do think that it behooves us to monitor our intake at *all times.*"

"*O-kay,*" Diane said as she lifted her glass of water and took a long sip.

Joanna and Beverly were smiling as they passed the breadbasket and butter around the table to the other women sitting there. Shortly after the salads had been served, it surprised everyone at Evelyn's table that she would not be able to stay for the rest of the luncheon because of an appointment. Without further ado, she picked up her belongings and disappeared through the dining room doors.

"What do you make of that?" Beverly asked to no one in particular.

Diane commented that there was no way anyone could make anything of Evelyn. Joanna unceremoniously proclaimed Evelyn a nut! Beverly stopped chewing and looked at Joanna with more than a little concern. In the all the years that she had known this woman, she had never heard her say something so rude about anyone. The fact that what she had just stated was something that was very true had nothing to with Beverly's concern.

The drive to Jill's house was always a pleasure for Joanna. It was a beautiful oasis in an overdeveloped area, and she loved to see what it had been in another time. Unfortunately, the drive today was a bit more troublesome. She didn't like the way Jill had sounded, she didn't like the way Jill looked, and she didn't like the fact she was the one that was supposed to give this woman support, encouragement, or whatever Jill might be looking for her to give. She didn't know if she were capable of giving it to her. Right at that very moment, she didn't know if she was capable of doing anything. As soon as Jill opened the door, the tears began to flow. The only thing Joanna seemed to do was hold her and keep repeating to her everything was going to be all right. Somehow this seemed to cause Jill's tears to come faster until Joanna insisted she get a drink of cold water. Temporarily this seemed to slow the tears, but as soon as Joanna asked her what this was all about, they started with the same intensity they had from the moment she had walked in the door.

"Jill. You're going to have to get a hold of yourself if you want me to understand what it is I need to do."

"I know, Joanna, I'm sorry. I just can't stand it when I let anyone down. I think I've let you and Beverly and now Diane down." Again the tears and now short sobs began to emit from Jill. Fear—no, maybe this was terror, Joanna thought as she helplessly watched this gentle, kind, strong woman dissolve right before her very eyes.

It had taken several more minutes before Jill was able to bring forth any coherent communication. During their conversations, Joanna had wished that she had continued to be unable to talk—then Joanna wouldn't have to take any kind of action about any of this information. Everything in Joanna was used up that afternoon. She knew Jill had done the right thing in getting her to hear about this latest development. She also knew, and had made it very clear to Jill, that she was going to have to take this to Tim Burke, and once she did, she had no idea how this would affect the investigation. How much more difficult was thing going to get? she was thinking as she drove toward her office. When this all started, she believed there was going to be a few weeks of looking into records, a few phone calls, and all the evidence would point or not point to wrongdoing by the Howards. That had been eight months ago, and instead of proving anything, the trail they were following was becoming more and more twisted and more complicated. She had learned a long time ago if didn't feel good and it didn't smell good, it probably wasn't good! There certainly wasn't anything that felt or smelled good about the Howards. Yet, here was a woman that she had worked with in the past that would stand up for anyone or anything if she felt it was the right thing to do.

"Oh, no," Joanna said to herself as she pulled into her parking space. "She is convinced that this is the right thing to do." How she wished Jill hadn't told her all that she had just been told. It was not only affected the investigation, it was going to affect her personal life.

Stopping at Vicki's desk, she picked up her messages. She went to her office and after a few more minutes of reflecting on her most recent visit, she picked up the phone. She heard herself say, "May I please speak with Mr. Tim Burke?"

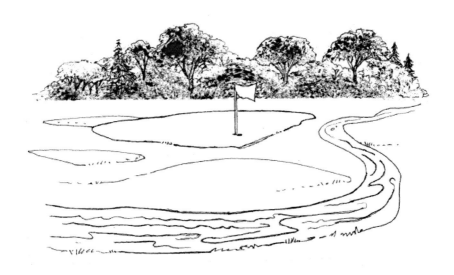

HOLE SIX
Par Three

Tolerance. Indifference. Or the reaction he had become accustomed to was disgust. Respect? Mac Shaw respected? Respected? Had he been sure of what she had said? She had even used the word "sir" when she first addressed him. Sir? *Sir?* Had anyone ever used that word when they had talked to him? Not that he could remember. She had. She had shown him respect and kindness, and unless he was kidding himself, she seemed genuinely interested in who he was. At one point in their conversation, he knew she understood. How? How could this attractive, seemingly intelligent female understand? He had to know. He had to know if this was real, or if she was just another one of those women that came and went in his life. Sometimes they wanted no more from him than free drinks; sometimes they were drunk and just wanted to be serviced by him. There had been a few times when one of them seemed to care. For whatever reason, the caring had turned into smothering or, worse, control. This was different. Their conversation had started out with the usual questions. This wasn't the first time he had been in a pawn shop, and he knew the drill. There was the usual discussion surrounding the item brought in for the pawn broker to evaluate. Some brokers were kinder than others, but all of them seemed condescending. Maybe it was because they were in the business they were in. Maybe it was because they wanted to feel superior to others. Maybe it was because they didn't like the business they were in. Whatever the reason, he had spent many years of his life dealing with these brokers, and this was the first time he left a shop feeling someone cared about who he was and, for that matter, cared if he drew his next breath. So it was. This unexpected, delightfully buoyant feeling had moved him into an area of life he had never visited until now. He had been smitten. The two of them were going to meet for lunch the next day. She had told him she would be most happy to have lunch with him. She had actually said those very words.

"I would be most happy to have lunch with you."

"Is tomorrow good?"

"I will have tomorrow afternoon off, so we could take our time and enjoy a leisurely lunch."

That evening he began to have doubts about his experience with the pretty girl in the pawn shop; maybe it had been nothing more than his imagination. He had to have been out of his mind to think a woman such as she could really care about someone like him. Maybe she didn't understand what kind of person he really was. That had to be it. She was some naive little country girl who had come to the big city and would be impressed by anyone who wasn't wearing a plaid flannel shirt, dirty jeans, and cow shit on their boots. Well. Tomorrow he was going to find out what she was really all about. There was one thing he prided himself in, getting to the bottom of another's character. He would flush out the real reason for this interest. Expose it. Then move on with his life. Because he wanted to have all of his senses on high alert, he would forgo the usual evening alcohol. Something was different, all right. He was going to find out exactly what it was, and he had to do it stone-cold sober. No hangover. No booze for tonight.

Even he was surprised at how much time he took to get ready for the lunch date. He had indulged in a shave and haircut. He wasn't sure he had ever had a shave in a barber shop. When he was given the mirror to inspect the barber's job, he was startled. He hadn't been clean-shaven in several weeks; he never cared about the length of his hair and seriously considered letting it grow and pulling it all back into one of those ponytails all the blue-collar guys wore. Yet when he thought about her, he didn't want to appear shabby. Deep in his gut, he could feel she wouldn't like and didn't deserve shabby. Looking at his reflection, he knew he didn't look shabby. No. He would never consider himself to be handsome, but he was looking at a well-kempt man who was nicely dressed and would be taking a very attractive lady out to lunch. This was all new territory for Mac. Right that very minute, he liked what the exploration of new territory was doing for him.

Mac knew in the first fifteen minutes this lunch date would be a turning point for him. The second she walked in the door, he had feelings he had never experienced. He wondered if he was going mad. As she crossed the room to join him, he knew he had never seen a woman this beautiful. When she spoke his name, he was certain no one he had ever encountered spoke it with the same melodic tone as she had just used. There was no doubt about it. He had most assuredly gone mad. So if insanity felt this good, he would just have to stay insane.

Before the salads had been served, he found himself talking to her as he had never talked to another human being. Maybe it was the intensity of those incredibly beautiful eyes. They seemed to probe his innermost soul. His responses to her questions had surprised him as he heard the intimate details he gave of his life. His failures. His dreams and his desires. He was being pulled into this deep dark pool of water. Yet. It was refreshing and he was not frightened of the depth. *If there is a God in heaven,* he silently prayed, *please let her be real!*

She had been real. She continued to be real, and she stood by his side at his first AA meeting. He knew he would have never attended if it hadn't been for her. She too was a member and understood what being a slave to alcohol meant. She had also bared her soul to Mac. As she told him her story, he felt anger, grief, and gladness for her. Once she had completed the telling, he knew if she had overcome the abuse, poverty, and addictions she had overcome, he could do the same. So his road to recovery would be with her hand in his.

He wasn't just existing—for the first time in his forty-two years of life, he was living. He began to see sights and sounds that surrounded him. He knew he would sound foolish to most people if he tried to explain how he had discovered the colors and fragrance of flowers, the beauty of a sunrise or a sunset, the repertoire of a mockingbird, or the laughter of a child. He made a vow to himself he would thank God, Sharon, and AA every day for the rest of his life for this sweet, sweet gift.

Now he was faced with the hard part. He didn't know how he was going to approach the subject, but he knew he had to tell her all of what was going on in his life. He wanted to do this. He hated to think about doing this. There had been several times he was about to open up the dialog when he felt as though his tongue had been frozen to the roof of his mouth. He had faced many things in his life and he had never considered himself a coward. To risk losing this woman frightened him more than anything he could remember being afraid of, unless it was having to hide from landlords who pounded on the door, wanting the back rent his mother owed. The fear of not knowing where they would live or what they would eat. His father had walked out on them when he had been in the first grade. He didn't remember much about him except his sternness. His mother had told him this was a trait left over from the military training his father had. Mac made up his mind he would never volunteer for the military, not if it was going to turn him into the kind of man his father seemed to have been. The last time he had laid eyes on the man was at his mother's funeral. Mac was shocked to see him at the funeral home. If it hadn't been for the other friends and family present, Mac thought he would have punched his dad out. His aunt pulled him aside to tell him his father was there to pay respects to his mother and he should let him do this. At the graveyard, his dad had walked up to him and told him there was an important matter he needed to discuss with him, and it could be of value to him. At first, Mac told him he was not interested in having

151 - LADIES LEAGUE FRONT NINE

anything from him, valuable or not. As he listened further to this old man who had fathered him, he felt a mixture of pity and curiosity. A few years later, he was informed of his father's death by an attorney in a neighboring state. He was told he would need to come to the attorney's office to receive his father's personal belongings. This seemed strange to Mac. His father seemed to live from unemployment check to unemployment check, and as far as Mac knew, he had absolutely nothing of value. The attorney was insistent he come to his office to deal with a legacy left by his father. A legacy? The guy had actually used the word "legacy." Upon arrival, he was handed a battered old briefcase with a small blue book and a dog-eared old calendar, along with his father's dog tags.

"Is this it?" He had asked the attorney. "I had to travel over three hundred miles to pick up this … this … legacy?"

Mac had laughed as the attorney was trying to explain that his father had paid him to follow the instructions he had been given. One point he had to be certain that was carried out was that Mac and *only* Mac would be the person receiving the briefcase. Further, in the event Mac was deceased, the briefcase and its contents were to be sent by certified mail to the state attorney general's office.

"Attorney general? What the hell?" Mac had muttered.

"Those were my instructions. I have carried them out. Good day, Mr. Shaw. My job is over."

Mac found himself unceremoniously escorted from the law offices of Blevins, Blevins, Blevins, and Krauss. I wonder who Krauss is? Mac thought to himself as he made his way out of the office building and got directions to the nearest bar.

The one thing he had definitely inherited from his old dad was the love of the bottle. He had started out as a journeyman with a local construction firm. He liked the work and found he had a talent for it, but his real talent seemed to be the drinking with the boys after a hard day at work. It wasn't long until he was dismissed from that job, and then another and another. That's when he opened the small briefcase which held his father's blue book. A few weeks later, he met Evelyn

Howard. After their meeting, he found the blue book had not been a bad thing to inherit. It had held his present job for him the last twelve years.

Now. Now. How could he admit to a woman he was rapidly falling in love with that he was a criminal? He knew the charges of breaking and entering. Stealing. Stalking. Intimidation. Oh yes, the little matter of perjury still haunted him. If he confessed, it could cost him dearly. This was all too much. He had to do some thinking. Soul-searching. Confessing. Wasn't that part of what the twelve-step program was all about?

Many years later, he would still be repeating the story of how he came to the conclusion he had to come clean. Clean with the woman who had become the love of his life. Clean with the agency that could have put him away for years of his life. Clean with his maker, who had become the Lord of his life.

Many days had passed since he had a drop of alcohol. He had expected to experience withdrawal, even delirium tremens. Nothing of that nature occurred. He was surprised, as were others in his group. Yet he still struggled with the course of action to take concerning his involvement with Evelyn Howard. Did he tell Sharon? If he told her, what would she think of him? What authorities would he go to if he decided he needed to report any or all of his part in this to them? Days passed, and the questions and stirrings became stronger and stronger. Then, on a Wednesday at exactly 3:00 Am, he awoke with the answer. He would tell her all he had done. If she were the person he thought she was, she would understand and stand by him. He knew what authorities he would be talking to. Before he spoke to either of them, he had to make sure of one more thing. That the blue book would be safe. He made sure it was.

It had been a cold, rainy evening when he met her with the sole purpose of divulging the entire truth. The weather seemed to reflect his very mood. When he stepped inside her apartment, he could feel the warmth and hominess of the small space. He marveled at her ability to create this atmosphere in an area of town that could only be described as drab. There she stood. Deep-set brilliant blue eyes looking through him all the while a faint smell of lavender assaulted his senses. Did she have any idea what she was doing to him? He was certain the answer to his own question was a simple no. She had proven to him many times and in many ways she was who she presented herself to be. That was the primary reason he was ready to take this next step. So the story began.

There were a few moments he was sure she would walk across the room and call 911. He knew if she chose to do this, he would have set on the end of the couch, waiting to be read his rights and have his wrists pulled behind him with handcuffs. She didn't move. When he had finished his tale, she kept her gaze as steady as it had been during the entire time he had been talking and simply said, "You know what you have to do, don't you?" Oh yes, he knew. He just wished he didn't have to do what he had to do. That is when he asked her if she would wait for him if the authorities decided he would have to be immediately taken into custody. Her response was all the courage he had needed. She reached for his hand and pulled him forward, giving him one of the most tender kisses he had ever experienced.

Mac had a lot of time to think about all the consequences of what he was about to do. He explained to Sharon he could not go to the local police. He didn't know who it was, but he knew there was at least one policeman that had been bought and paid for by Evelyn Howard. He had decided the best law enforcement would be none other than the FBI. This is where he needed her help. She agreed she would be the one to make the initial contact. For the last few weeks, he instinctively knew he had to keep a low profile regarding his activities with Sharon and his AA meetings. He was certain Evelyn was unaware of the changes that had recently occurred in his life. In fact, she had been driving up the lane near where he was trimming a hedge, and when he saw her he gave what he thought was a pretty good performance of a drunk. He could tell by her reaction his act had been convincing. He had wanted Sharon to make the phone call and have nothing more to do with this entire mess until it was resolved one way or another. She let him know that was not part of the deal. She was proud of him. She was going to stand by him. She was in love with him. This was the first time either of them had used the words. "I love you." He did what he had wanted to do from the first time they met. He walked over to her and brought his mouth to hers with a heat and intensity the two had never before exchanged in their relationship.

It had been easier than either of them thought it would be. She had called the regional FBI office. She had waited until a man who identified himself as a Mr. White came on the line. She spoke for a few seconds, but she was positive when she said the name "Howard," the entire interest from this Mr. White became intense. It was then he wanted a number to contact her. He would be back in touch within the next hour. Would she still be at this number?

Jacob put the phone carefully back in its cradle and sat motionless for several seconds. He was trying not to become too hopeful. The agency had been working on this Howard mess for years. He had personally been involved in the case for the last two. He had witnessed some slight-of-hand operations before, but this Howard woman was the best. Tim was out in the field today, but he felt certain when the captain heard the details of this contact, Tim's day as well as his would take a decidedly different turn.

Sharon and Mac tried everything they knew to take their minds off of waiting for the phone to ring. They had tried to watch an "I Love Lucy" episode, but even Fred, Ethel, Ricky, and Lucy couldn't keep their minds off the silent phone. Mac was unusually quiet. Had he done the right thing by having Sharon make this call? Maybe he was a coward after all. Was he hiding behind a woman's skirt? If anything happened to her because of what they had just done, he knew he couldn't go on living. That's it. That has to be part of the deal. He would meet with them, but he didn't have to tell them anything unless they agreed to keep her out of danger. If that caused him to have to go to jail today, then so be it! Right now all that mattered to him was the welfare of the woman he was madly in love with. Whatever happened to him was what he deserved.

Tim had made it back to the office in record time. He had been waiting for something like this to happen. He had graduated from the FBI Academy in the same class as Jacob. After finding their assignments would take them to the same region, they were thrilled. They had connected the first day they had met, and the depth of their trust in each other couldn't go any deeper. Giving your partner the responsibility of holding your life in his hands in any given situation was as big a step in trust as any human could give another. Yet, here were two men who did this on a daily basis and thought no more of it than what they would order for lunch. Jacob had considered all of this while he was still in the Academy and knew this was a part of the job for any law enforcement officer, soldier, pilot, sailor. This was what warriors had to do.

Jacob admired his captain for several reasons, but his efficiency was something to see. By the time he and Tim sat down in his office, he told them where the call had been made. The name of the woman who had made the call. They believed she had made the call on behalf of her boyfriend. As it turned out, the boyfriend was none other than Mac Shaw, the long-time employee of the Howards.

"Whoa! I think we may just have the break we've been waiting for." Tim was as excited about this information as he would have been if he had been told he had the next month off with full pay. Jacob was waiting for the impact of what the captain had just said to sink in. It was obvious to anyone in the room that Tim had already decided they were on their way to doing what they did best. Fight crime. Jacob was more on the cautious side. He had been led down alleys before, and he wasn't sure this wasn't some kind of setup. Part of what made the two men such good partners were these very differences.

"Sir. I told her I would call her back within the hour. I don't want her to run." Jacob knew he was walking on shaky ground with the captain, yet he felt he needed to keep his word with this woman. He wasn't convinced she—and now as he had been told by his captain, her boyfriend—wasn't ready to bolt if he didn't keep his word.

"I understand your concerns. I want you to call her back now. Here in this office, and this is what you're going to tell her." The captain's tone of voice filled the room with authority.

Jacob followed his orders. The call had been made, the time and place for the meeting had been decided. After meeting with them, Jacob couldn't help but like these two. He believed the entire story, and that was unusual for him. As much as he wanted to put an end to this case, he found himself wanting the best for the two people he had just met. Tim interrupted this thought with a jolt. "Man. Will you pinch me? I *cannot* believe what a break this has been for us." Tim was still on a high from the event.

Jacob was used to his reaction. Jacob's mother's oft said proverb popped into his mind: "There is many a slip between the cup and the lip." Jacob was wondering how many slips there might be, before they could stamp "case closed" on this one.

Mac had held back. He had one thing, and one thing only that could help him when all this started coming down: the briefcase that held the blue book, the calendar, and the dog tags. No one—*no one*—knew where the briefcase was hidden, and no one was going to know until it needed to be revealed. Jacob would be contacting him within the next twenty-four hours to give him further instructions. No one had used the term, but Mac had become a mole. This was the thought Mac had has he was putting the bricks back in their place, the bricks that hid the briefcase. At that moment, a small silverfish scurried up the side of the wall. Mac watched as it darted, and then stood still. When this small insect sensed it was not going to be harmed, it moved into one of the tiny dark crevices of the wall. Yes. That was exactly what he was going to do. He would move quickly, silently, and stand perfectly still until he sensed all danger had passed. Unlike the silverfish, he wouldn't hide

157 - LADIES LEAGUE FRONT NINE

in some dark crevice. When this was all over with, he would come out in the full sunshine, because that would be the day he became totally free. That also would be the day he would hand his newfound freedom over to the woman he loved.

"Look. I don't care what you want to be called. It seems to be an unusual name. Then I guess all code names are unusual. I'll tell the captain, and it'll be the named used. Are you clear on how to contact us should the need arise?" Jacob retrieved the bottled water from the vending machine. Stepped aside to allow another traveler access. The two men strolled toward the picnic area. Mac was fascinated as he watched Jacob. He asked a man what kind of breed his dog was, picked up a sandwich wrapper that was laying on the sidewalk, and tossed it into the trash. When Mac assured Jacob he knew exactly when and how to make contact, Jacob opened his bottle and took a long drink before he gave Mac further instructions. A passerby would believe these two men were discussing football scores, if they were noticed at all. This was deliberate. Mac had been given instructions on how to dress, what to drive, and exactly what time he was to arrive at the rest stop.

"Hey. Good to see ya, buddy. Take care." Mac gave a small wave, got into his pickup truck, and drove away. It was only then that Jacob returned to the vending area to toss his bottle into the recycle bin.

"Good morning," the man in the janitorial uniform addressed Jacob as he passed him on the way back to his car.

"Good morning, and how are you today?" Jacob responded as he looked into the eyes of his good friend Tim Burke.

"Why I'm fine, sir. Just fine."

The first one-on-one meeting with Mac, Jacob had walked away impressed. This man had been living his life inside of a bottle. That had been the *only* hold Evelyn Howard had on him. Jacob prayed Mac would stay outside of the bottle, at least until they finished their job. No. That wasn't true; Jacob prayed that Mac would stay out of the bottle for the rest of his life. He was a good man and deserved some happiness after all the years of existing inside this self-imposed prison. Evelyn Howard had stood guard over this prisoner, never suspecting he might reach for the keys to his cell. If Mac was going to be as instrumental in solving this case as it appeared, Jacob would do everything in his power to see he was given every break the legal system would allow. Mac had been most cooperative in giving information concerning his role in Evelyn Howard's schemes. His role as handyman had been a front for what she had really been paying him to do. Yes. He had been the one to enter Joanna's house; yes, he made the phone calls to intimidate her. He repeated what Evelyn had told him: "That attorney bitch has to learn her place in this town. I'm tired of having her block our every move." That was the reason for her instructions. He had even made a few calls to a woman by the name of Diane. He hadn't remembered her last name because Evelyn had given him her first name and phone number and told him to make a few calls. In Evelyn's words, she needed to be driven back to her little rabbit hole. That was all she had told him. He wasn't sure why she wanted this done. Mac had been forthright in recalling events, yet something wasn't adding up. He didn't know why he felt the way he did, and he would have been hard-pressed to explain to anyone, including Tim, why he felt the way he did, but he was sure Mac was holding out on something. He couldn't imagine what it was, but it was there. He was making his way through the interstate traffic as he tried to place this concern about Mac withholding information when another troublesome thought came into his head. He hadn't seen Joanna in several weeks. She had hovered over him after his hospitalization. When she first came to visit, he had been convinced the doctors and his friends were withholding how serious his condition was. He woke up one night while still in the hospital, convinced that when they went in to remove his appendix, the surgeon had found he was full of cancer. He had heard about these kinds of things. It had taken three nurses, a call to the doctor, and a big shot of some kind of drug in his ass to calm him down. Looking back on this, he realized much of his reaction could be attributed to Joanna. Every time he looked at her, she had tears in her eyes. She was bringing him flowers, food, and magazines, and asking if there was anything else she could to do. He had enjoyed the attention in the beginning, but by the third day he was starting to worry; by the fourth day, it was the shot-in-the-ass time and a good long lecture from the doctor. Once the shot had worn off, he had time to reflect on all of it, called Joanna, and had been very candid about her visits and what kind of anxiety it had created for him. Her reaction was typical Joanna. She gave her deepest apologies, inquired on how he was doing, and thanked him for being so truthful. He knew her well enough to know by the tone of her voice she was shutting him down. He had been correct. There were no more visits, flowers, magazines, or phone calls. A few weeks after he had been discharged from the hospital, he had called her office and been told she was in court. He had asked that she give him a call when she had the chance. The call had never come. Now he needed to talk to her. He hoped she would want to talk to him.

Saturday was the day Joanna set aside each week to catch up on her to-do list. Some Saturdays were busier than others, but today was one of those days she decided to steal some quiet time and enjoy the day. When she heard the doorbell, she reached for her purse, expecting it to be the paperboy. When she opened the door to find Jacob starring down at her, she was speechless.

"Is it okay if I come in?" he spoke these words with a faint pleading in his voice and most definitely a pleading look in his eyes.

If her heart hadn't stopped, it had at least skipped a beat before she could respond. "Oh, of course. Of course," were the only words she could find as she continued to stare. After a few more seconds, he told her if she really meant what she said, she would have to step aside so he could do just that.

Once they had seated themselves, coffee had been offered, the "how are you feeling?" question had been answered, Joanna looked him directly in the eye and said, "So. What brings you here? I know this isn't just a social call."

Jacob couldn't help but admire and be distressed by Joanna's statement. Again. She was right on target. It was not just a social call, but what she failed to realize was it was a call for help. He had known for some time she was one of the very best friends he had ever had.

She was miffed at him for the moment, but she would step up and help him work through anything he needed to work through, and he needed to work through his thoughts and feelings about Mac, the senator, Evelyn, and Jill. He also wanted an update on the Matthews'. After a few more niceties, the conversation turned to what needed to be discussed. Joanna acknowledged indeed she had not appreciated his call to her about her visits, gifts, and offer to help in any way she could help while he was in the hospital. Had not Tim hovered over him as well, and had Jacob called him with the same request? She knew he had not, and had he considered that part of his anxiety may have been of his own making? Had the doctor addressed this possibility? She had made some very good points and raised some questions in his own mind. Why hadn't he made the same phone call to Tim? Many hours and days after he left Joanna, he wrestled with the questions she had raised.

Once the discussion left the concerns surrounding his hospitalization and turned to the Howard investigation, Joanna did what she did the best. Listen. Weigh the evidence. Advise. He had always been fascinated by this woman's deduction abilities. He remembered the day after she had found her lover in bed within another woman. Set his belongings on fire. Walked into their class and impressed every student in the class along with the professor with her ability to argue and win the case, all the while her client had been her ex-lover. She amazed him then, and she amazed him still.

He liked her ideas about how to use Silverfish. She agreed with him, Mac was holding back on something. She also agreed it shouldn't be an issue at the moment. Mac would have to be tested, watched, and stay under surveillance. Until Jacob felt it necessary to exert any pressure on him the matter should be left alone. When the subject had turned to Beverly, Diane, and Jill, Joanna expressed her concern for the safety of these women. Jacob reassured, as best he could, that every precaution was being taken to protect each of them, even though he seriously doubted any of them were in any kind of danger.

"Easy for you to say." Joanna had responded to Jacob's last statement with a raised eyebrow and a look that told him she didn't buy any of what he had just said about none of them being in any danger.

After he left Joanna's house, he mulled over the events of the past week. There had certainly been a break in this case, but he continued to be concerned. He didn't share these thoughts with anyone, certainly not Joanna. He was more concerned about all of these women than he had ever been. He had tracked this Howard woman's activities for the last two years, dug into the research done by former agents, and had come to one conclusion Evelyn Howard was a woman capable of anything if someone got in her way. Every one of these women were standing directly in Evelyn Howard's way. This worried him a great deal.

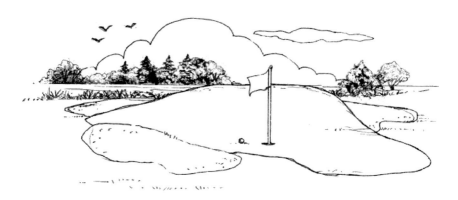

HOLE SEVEN
Par Four

Something was wrong about all of this. *Yes,* Jana thought, *something about all of this is very, very wrong.* When Evelyn had first approached Beverly about the show, Jana would have bet her last dollar her mother would turn her down flat. Instead, she not only agreed to provide the fashions, she allowed Evelyn to actually give opinions on what Beverly was to use in the show. Unbelievable. The one discussion she had with her mother about all of this had also been a surprise.

"Now, Jana, I know that Evelyn and I have had our differences, but this is an opportunity for us to show the ladies in the community what we can do." Jana was pretty sure she had held her mouth open for more than a few seconds. When she finally got around to closing it, her mother had left the room. First, Jana knew as well as anyone who shopped in the community that Beverly had created a dress shop next to none. Secondly, unless her mother was on some drug she wasn't aware of, Beverly had never been able to stand the likes of Evelyn Howard, yet now they're going to collaborate on a fashion show? As Jana helped her mom unpack, inspect, and hang up the clothing she asked, "When do you think Jill will come back and help out around here?" Jana was more than a little puzzled by Jill's sudden inability to work in the shop. In fact, now that she thought about it, there were a lot of things not adding up for her. She couldn't put her finger on it, but ever since her mom had returned from the golf school, things had been strange. Now this thing with Jill. The day Jill had come to the shop to talk with

Beverly, Jana had briefly interrupted their meeting to give her mom a message. One glance at Jill told her whatever was going on in this woman's life was not good.

That evening Jana had approached her mother about Jill, and for the first time Jana could ever remember, her mother refused to discuss anything with her. In fact, her mother's exact words were, "I will not discuss the situation with you," and then she had abruptly changed the subject. The thing disturbing Jana the most was the distance which seemed to be developing between her mother and herself. She had felt in these recent weeks her mother was shutting her out. She had never felt this before, and she didn't like it.

"Jana. There isn't anything the two of us won't be able to handle around here. Jill needs some time to herself. All of us need time to ourselves once in a while."

"Mom. I don't mind doing more than my fair share around here. You know that, don't you? I just wish you'd tell me what's going on." The pleading in Jana's voice stung Beverly. She knew the events surrounding the Howards were taking a toll on everyone, and that included her beloved daughter. She also knew she would protect this young woman with every ounce of energy she had left in her body.

For this very reason she heard herself say, "Jana. My goodness, don't make a mountain out of a molehill. Jill will be fine; I'm fine; the fashion show is going to be fine. Now, stop this incessant questioning."

That was all Jana could stand to hear. She didn't know what was going on, and that was fine with her. However, she was not going to be treated like a child, even if the one giving her this treatment was her own mother. "All right, all right. I won't say anything more, ask anything more, and I won't be a bother to you anymore!" The last words were spoken as she slammed the door.

Beverly rose to follow her daughter, and then sat back down with the sweater she had just unpacked resting in her hand. *When will, and how will, all of this end?* Jill had become a basket case. Joanna was hanging on by a thread. Everyone had worried about Diane, and at this moment she seemed to be the one of them that was the least disturbed. She was glad that tonight she was having dinner with Joanna. The two of them had a lot to talk about, and at this very moment she needed some reassurance herself.

For the first time in a long time, Beverly felt down. Jana had left the shop early in the afternoon. She had told Beverly she would come in early the next morning to unpack the rest of the items that would be used in the fashion show. Her tone and her manner had remained cool. Beverly knew her daughter was confused about all that was going on around her; worse than this, she was hurt.

The first words Beverly spoke as Joanna opened the door were, "I can't take this much longer!"

"And good evening to you, too." Both women would have laughed at this any other time. Neither of them felt like laughing tonight. "The first order of business is to open the wine, eat some of the cheese and crackers I bought, and put our feet up. Not necessarily in that order."

Beverly was feeling a little better by the time her visit with Joanna was over. Neither of them saw what happened to Jill coming. In fact, Beverly had told Joanna she would check on Jill. Since it was relatively early in the evening, she would make the visit before she went home. As she turned her car in the direction of Jill's house, she was mulling over some of the recent developments in the Howard investigation. Some of the information Joanna shared with her this evening was encouraging, curious, and a little humorous. "Who in the world gave this informant the name Silverfish?"

From what Joanna was given to understand, the informant had given himself the name.

"All of this is getting stranger and stranger. Have you any idea how much longer it's going to take the agency before they have enough proof to make their move?"

She was thinking out loud when Joanna responded. "Beverly, I think they're just waiting for a couple of pieces of hard evidence. Then, I think they'll move. Please understand. This is my read on things. Absolutely nothing confirmed."

"Yes. Madame Attorney. I will not hold you responsible if this thing isn't over within the next twenty-four hours!" That was as close to real laughter as the two women would share tonight.

As Beverly turned onto Jill's lane, she had a strange feeling. There was something amiss; she just couldn't make out what it was. Then her headlights fell on something laying in the middle of drive. "Oh, no! Oh, no!" Beverly knew she was screaming but couldn't help herself. Then in spite of, or because of, her screaming, the largest raccoon she had ever seen in her life looked or sneered in her direction and ambled to the side of the lane. "This shit is really getting me down!" Beverly spoke with newfound conviction.

When Jill opened the door, Beverly could see her dear friend wasn't much better off than the last time she had seen her. "What's happened? Have they made arrests? Is he all right? Why are you here?" All of these questions had been strung together to form one sentence.

"Honey. It's okay. Everything is okay, except for that damn raccoon you have out there in your driveway!"

"Raccoon? Raccoon? What are you talking about?" The look on Jill's face suddenly struck Beverly as the funniest thing she had seen in weeks. The answer to Jill's question was one big horse laugh. For a few seconds, Jill was irritated as she watched her friend laughing, and then all her emotional conflict gave way, and she joined Beverly in the hardest laugh she had enjoyed in weeks. The two women talked with the depths of friendship which only occur with the right mix of strength, maturity, and caring for one another.

"Beverly. I had no idea how I felt, or I would never have told you or Joanna, and certainly not Diane, I would be part of this. When Joanna first broached the subject of reconnecting with Jim, I actually thought it would be fun and I would be doing a service for … for … who did I think I would be doing a service for?"

"Jill, you and I both knew at the time and still know how underhanded the Howards have been. Maybe it's only Evelyn that is behind all of this. I don't know, Joanna doesn't know, and apparently the FBI doesn't know, or there would have already been action taken. So stop beating yourself up about the fact you discovered feelings for the senator." Beverly assured her for the hundredth time both she and Joanna completely understood, and given the same situation, they both felt they would be struggling in the same way she was struggling. As for Diane, it wasn't something she needed to know and therefore she had not been told anything.

"I couldn't believe he would come out here. That was so risky. Here he is running for office, married to a woman that is capable of Lord knows what! Then in the middle of it all he shows up at my door!" Jill stood and began walking around the family room, holding the stem of her wine glass with the grip of the damned. "Beverly. I had no idea how I felt about this man. You do believe me, don't you?"

With the brutal honesty Beverly was known for, she replied, "Jill. I didn't think you cared all that much about him when we were all going to school together. In those days, everyone had to be going with someone, and I thought he was just one of the many guys you dated while we were in school. How in the hell would I know you held these deep-seeded feelings for the man? If you remember, my dear, you were the one who gave him the old heave-ho!"

Good old Beverly comes through once again, Jill thought as she reflected on the words her friend had just uttered. Of course she was right. Jill had been so certain twenty-five years ago she was doing the right thing, it never occurred to her she was burying her feelings. Now as these feelings resurfaced, she all too late realized they had been buried in very shallow ground. This was a fact that started raising its ugly head at the Matthews' fund-raising event. Then, last Tuesday night when Senator Jim Howard had come to call, all of those pitifully buried feelings rose from the dead and threatened her very way of life. He had waited for her to make an appointment with him at the office. When days went by and he hadn't heard from her, he decided he would face his dilemma. That was exactly what he had called this, a dilemma. She wondered if he had looked the definition of the word up in the dictionary. She had been less than candid with him in their meeting. The only thing she was certain of was the fact she still cared very deeply for this man. Yet he could have turned into one of those charming criminals who sweep women off their feet, use them, and once their use is over, the body is found in a cornfield months later, and the police are consulting dental records. What she knew about Senator James Howard was twenty-five-year-old knowledge. It certainly didn't bode well that he had married Evelyn, and worst of all, had stayed married to her. He had indicated to Jill he had become a prisoner in his own house. *Yeah right,* Jill had mentally added, *and my wife doesn't understand me!* Joanna had wanted Jill to leave her house and move into temporary living quarters. Jill would have no part of it. She had her pets to consider, and she was not the least bit frightened. After further discussions with Jacob, Joanna backed off the idea because Jacob had assured her they would be doing constant surveillance at Jill's house and no one at the agency thought it a good idea for Jill to suddenly disappear. It had also been determined that Jill would not be made aware of the surveillance given the latest development between the suspect and their collaborator. Jill. Beverly watched helplessly as her friend tried to make sense of what was going on around her, what was going on within her, and what was going on with a man she now determined she loved.

"Would you like for me to spend the night? Since it's nearing the witching hour and since I'm a witch, I was thinking a sleepover might be in order."

"Oh would you? Would you really mind? I could sure use the company. It would be a nice distraction for me."

"Thanks, Jill. If there is anything in this world I want to be, it's a distraction! Where do you keep your ashtrays?"

Jill smiled as she pointed her toward the bar in the family room. "The light switch is on the right side of the doorway," she called out as Beverly was leaving the room.

"I don't need a light switch; I remember where the bar is."

Jill was just about to ask Beverly if she would like something to drink when Beverly walked up to her, grabbed her by the arm, and told her she needed to call the police. All of these instructions had been given to her in a stage whisper. "Go into your bedroom to make the call because I don't want them to see you using the phone."

"Them? You said them?" Jill didn't know if she had spoken or screeched; she didn't really care. She continued, "How many are out there? Two, three, a National Guard Unit, Lord knows a senator might have enough pull to get a National Guard Unit!" Now Jill was certain she was screeching.

"Pull yourself together, *woman*! This is no time for you to freak out on me!" With this newfound authority, Beverly took charge of making the phone call, lighting a cigarette, and instructing Jill where she was to sit and how she was to behave until the cops arrived at the front door and told them of the arrests they had just made.

The two women were sitting across from one another, trying to act as normal as either of them could remember ever being. Jill watched Beverly smoke cigarettes as fast as she had ever seen anyone smoke. At one point, Jill told Beverly she might want to slow down because she wasn't sure but she thought her smoke alarm might go off, and that would certainly alert whoever was out there things were not going on in a normal fashion. It hadn't been a week since his visit, and here she sat with her friend the smokestack, men prowling around her property, police on their way, and, oh yes, a dog she thought was a good watch who was sleeping peacefully at her feet. "You sic 'em, Brutus!" she said as she reached down to rub Lebo behind his ears.

Beverly was quiet except the exhaling sounds she made. Her eyes were trained on the door. "Do you have any kind of a gun?" Beverly's question had startled her in more than a few ways.

"I have an old shotgun upstairs."

"You might want to get up there and bring it down here."

"All right. Have you seen something else out there? Beverly? Beverly?" The sound was unmistakable. Lebo sprang to his feet and charged in the direction of the sound. Beverly and Jill were moving in tandem to the door. Beverly recognized the young uniformed policeman. As the officer was about to ask questions of Jill and Beverly, headlights began bouncing behind him. Jill didn't think much of this until she watched Joanna step from a car that she didn't recognize, with a man she recognized as Jacob. As they made their way to where the young policeman stood, Joanna brushed past him as Jacob pulled the officer aside. Joanna stepped inside, taking Jill by the hand, turned to Beverly, and directed both of them to the family room. Once the three women were seated, Joanna began the explanation. On their drive over to Jill's house, she had mentally tried to prepare herself for what would await her once the two of them had been told the truth. Now, after she and Jacob had been sitting with the two of them for more than an hour, she knew there would never have been enough time to prepare for these two.

"Joanna. You mean to tell me you knew there were FBI agents out there prowling around my house and you didn't bother to tell me? Why? Did you think I would be that untrustworthy?"

Before Joanna could respond to Jill, Beverly had broken in with her tirade. "You know, Joanna, you and those guys out there did a very risky and dangerous thing. I had just asked Jill if she had a shotgun. She did! She would have used it, too! Then, whose fault would it have been? Mine? Jill's? Yours?"

Again, before a response could be made, there chimed in a fourth voice; this time it was male and the owner of the voice was Jacob. "If one of the men had been shot, it would have been considered to be in the line of duty. No one would be guilty of anything."

Joanna and Jacob had spent another hour calming the two women down. When Jill had offered to make them coffee, they both refused but felt a sense of relief. At least Jill looked like she was on the road to forgiveness. It was going to take Beverly a few more trips down this road before she would get there.

As Jacob was driving Joanna back to her place, he shared his assessments of the two ladies. "I can see what you've been trying to tell us. We should have informed Jill about our surveillance. However, she threw us a curveball last week, and I think the decision to go forward without her knowledge was a good one. As for Beverly. Why in the world do you worry about this lady? She's as tough as nails!" Joanna could hear by the way he had spoken of Beverly that he really liked her.

"Beverly isn't as strong as she lets on. Don't get me wrong, she has great courage, but I think she hides a lot behind that rough exterior of hers."

"Jill. It's nearly five o'clock in the morning. Want to go and find some breakfast?" After Joanna and Jacob had left them, they continued to hash over some of the most recent developments. Jill had assured all concerned that it was perfectly okay for the agents to continue their surveillance; in fact, she felt comforted just knowing they were there. If the senator did show up on her doorstep again, they would be among the first to know. She wouldn't have to call Joanna. The last statement was supposed to have been funny, but no one in the room laughed. Jill was deep in these thoughts when Beverly had asked her the question. "Oh. I'm sorry what did you just say?"

"Would you like to go and find some breakfast?" Jill stood up, grabbed her purse and her keys, and said, "Let's go."

The word "exhausted" seemed to have been used a lot lately. Beverly knew by seven o'clock in the morning this word applied to her as it may have never applied before. Physical, emotional, and mental exhaustion engulfed her most inner being. Screw the fashion show, Evelyn Howard, for that matter the FBI, and, oh, she almost forgot, her shop. "Damn."

"What's wrong?" Jill had the nerve to actually ask the question.

"What's wrong? Let's see. The fact I've been awake for the last twenty-four hours; the fact I thought the two of us were probably going to be murdered; the fact I am working with some grazed, greedy woman I cannot stand the sight of. Or Jill, maybe it's the fact my only daughter is barely talking to me! Now that I have given you all this information, you tell me what you think might be wrong." Nothing was said between the two women for several minutes. Jill realized Beverly's outburst had actually been what she needed. For the first time in days, she began to see that the world did not revolve around her, the senator, or, for that matter, Evelyn.

"Beverly. I am so sorry. I have been thinking only of myself and my problem. You need to get home and get about two days of sleep. You also need to have a talk with Jana. I don't care what Joanna has told you to do. Look what happened to the two of us just a few hours ago. Get some sleep, and then talk to Jana. Tell her whatever you want to tell her about me. I don't care anymore. Whatever happens, happens."

Beverly looked at Jill with curiosity. Was this the same woman who had dissolved before everyone's very eyes only a few days ago? Did she really think she had suddenly become this ... this what? Beverly was searching for a word that would describe what she was feeling about Jill's sudden change of character or, for that matter, what she was feeling about any of this. The only thing she was sure of was that she wanted to get home and get to bed. She wanted to have the relationship she and Jana had enjoyed since her birth to return. She wanted to get the fashion show over with. Most of all, she wanted to *not* have to deal with Evelyn Howard for the rest of her life!

"Jill. You're absolutely correct. I need to get home and get some sleep. First, I need to call Jana and tell her she needs to open and close the shop today. Yes. I most certainly need to have a talk with Jana. I'll see if she can make it over for supper tonight."

The two women got up from the table to pay their bills as Silverfish, who had been listening to their conversation, watched.

When she opened her eyes, she was trying to figure out where she was and if she was going to be late opening the shop. Near panic set in before she realized she had already talked to Jana, the shop would be opened, and she and Jana were going to enjoy a home-cooked meal at her home. The time on the clock read 3:00. "Well, I hope it's 3:00 pm and not am," Beverly said to herself as she made her way to the bathroom to grab her robe. The reflections of the sun and shadows told her indeed it was in the afternoon. She loved her small cottage in Old Town. There were large oak trees in the front yard with a beautiful boxwood hedge acting as a fence to her beautifully landscaped lawn. The house had been built in the late twenties or early thirties. Four years before, it had been renovated by a couple named Ted and Bob. They had told her at the closing this was a passion of theirs. Buy these "old darlings" and bring them back to their splendor. Those had been the words of Bob, with Ted nodding in agreement. She had told them she was glad they had this passion because she had been the beneficiary. Indeed she had been. The rich hardwood floors, the new-paned windows, granite countertops, and modern bathroom fixtures gave her the best of both worlds. The outside reflected the period of gingerbread wood work above the wraparound porch, while the updated interior gave her the conveniences of modern life. Beverly sat on this porch in the summertime and imagined young girls with their long hair in finger curls and huge pastel bows sitting on the top of their heads, playing a game of jacks while a large Lab sat by their side. She knew this was not just her imagination. Bob and Ted had uncovered some old tin photos when they were doing the restoration and presented them to her at closing. The two young Victorian-dressed girls were in one of the photos. It was a wonderful place to live. That very thought stupefied her. When Robert died, she really didn't care where she lived or if she lived; she could never have believed she would live and actually feel content. Yet, here she was, feeling all of this. Except, of course, for this Howard mess. One thing she determined after last night's experience was she would not let the relationship with her daughter suffer. No. Jill was absolutely correct. This thing was not going to harm her daughter in any way. Not physically, not mentally, and not emotionally. So tonight was going to be a very good night for the two of them.

The dinner had been wonderful. Cooking was one of Beverly's pleasures that had just recently returned. The texture of the foods, the smell, and presentation was a form of art for her. Tonight may have been one of her more memorable works. Jana had marveled at what was presented; the appetizers had been outstanding; the chilled shrimp had been perfect and was served along with baked brie. When she brought out the main course, Jana's eyes grew wide. She had no idea her mother knew how to make beef Wellington, much less make it better than any she had ever experienced. "Mom. You should sell the dress shop and open a restaurant."

"No. No. My child. One reckless adventure in life is enough!" Beverly had responded with more than a small amount of conviction.

The polite conversation continued for a while, and then Beverly looked Jana squarely in the eye and began the story. There were no questions and no interruptions as Beverly worked her way through the entire saga of the Howards, Diane, Jill, and Joanna. When she told her what had happened the night before, Jana blanched.

"Mom. I don't want you hurt. I don't care what else happens. I don't want you hurt." Beverly could hear the fear in her daughter's voice. As she tried to reassure and comfort her, she wondered what she had gotten herself into. When she told Jill to get her shotgun less than twenty-four hours ago, this thing had become larger than any of them had imagined it was going to be. All of this was going through Beverly's mind as she looked at her daughter and was glad she had shared all there was to share. Yet, she was worried as well. How could she forget the advice of her brother-in-law? He was the one that had to tell her, her beloved husband may have been a homicide and not an accident victim. That was the day she had gone to her room and moved only when someone told her to. It was a time in her life that had become a dark blurred memory. Jana stayed by her side. She encouraged her in every way imaginable. Waiting on her hand and foot, fixing meals, cleaning the house, and maintaining constant contact with Hugh. Once she began to climb out of the black abyss, Jana had been on one side of her, while Hugh had been on the other. Holding, encouraging, pulling, and pushing her to begin living again. Because of the two of them, she had the courage to fight and win the battle of the lease for her dress shop. This is when Hugh had given her the advice, the application for a gun permit, and the small handgun.

Several hours had passed since Jana left. Beverly watched the late news, smoked more cigarettes than she wanted to admit, and decided she needed to talk to Hugh. She heard the answering machine's mechanical voice, and left the message. "Hugh. This is Beverly. Call me."

Damn! Hugh thought as he heard Beverly's voice come over the machine. *I knew this was going to happen. I knew it! I knew it!* Hugh had been worried for months about his sister-in-law and this Howard investigation. This couldn't be good news. These idiot politicians and their idiot plots! However, the Howards worried him more than a little. Evelyn was much more troublesome than the senator. She had been raised to understand the power of money and the power of government. Those two elements added up to a dangerous equation; mix in Evelyn Howard and the equation had the potential to become lethal.

The two had talked for hours. There were very few people in Beverly's life who earned the trust she placed in this man. His concern for the welfare of her and for her family was the same he held for his wife and children. The reverse was true for Hugh. He knew whatever she saw or heard was a clear unvarnished report of events. Sometimes he had wished some of his agents had the same ability.

The next morning was a beautiful day. Beverly had set the alarm so she could open the shop and finish unpacking the inventory for the fashion show. She had told Jana the night before not to worry about arriving until she felt like it. When she reached the parking lot, she didn't like what she saw. Directly in front of the shop door was Evelyn Howard's car, or a car that looked exactly like it. "Well. Friggin' good morning!" she said out loud as she fumbled with the keys to the shop.

"And a friggin' good morning to you," came a response from behind her. She turned to see Evelyn Howard approaching with a cup of carryout coffee in her hand, a phony smile on her face, and a cold look in her eye.

Beverly returned the stare and the phony smile as she said, "Why, Evelyn, how good to see you. What brings you out so early in the morning?"

Again, Evelyn was set off-balance by Beverly's response. No matter how hard she tried to believe she had the upper hand, it was times such as this that brought the truth to the surface. Beverly did not think she was someone special; in fact, it was clear to anyone who knew these two women that Beverly didn't even like her, and very many times she was hard-pressed to tolerate her. At this moment, Evelyn would have appreciated tolerance because the look Beverly was leveling at her showed something that made Evelyn extremely uncomfortable. Within a few seconds, Evelyn regained her composure and began to discuss the fashion show. Had the dresses arrived? Had she talked with the models about the fittings? Was there anything she could do? Beverly answered all of the questions appropriately; in fact, there had been a few times during their discussion Beverly had actually interjected a small bit of humor. This had always dumbfounded Evelyn. How could someone who obviously abhorred another find humor in the interaction of the two? Even Evelyn had to admit Beverly was a mystery.

So be it! Evelyn thought as she turned to leave the shop with the requests for the fashion show for Beverly to work out. She didn't care about Beverly. She didn't care about the stupid fashion show, other than what it would provide for the campaign funds, and she sure as hell didn't care about Jim Howard, except for what he could provide for her in the way of making money and giving her the control of that money. Someday she wouldn't need him for that, and if things worked out the way she hoped, that day could be very soon. With this last thought in her mind, she broke into a wide grin as she pulled out of the parking lot.

Try as hard as she might, Beverly couldn't get Evelyn's visit out of her mind. She was concentrating on the schedule for the model's fittings when the sound of a whirlwind blew open the shop door. In spite of herself, Beverly was happy to see Patty. It always fascinated Beverly the way Patty could hold a one-sided conversation. The listener was just a listener. Beverly was certain the only words she had spoken during Patty's twenty-five-minute visit were "oh," "sure," and "we'll be there." By her calculations, she had been allowed one word every five minutes. All the things had taken place these last few weeks had pushed golf far from her mind. It seemed impossible it was already time for the member/member tournament. She had been looking forward to this event, and until Patty dropped by, she had completely forgotten about it. She decided she would discuss this with Jill. While all of them had been at golf school, they had talked about the partners for member/member. The original plan had been for Jill and Beverly to play the event with Diane and Joanna. Patty had accepted Mildred's invitation, and so it had been set. Had this just been four weeks ago? Impossible. Absolutely impossible. It must have been three months ago. How could so much have happened in such a short period of time?

"Hey. Annie Oakley. How are you this morning?" Jill asked as she opened the office door.

"Me? Annie Oakley? You're the one that owns the shotgun." Beverly lifted her head from the pile of dresses she had been working on. There had been a transformation that had come over her good friend. She looked younger than Beverly had remembered Jill looking since her makeover for the Matthews' fund-raiser. Before Jill could respond to Beverly, she added, "Jill. You look wonderful." This statement had surprised and pleased her, and then she broke out in one of the widest smiles she possessed.

"Beverly. My dear, dear friend. That is one of the best compliments I have ever been given by anyone. Thank you." The two women gave each other a quick hug and began to busy themselves with the tasks at hand. Jill was bringing Beverly up-to-date on her latest reflections. "The other night was a good slap in the face for me," Jill had stated. "I'm not sure who this Jim Howard really is. I'm not sure it is important for me to care who he is or, for that matter, who he was. The only thing I care about right this moment is that I cooperate in any way I can and bring an end to all of this."

"Amen, brother," Beverly all but shouted, and then added, "It's good to have my old friend back."

"Hey. Wait a minute. I thought you just told me how wonderful I looked."

The rest of the morning flew as the two of them worked scheduling, steaming the newly arrived garments, and discussing the member/member tournament. Jill had expressed the same surprise Beverly had felt when she was told the tournament was only a week away. Jill was going to give Joanna a call later in the afternoon to see if she still had this on her schedule. Beverly would call Diane during her lunch hour to see if she was still available.

"You know. I haven't heard anything from Diane in several days. I hope things are all right with her," Beverly said off-handedly.

"I think she and Steve were going to some kind of meeting. Remember she was talking about going to Mackinac, Michigan?"

"Yes. I do remember that. She told us the last time we all played golf together. Do you remember when she said they would be back?"

"Did I hear my name being called in vain?" Diane asked as she popped her head around the corner of the office door.

"Speak of the devil, and here she is!" The conversation began in all directions, with three women talking at once. Diane had just returned from their trip. She had many things to share with the two women. No. She had not forgotten the member/member. No. she hadn't heard about Joanna's friend going to the hospital. When the question was asked about the Howards, both Beverly and Jill decided the three of them would get an order for carryout and eat lunch in. Jana was taking care of the shop while the three of them ate in the office and updated each other on the latest developments. When a new piece of information was shared that one of them had not heard, there would be a follow-up of questions, ideas, speculation of what or how this new piece to the puzzle fit into the Howards doing business with Phil Matthews. As Beverly listened to the other two talk, she lost herself in the knowledge she had been given by Hugh, and how she would keep all of this to herself for the protection of the women in the room and her own sweet daughter.

Beverly was pulling her car out of the parking space and humming that old song. She couldn't remember all of the words, only, "What a difference a day makes. Just twenty-four hours." The day had held many surprises. Patty had been the first surprise. She hadn't realized how good Patty's visit had been for her. Her talking, her genuine smile, the goodness of this person came through in spite of the constant chatter. Jill's quiet, calm resolve had shown through the minute she entered the room. This had been a comfort and a boost to Beverly. Diane's visit and the new information she had to share, which Beverly would be sharing with Hugh. Of course there was her wonderfully generous and loyal daughter, holding down the shop in the midst of confusion. "Beverly.

You're one fortunate woman," She said this out loud as she drove up to the fast food speaker to order a burger and some fries.

The week had been packed with a thousand things on her to-do list. It seemed incredible to Beverly that middle-aged women who were going to model in the fashion show actually became prima donnas. She was close to telling one of the women (that had been handpicked by Evelyn) that she had given more thought to the problem and she really didn't need her in the show. Beverly had already had the waist of this woman's dress taken out as far as the material would allow. After all of this, the woman insisted the wrong size had been sent. Beverly knew this woman had gained ten pounds since the fittings and wanted to tell her she looked like ten pounds of potatoes in a five-pound sack. Jill had been in the room at the time, and when she saw the color of Beverly's face change from soft pink to bright red, she stepped in with some sage advice. "Why don't we all get some rest and come back in the morning to finish picking out the accessories? I'm sure the right color of scarf with some 'fun' jewelry will draw the eye away from any problem areas." The woman started to whine about the next morning not being a good time for her, and if she had known how much time all of this would have taken, she wasn't sure she would have agreed to model, and she had to get ready for her trip to Europe, and on and on and on. Jill led her out of the shop, all the while agreeing, cajoling, and placating her. Beverly was telling Jana the only reason the woman didn't want to come back in the next morning was because it interfered with her two-hour feed! As frustrating as all of this was, it felt good to be busy doing the things she knew how to do instead of telling Jill to get a shotgun. Neither Beverly, nor Jill, nor Diane had heard anything regarding the Howard investigation. Joanna had told Jill she still planned on playing in the member/member. When Jill asked if there had been any new developments, Joanna had told her it had been very quiet. Jill heard nothing from the senator, and this didn't seem to concern her in the least. Diane had attended another lunch meeting with Karen. There had been a little more information on that front, but Karen had cautioned Diane to take what she told her for what it was worth, because Phil had been drunk out of his mind when he had told her about his plans with the Howards.

Beverly had just finished her dinner and was going to her closet to select the outfit she would wear in the member/member the following morning. She wanted to look especially stylish; all the women in the league would either have purchased new golf outfits or wear their best ones. There seemed to be some unwritten rule about dress when it came to the Ladies League tournaments. When Diane had stopped by the shop, she asked Beverly her opinion about what she thought she should wear for the tournament. "Amazing," Beverly murmured to herself. Not more than six weeks ago this same woman had wondered what all of the fuss was about. *It's a game you play outside in the heat, you sweat, you get sand all over you, and you think I should spend good money to dress up?* Now it seemed Diane wanted advice on what to wear.

"If I can't play the game very well, I might as well dress the part," was the remark she made to Beverly while selecting a very tailored and expensive pair of golf shorts, shirt, and matching shoes. So the bar had been raised, and Beverly knew she would not drop beneath it. She brought three different outfits from the shop and decided on the khaki-colored shorts with the matching polo shirt. She was as puzzled as Diane about why it seemed important to all the ladies in the league to look their best on tournament day. She really didn't care about the reason. It had been good revenue this past week, and she for one would vote to have more tournaments.

The clubhouse parking lot was abuzz with all the ladies sporting their finest. The chatter, the laughter, and the sound of golf clubs clanking greeted Beverly as she stepped from her car. It had turned out to be a perfect day for the event. There was a slight breeze blowing from the west, a few puffy white clouds rolling across the sky, and the predicted high was seventy-eight degrees. "Wow," Beverly said out loud as she crossed the parking lot, "this is going to be a gorgeous day." She was asking Jim if her partner had signed in, but before he could answer, Joanna stepped up beside her and informed her that she and Diane would not be in their foursome. It had something to do with the pairings the pro shop had made. No. Joanna had not seen Jill, nor had she seen Diane. At this point, Mildred joined the two and told them Jim had explained to her the pairings were always done by the pros when there was tournament play. Joanna and Beverly assured Mildred this was not a problem and to please not worry about it. All of this had just finished being discussed when Diane walked up to their group without so much as a "good morning," "kiss my ass," or "what's new?" She launched into her not understanding why the four of them couldn't play together. This sent Mildred into a tailspin, something she could easily do, so off and running she went about the pro shop, etc., etc. As soon as Diane began to show some reasonable sense of understanding, Jill walked up with the same look of confusion Diane had just shown, and so the explanations once again began. It was at this point Beverly glanced in the direction of the ladies' locker room. There stood Evelyn Howard with what Beverly would describe later as a look of disdain written on her face. She approached the group, never taking her eyes off of Jill. This puzzled and concerned Beverly.

The only comment she made as she walked passed all of them was, "Hope all of you play well." Beverly's eyes followed her as she made her way out of the pro shop. *How in the world could such a short fat lady leave such a chill in the room?* Beverly all but said these words out loud.

It had been years since she and Jill had played in a tournament, and this was first tournament play for Joanna and Diane. Beverly couldn't help but be concerned for Diane; she knew Joanna was given a certain amount of respect by the other women in the league because of her law practice. Beverly had overheard one of the league women say to her cart partner one day, "You've got to be nice to her. You never know when you might need a good attorney." She knew Shirley Knight slightly better than Judy Rhoads. They had already started the bowing and scraping act for Joanna, while Diane was being ignored. This had all taken place while they waited for Jim to make the announcements. Beverly had deliberately made a show of going over to Diane's cart and talking loudly about how nice Diane looked in her outfit. Diane nearly blew the whole thing when she started to say something about Beverly selling it to her. Beverly had pinched Diane, who then only yelped, "Ouch!" as Beverly led her away to the water station to explain some things to her dear friend. She knew the other two women well enough to caution Diane. They came into her shop from time to time. Neither purchased much, if anything, and both acted as though she and Jana were their personal handmaids. They never attempted this with Jill. The citizens of the community held a great deal of respect for Jill. Up until the time of her husband's death, they had operated their horse farm for the benefit of autistic and physically handicapped children. Their contribution to the community had not been forgotten, and Jill was regarded with a great deal of respect by the city fathers. Women like Shirley and Judy would never want to go against the grain of those they perceived to hold status. People considered to be of lesser importance by these two were minimized and ignored, if not made fun of. After interacting with the two of them for the last several years, Beverly had concluded neither of them were very nice women. Diane was a nobody to them, and they would make sure she would understand her place before the nine holes of golf had been completed. Neither one had any idea what would await them on this fine tournament day. It would be weeks later before Diane found herself laughing with Beverly, Jill, and Joanna over the day's events. Up until that time, Diane had seen absolutely nothing funny about any of it. Yet, as she listened to the chronological description of what had taken place, she saw how funny all of it really was. The only thing Diane regretted doing was stooping to their level. Yet, the other three women assured her she had done the right thing, and may have actually helped others that found themselves in a foursome with the two of them.

There were several new members that had never played in a tournament event. Mildred's suggestion to Jim had been for him to go over the format of the game, explain the necessity of exchanging the official score cards, and since this was a two-best ball competition, explain why it was important for a player to pick up their ball if they knew it wouldn't count in the interest of pace of play. Diane remembered hearing the "pace of play" phrase, and next to the word "whiff," it set her teeth to grinding. Adding the fact that Beverly had given her the heads-up on the other two women she would be playing with had given her nerves the tautness of forty-gauge wire. Beverly failed to realize Diane already had a slow burn going for these two, and she had just thrown gasoline on the smoldering flame. The foursome had started on hole number one. By the time they had gotten to the green on hole number three, this flame had gone from smoldering to flickering. It was on the green of hole number seven that anyone on the golf course, inside the clubhouse, or, for that matter, motorists on the street could see a three-alarm fire had erupted. Diane had dealt with this type of individual before. *How I wish I could buy them for what they're worth and sell them for what they think they're worth.* This was a phrase she had heard her parents repeat to each other on more than one occasion. What she never understood was why anyone became so concerned with only themselves. She was mulling this over as she watched first Shirley and then Judy take turns trying to impress Joanna, all the while ignoring her. They had not met her before and officially they still had not met her as they approached the tee box on hole three. She watched all three women tee off before she walked up to the box, put the golf tee in the ground, stood for a few moments, and then walked off the tee box, approached the cart of the two, stuck out her hand and with a grin as wide as she could manage said, "Hello. My name is Diane Stoner. I presume you are Shirley Knight, and that would make you Judy Rhoads?" Never taking her hand away or taking her eyes off the faces of the two until Shirley finally responded with a faint "glad to meet you," Judy began to giggle nervously while her face grew a bright red. Once Diane decided the introductions had met with her approval, she walked back to the tee box and proceeded to hit the best drive that she would hit for the day. Joanna said nothing as she waited for Diane to return to the cart. When she put her foot on the gas to drive to the next shot, anyone within a mile radius could see the huge smile spread across her face. The conversation between the four women was at a minimum for the next few shots. Only when Diane was hitting her fourth shot did Judy let out a laugh as Diane's ball landed a mere three feet from where it had been. Joanna would later tell everyone she had never seen a laugh stick in anyone's throat before, but she had witnessed it that day. Diane didn't move; she didn't even look like she was breathing; she just stared at Judy until the look on her face turned from a smirk to a look of something between shock and fear. Judy waited for a response from her dear friend (who always seemed to be quick with some kind of putdown), but then realized nothing was coming from Shirley. She attempted a feeble reply about how she and

Shirley had hit this same kind of shot so many times, she couldn't help but laugh. "Isn't that right, Shirley?"

At this point, Joanna broke in with the comment that none of the women in the nine-hole league could be that good, or they would be playing in the eighteen-hole group, wouldn't they? This statement seemed to move Diane from her frozen position and allowed Shirely and Judy to move their carts in the direction of their next shot. "Don't pay any attention to these two. To pay attention to them gives them some validation, and neither of them deserve validation." Joanna's statement helped assuage Diane's feelings until she was walking off the green of the seventh hole. This is when Shirley decided it was time to tell Diane she had been mistaken about the score she had given them on the sixth hole.

"After reviewing the strokes you took on the sixth hole, we decided you had an eight and not a seven for your score."

Diane stood motionless as she heard Joanna's voice interrupt the silence of the group. "How so?" was all she said.

Following this question came a few sounds of someone clearing their throat and finally a weak response from Shirley. "Well. We believe Diane didn't count a stroke."

"That is a foregone conclusion? Where do you think she erred?"

Before Shirley or Judy could respond, Diane not only found her tongue but her temper, and both of them had been turned lose. "Wait just one minute. Since I am the one that is supposed to be in error in this matter, let's include me in the discussion. You're telling me the last hole we played, number six and not number seven, is where you think I scored an eight and not a seven; is that correct?" She was glaring directly into Shirley's eyes until Shirley decided the most important item in her life was the score card she was holding in her hand. In a feeble effort to come to the aid of her cohort, Judy began to offer an explanation of why they felt Diane had in fact scored an eight instead of a seven.

At this point Joanna, the logical one, simply said, "Let's review." Well, review they did. At least that's what Judy and Shirley thought they were going to do. It seemed they thought, or knew, Diane had taken an extra stroke in the middle of the fairway. How or why they thought they knew this was never clearly understood, not even by the two of them.

Try as Diane might, there was absolutely no possibility she was going to maintain any decorum after she pointedly asked Shirley if they were questioning her integrity and Shirley's answer had been, "We are not questioning your integrity, but we are questioning your math."

The first response Diane remembered making was to the effect that it would be hard for anyone to question someone's math skills when they had none of their own. There were so many things she wanted to say, but even she understood there was a certain amount of decorum that needed to be maintained on the golf course. After all, it was a gentleman's game. Apparently it was not a lady's game! Joanna's legal skills had kicked in as soon as she saw the emotional state her partner had entered. Shirley and Judy's attitude could only be described as "backpedaling" while Diane tried to control her own meltdown. So the eighth and ninth holes were played with forced civility within the foursome. All four of the women knew as soon as they hit the dining room all of their stories would be told, and before the dessert could be served, the room would be divided into the Joanna/Diane side and the Shirley/Judy side.

While Diane was driving home, she remembered the words her dear friend spoke when she was trying to talk her into joining the nine-hole league. "They're just a fun group. None of them take the game seriously."

HOLE EIGHT
Par Four

   She had ceased being intimidated years ago by the smell and feel of wealth. Yet, as she sat in the Adams/Turner/Wade Law Office, she felt intimidated. The starched pleasantness of the receptionist gave her little comfort. Karen smiled at the professionally attired young woman who had just offered to bring her a beverage. The same moment she was declining the offer, her smile widened as she thought about the old tired line from a hundred-year-old joke: "Coffee, tea, or me?' The dark leather couch on which she sat, the original oil paintings of the city's skyline, the music playing softly, the richness of the wood furnishings—all of it was in exquisite taste. For some reason, she felt amused and not intimidated by any of it. So why did she feel this way? What was it? Afraid Mr. Adams had already agreed to represent Phil? Maybe. No. That wasn't it. She had good reason to believe Phil had not yet made his move to start divorce proceedings. So why this feeling of inadequacy? She was searching for an answer to her question when her eyes fell on the bookcase across the room from where she was seated. Of course. Of course. It's the same old thing. I don't think I'm smart enough. How many times she had heard herself explaining the reason she had to drop out of school. The excuses—yes, that's all they were. Excuses for why she didn't return to school and finish her degree.

Her latest reason was an honest admission. She hadn't returned to school because Phil had told her he wouldn't tolerate her leaving their children to pursue some overpriced degree. For some reason, she had never wanted to share this before now. The first time she heard herself admit the "why." She felt ashamed. Ashamed of herself for selling out to a man that had grown into someone she didn't want to be around, much less continue to share life together. Looking back on the years she had spent with Phil, she saw a pattern in his behavior. He wanted to control everything and everyone. On the surface, he seemed a generous and giving man. He was not. Early in her marriage, she learned that any time Phil gave a gift, did a favor, or loaned anyone something of his, he expected a payback. It didn't matter how small the payback was; the only thing that was important to him was the payback would be paid when, where, and how he wanted it. So that's what she had done most of her married life. Pay him back for the homes they lived in, the clothes she wore, the lifestyle she enjoyed. The biggest payback for her had been the inability to finish her education. How could anyone really understand what she had gone through? Her own mother constantly reminded her of how fortunate she had been to marry a man like Phil. When she stopped to assess her life, she came to realize that outside of her children, there was really no one she felt close to and she seriously doubted any of her so-called "friends" felt close to her. All of this was going to change. Today she was taking the first step on a new and unknown path. Today was the day that "paid in full" would be stamped across her marriage license.

Diane had assured Karen she would say nothing to Steve about the steps Karen was going to take. There had been more than a few reasons Diane had made this promise. Never was there a time when she felt divorce was something to be joyous about. She had gone through one of her own, and many times she had said she wouldn't wish a divorce on her worst enemy. Yet, when Karen had asked to meet with her and made the announcement, she would have been lying to herself and anyone else if she had not admitted that deep down she was thrilled to hear Karen make the statement. She didn't mention any of this to

Beverly, Joanna, or Jill. Once during the member/member tournament, she had toyed with the idea of telling Joanna. Somehow the timing of the telling was off. Now, she wondered if she had made a mistake in keeping the information to herself. No. A promise was a promise. She would wait until she heard from Karen before she told anyone anything about what she knew of the Matthews' and their possible divorce.

The farthest thing from Phil Matthews' mind was a divorce. He had just finished a phone conversation with Evelyn Howard. It was three o'clock in the afternoon, and he felt he deserved a celebratory drink. When this deal went through, he was going to be one wealthy man, and he and he alone would be the victor. His whiny-ass business partner Linda and her arrogant husband would know who they had been dealing with all these years. As for Steve and Diane, they would finally know their places. Oh, how sweet all of this was going to be. These were the happy little thoughts running through his mind as he walked over to the credenza in his office, pulled out a large bottle of bourbon, and began to pour. When he finished dealing with his pitiful business partners, then and only then would he deal with Karen. In the meantime, he would keep her from suspecting anything until he was ready.

Mr. Wayne Adams Esq. had just escorted his newest client to the private elevators of his spacious office. As he sat down to review the information he had just been given, he began to smile, which turned into a very large grin, which turned into a chuckle. By the time his secretary opened the door to his office, he was laughing out loud. When she announced he had another client waiting to see him, he told her it would be a few moments. As he said the word "moments," he let out with a guffaw that startled the otherwise composed secretary. This only caused a few more guffaws, followed by some more "I'm sorry." Finally, he was able to compose himself, but couldn't keep the smile from returning. Never in his wildest dreams did he believe he would ever get Mr. Phillip Matthews by the short hair. There was justice after all. Sometimes it came in strange forms, but justice was justice, and he knew he was going to do everything in his power to see Karen Matthews got the best divorce settlement this state had ever known.

The visit with Mr. Adams had left Karen feeling emotions she hadn't felt in years. Fear, anxiety, relief, excitement, and anger were some of the emotions that began to surface as she started her descent inside the private elevator. Mr. Adams had given her a list of things she needed to do before her next visit. Her next stop would be at the First National Bank of Old Town. She had been remiss in this area of her married life. Phil was the one that handled all of their finances. Once every year, she had to sign the joint tax return, and this was the only time she saw anything that gave her an idea of what their annual income was. She clearly remembered the first time she saw a six-figure income on the return and expressed her surprise to Phil. She also remembered his reaction when she had the nerve to comment on the amount. "Just sign the damn return and leave the rest to me and our accountant," Phil had said with no small amount of annoyance in his voice. Wasn't it strange she could recall his exact words, the sound of his voice, and the look on his face as he had once again demeaned her? What a stupid little fool she had been. What a stupid little fool.

"Good afternoon, Mrs. Matthews. What can I do for you today?" Karen always waited for Kelly's window to open up when doing any banking. Not only was she one of the most efficient tellers, but her mother had worked with Karen on a community foundation project. Karen had found her to be one of the most refreshing people she had encountered in years. When Clara Ashton mentioned her daughter was a teller at First National, Karen had told Clara she would be the only teller she would see from that day forward.

That had been three years ago, and Karen had kept her word. "How are you doing, Kelly?" Karen asked with genuine interest in her tone. "And how is Matt doing?" Matt was Kelly's only child. After a very difficult pregnancy, he had been born two months prematurely. His stay in the hospital and the medical bills surrounding his birth had been more than Kelly and her husband could handle. Karen had seen that the balance of the outstanding medical bills was taken care of. It had been Karen's request the donor remain anonymous; however, Kelly had a close friend who worked in the hospital's billing department, and revealed Karen's name to Kelly.

"He's doing great. Can you believe he is going into preschool this fall?" "Isn't that wonderful? They grow so fast. Hold on to every moment you have with them."

"Mrs. Matthews, I know I've told you this before, but I still can't thank you enough for helping us out with Matt's hospitalization."

"Kelly. You just pass it on. There will come a day when someone will need your help. Like I've said before, just pass it on."

"I plan on doing just that. Now. How can I help you today?"

Karen hesitated a few moments, cleared her throat, and then spoke in a softer tone when she asked for copies of their bank account. "If possible, I would like copies for the last year." Kelly smiled a wide smile and assured Karen she could do just that. It was only when Karen returned to her house and opened the statements that she saw that Kelly had indeed "just passed it on." She and Phil had a joint account; however, the documents Kelly had just given Karen included a copy of Phil Matthews' private account, an account that up to this very moment Karen hadn't known existed. There had been several checks written from this account in the amount of five thousand dollars twice monthly. From the statements she held in her hand, there had been no less than seventy thousand dollars written to cash.

Diane had just finished putting away the groceries when Karen's call came. She didn't hesitate when asked if she could meet Karen at the same small cafe north of Old Town. Excitement with a mix of anxiety filled Diane as she walked into the room. Karen had already arrived. A glass of iced tea sat in front of her while cigarette smoke swirled above her. There were some country-western tunes playing in the background while a couple of good old boys were joking with a young waitress. Diane slid in the booth across from Karen. Before either of them spoke, a more mature waitress was asking Diane what she wanted to drink and if she wanted a menu. Once all questions had been answered and their orders for food had been given, the two women sat staring at each other. Diane had the same stabbing in her gut she had experienced when she knew she would be going through her divorce. She waited for Karen to speak, and speak she did. They had been in the cafe for an hour and a half. Much of what Karen had to tell Diane was nothing Diane had not witnessed herself. However, when Karen talked about the bank accounts, how Phil had been writing checks from this account to "cash" for five thousand dollars twice monthly, Diane could feel her breathing become more difficult. When Karen reached in her purse and pulled out a copy of Phil's private account and handed it to her, she was sure her breathing had stopped.

"Give this to anyone you think needs to see it, and with my blessings. You know how to get in touch with me." With this last statement, Karen held her gaze on Diane until she felt Diane had understood her meaning. The two women were quiet as they made their way to the parking lot. It was only when Karen reached the handle of her car door did either of them speak.

"Diane. I don't know what is going on. For a very long time I have felt I was a useless, stupid, middle-aged woman. Maybe for the first time in my life, I have come to realize I am neither stupid nor useless. You do what you have to do. Keep me informed."

The only words Diane could utter were a simple, "I will."

As Diane made her way through rush-hour traffic, she was trying to decide what she needed to do first. Should she sit Steve down and tell him all she knew about the Matthews/Howard mess? Did she call Beverly, or should she call Joanna? Where should she keep these bank statements? How did she get in the middle of this mess? She found herself turning into the parking lot of Beverly's boutique; at that moment she knew what her plan of action was going to be. She also knew she was not going to keep any information from her beloved husband any longer. Things had gotten too complicated for him not to be aware of what she knew. If Beverly and Joanna had a problem with that, then they would just have to have a problem with it.

As soon as Beverly looked at Diane, she knew something had happened and things were not going well for her dear friend. Jana was summoned to help assist the customer Beverly had been helping. Diane had already made her way back to the office and was pacing when Beverly opened the door. "What is it? What is wrong?" Beverly was truly concerned for Diane, who already had tears welling up in the corners of her eyes.

"Oh, Beverly. You're going to have to tell me what to do next. Who do I talk to? Who do I give this to? What do I do?" Before Beverly looked at the pieces of paper Diane was holding in her hand, she pulled her close, and with the same touch she would have given Jana, she gave her a hug.

"I don't know what's happened, but it's going to be all right. It's going to be all right."

The words, the hug, the sound of Beverly's voice only lent to more tears. When Diane felt she was composed enough to talk, she asked Beverly for a tissue, blew her nose, and laughed when she saw the expression on Beverly's face at the sound of her nose blowing.

"Now. That's quite a honker you've got there!" Beverly proclaimed as Diane laughed harder. The news of the visit with Karen Matthews was something Beverly had not expected. Certainly not copies of her husband's bank statements. There had been a few times during the telling of the afternoon's event Diane had with Karen Matthews when Beverly wasn't sure she wasn't on the verge of tears.

"Look. It's nearly six o'clock, and Steve has no idea where I am. I really need to get home. Will you see this gets to where it needs to be?"

"I'm going to call Joanna as soon as you leave. She'll know best what steps need to be taken, and we/I will be in touch with you. Now *get*! Get home to that man of yours." No one had to ask Diane twice. She was out of the door, in her car, and pulling out of the parking lot before Beverly had finished dialing Joanna's number.

"As interesting as all of this is, I'm not sure any of it will help our investigation." Jacob looked first to Beverly and then Joanna as he saw the look of disappointment fill both of them. "If. *If.* These checks had been written to the senator's campaign fund, or better still, to the person of Evelyn Howard, then we might have something we could sink our teeth into, but these checks were written to cash, and there is absolutely nothing wrong with anyone writing checks from their personal account to cash. In fact, you can write a check for nine thousand nine hundred and ninety-nine dollars and ninety-nine cents every time you write a check and not one red flag will come up. Write a check for ten thousand and the bank examiners' will be all over it." Jacob could tell by the look in Beverly's eyes that he was going to catch the brunt of the telling of this latest piece of news. Surprisingly, the onslaught didn't occur. She walked across Jill's family room, picked up a table lighter, and with her typical flourish, lit a cigarette before speaking.

"Jacob. This Silverfish person, is there any way he could help?"

It never ceased to amaze anyone that knew her what insight she had. Maybe it was raw intellect, intuitiveness, the luck of the Irish— whatever it was, Beverly had it. *Of course. Of course.* Jacob was thinking to himself. Silverfish was exactly the one he needed to talk to. If anyone was going to help with this latest development, it would be Silverfish. "I think this is something we need to look into." Joanna looked at him with a little more than curiosity; this was not a response she had expected and it was most certainly not a typical Jacob/agent response.

Beverly responded with a simple, "Good." The discussion was over.

Mac knew the convenience store would be his weekly contact. There was a payphone outside near the gas pumps, but not so close that anyone could listen to his conversation without him being able to notice them. He understood anyone in the agency that needed to contact him would be through Sharon. He had resisted this vehemently, but once again, Sharon had convinced him this was a safe and sane thing to do. He was somewhat surprised when he got a call from Sharon telling him the party would be held at the Stratford apartments and to bring his own bottle. This was the code for Mac to know Jacob needed to meet with him. Everyone believed Evelyn still thought him to be a hopeless alcoholic, and a call from a woman telling him where the next party was going to be seemed good cover. This was all done in case she had the phone in the carriage house bugged, and she indeed did have it bugged. He made the call from the convenience store payphone and waited to hear what his contact had to say. Jacob had sounded a little more tense than Mac had heard him sound before. Once the time and place had been established, Mac went back to the carriage house with more than a few thoughts running through his mind. Although Jacob had not given him any details of what the meeting was about, he knew he had new information about his employer's activities, or the contact would not have been made. This excited him; this troubled him. What did Jacob want? How would he respond to what the Feds wanted? As he climbed into the seat of his pickup truck and his eased into the traffic, it began to hit him. This may be the beginning of the end of the life he had lived for the last twelve years. He knew his decision to contact the Feds had been a turning point and one that he had taken because of Sharon. He now knew what he was about to do would also be a turning point for both him and Sharon. He didn't really care so much about what happened to him, although he was frightened; he cared very much what happened to her, and he had to weigh every step he was about to take very carefully.

Once Beverly was satisfied she had done her part in passing the bank records to Jacob, she left to keep a dinner date with her daughter. Joanna asked Jacob if he had time for some pasta; she would do the cooking. He gladly accepted the invitation and would meet her at her house after stopping by the office. As he sat down in the overstuffed chair with a copy of the latest news magazine, he became aware of the sounds coming from her kitchen. She was humming softly. The aromas of baking bread mixed with the spices from the sauce and steam coming from the large pot on the stove was giving him a feeling of coziness and warmth. He could see Joanna moving with adeptness as she tended to her tasks. He didn't know how long he had been sitting there taking in the sights and sounds of this ordinary meal preparation. He wondered how many men went home to something like this every night and never noticed how fortunate they were to have someone waiting for them to prepare food and create an environment he was enjoying this very minute. *Get a hold of yourself, big boy.* Jacob mentally shook the sights and sounds while desperately trying to focus on some item about recycling. Just as he was beginning to get the gist of what the author was trying to convey to the reader, Joanna was telling him that the dinner bell had just rung. "You okay?" she had asked with concern in her voice.

"Oh. Yes. Sure. I was just caught up in the article I was reading."

"Really. What was the article about?"

"Oh, recycling." As soon as the words were out of his mouth, he would have given anything if he could pull them back.

"Recycling? Is this the same man that has a trash bag a month because he is never home to use anything, and you've become interested in recycling?"

Ignoring her statement, he countered by asking if she would like for him to seat her at the fine Italian table she had just set for the two of them.

"Why, thank you, sir. Recycling?"

Once he took the first bite of pasta and rolled his eyes while letting out a long and loud "umm," the entire recycling episode was forgotten. The conversation turned once again to the Howard mess, which seemed to be the description given to this investigation by anyone that was involved. Jill had heard nothing further from the senator. In fact, she was going about her life as she had been doing for years. Months before, she had planned a trip to Colorado to visit an old classmate of hers and would be gone for two weeks. Just before she left town, she called Joanna and told her if they needed to use her house please feel free to do so. She had even offered to let the agents stay there while she was gone. Joanna assured her she would pass the information to Jacob, but she had added, "I don't think I'll tell him about letting the agents use your house. I have seen some of these guys and they think nothing of tossing the wrapper from their latest fast food purchase on the middle of the living room rug." So, Joanna had been given the keys to her house along with the security code numbers. This had struck both of them as being ironic. Not more than three weeks ago, Jill didn't know that agents were surrounding her house, and now she had offered them a place to stay.

After the dishes had been removed from the table, Joanna asked him if he would like to have coffee by the fireplace. This invitation was readily accepted. At first, they both sat quietly sipping their coffee and watching the flames flicker through the ceramic logs in the gas fireplace. Then, with no warning, he stood from where he had been sitting and began to pace. This was not something he often did. He was silent, but the quieter he was, the more he paced. Joanna was about to remark on this behavior when he began to open up about his concerns.

"Joanna. I don't know what Silverfish is holding back, but he is holding something back. I don't like the feeling I've had from our first meeting. I just wish I could put my finger on it." Joanna sat quietly as she waited for her friend to expand upon this latest revelation. For the next few moments, his pacing only increased in speed and intensity.

"What time are you supposed to meet?" Joanna knew the time that the two were to meet; she just wanted to get Jacob to focus on the job at hand.

"Oh. Oh. Ten-thirty. I told him ten-thirty. I guess I had better be on my way if I'm going to keep my appointment."

"Jacob. Are you all right? I mean, you don't seem to be the usual 'in control' guy I've come to expect to see before he goes out on some assignment. Then again, I guess I've never seen you go out on assignment." With this last statement, Joanna let out a small giggle. Jacob gave her a side glance that cut the giggle short. "Jacob. Listen, do you think you'll be safe? I mean, are you feeling that this Silverfish might be setting you up and is going to do any harm to you?"

He turned to face her as she asked this latest question. He could see the furrow that was deepening between her large beautiful eyes; the glow from the fireplace created a halo effect around her curly red hair. Now it was Jacob that began to smile. "No. No. I don't believe Silverfish would ever put me in harm's way. He's this regular kind of guy that really wants to turn the way he's been doing things around. In fact, I'm personally pulling for him."

Joanna watched Jacob's expression as he spoke of his informant and knew that he indeed liked the man. "So. Why are you so concerned? I mean. If you think he's such a regular guy, why do you think he's not being straight with you, and more importantly, why do feel so sure that he is no danger to you?"

"Oh, Joanna. I wish you could meet him, know who he is, and what he does, then you'd understand what I'm trying to tell you."

She looked at him for several moments before she responded. "I wish I could meet him too." He stepped close to her as she spoke these last words, pulled her close, and brought his lips to hers. There was no resistance, just softness and warmth that emitted from her and surged through him. He held her for a few more moments before stepping back. What had he just done? What in this world was going on inside him? He wanted to make love to his best friend. He had to get out of here and fast! All the while, these thoughts were whirling in his head as she stood motionless, not saying anything, just standing there, looking more beautiful by the second.

He finally managed to find his voice. "I really need to be on my way," was all that he could choke out while he walked toward the door.

"Oh. Of course. Of course." Joanna recovered enough to respond. Just as he was stepping through the threshold, she called his name. "Jacob. Please be very careful. Please take care of yourself."

He didn't have the strength or enough sanity left to respond to her other than a feeble, "Don't worry about me. I'm a big boy."

She listened to the sound of his steps grow dim, heard the engine of his car start, and walked to the window to watch him drive away. She had slept with men that had never made her feel the kind of intimacy she had just experienced with this man after one kiss.

As he was pulling out of his parking space, he knew he had never felt this kind of intimacy in all the years he had been married.

Silverfish pulled the brick he had carefully marked from the wall. Immediately, it opened the hiding place of his past, present, and future. He carefully opened the blue book. Somehow, holding this book gave him security. He wasn't sure he could part with this security, even for Sharon. This book and all it held could bring him many things. Early in his life he had learned not to trust what anyone said, promised, or did. Once he had inherited the blue book and found out the kind of control it could give him, and had given him for the last twelve years, he wasn't convinced he should hand it over to anyone, not even if they were promising him freedom. He wasn't aware of how long he had been standing there, looking at the pages of dates, times, and amounts of money that had exchanged hands. The latest entry he had made was the bank's routing numbers along with the checking account number of a Swiss bank account. This entry was something he was sure his contact wanted. How and why they knew about these transactions was something he couldn't understand or care about. What was important to him at this point was that whatever he did it would be the best for Sharon and himself. He placed the blue book back in its hiding place with the same reverence a rabbi would handle the Torah. He knew exactly what he was going to do and how he was going to do it.

The meeting had been set up at another rest stop along the interstate. This time, it had been moved west of the town. There were a few tractor-trailers parked on the truck side of the parking lot. Fewer cars were parked on the opposite side of the building, which housed the restrooms and vending area. Jacob watched as the pickup truck pulled into a parking place. He watched Mac carefully close the truck door and make his way to where he was standing. Jacob could tell by his approach something was different. Again. He couldn't explain to anyone what he was picking up on, but it was there, as sure as he was standing in front of the vending machines. The first words out of Mac's mouth riveted Jacob. He knew he was taking a risk, and perhaps a big risk, but he did exactly as he was told to do. Two of the truckers got in their rigs and pulled away. A security guard left the rest stop. None of the men liked what they had just been instructed to do, and that was to leave one of their own without cover.

Once Mac was convinced it was just the two of them and Jacob had not been wired, he began to lay out what he wanted. Jacob listened intently to this ordinary-looking man talk about how they should proceed. He knew on an intellectual level he should be concerned for his own safety, and more importantly he should weigh the possibility Evelyn Howard was behind this latest development. These thoughts were ever present as Mac continued to lay before him a plan that held a lot of merit and held a lot of risk. As odd as his voice sounded and as strange as the words he spoke seemed to him, he heard himself say, "I think I can sell it to the captain."

"Good. How long do you think your sales job will take?"

"I'll be in touch with you before this time tomorrow." With that simple question and the simple answer, the two men parted. Jacob walked toward his car after selecting a pack of peanuts from the vending machine. Mac walked into the men's room as though this had been his objective from the moment he had arrived at the rest stop. A casual observer would not have suspected anything out of the ordinary. The woman carrying the bag of trash from the ladies' room knew this had been no ordinary conversation. As she watched both of the men leave the rest area, she reached into the pocket of her jacket, and pulling out a small transmitter, reported all was clear.

"I don't get it." Beverly was saying this out loud to herself as she put the phone back in its cradle. *She has to cut our dinner short because she has to rush home and finish the month-end financials. It's eleven o'clock and she won't answer? This doesn't make sense. Oh, well. Maybe she has a secret lover. Lord, I hope he isn't married.* With that happy thought, she walked over to turn the local TV news station on. Somewhere between the weather and the sports she fell asleep, only to awake to a strange movie about superheroes. As she made her way through the mental fog in the direction of her bed, she reminded herself to ask Jana what the big hurry had been this past evening. Yes. She would ask her that question first thing in the morning.

For the entire night, she kept awaking to the thoughts of her daughter. Why couldn't she get some uninterrupted sleep, she kept asking herself as she awoke every hour on the hour.

Diane and Steve were ready to go to bed. It had been a long day for the both of them. Diane knew all she had to share with Steve was going to be difficult; she just had no idea how difficult it was going to be. She began her story with what Karen was in the process of doing. She tried to explain the whole Beverly, Joanna, and Jill connection with Karen and Phil. This had been a daunting task. The more she tried to explain, the more complicated it seemed, and at some point, it seemed very complicated even to her. "Please. Please. Bear with me." She had pleaded at one point. "This is something I could not make up, and it is certainly something I would not bring to you if I didn't think you needed to know all there is to know about this."

After this proclamation Steve began to see what and how serious the information she was trying to impart to him really was. Finally, he pulled his wife next to himself, kissing her on her forehead, and simply said, "Let's go to bed and see if we can get some sleep."

Neither of them slept well.

Jacob had left the rest area with more than a few concerns. The first thing he was hoping was that Mac was being straight with him. If this man had just been trying to set him up, the complications were endless. If in fact he was bringing all of this to a conclusion, then the man was just short of brilliant. He had a lot on his plate at the moment, and the biggest portion was the meeting he had with the captain at 7:00 am. It had not gone well with the captain when he was told that all of the backups were asked to leave the rest stop. He reluctantly gave approval, but the captain knew he had kept a backup in place.

As full as Jacob's thoughts were about this entire Howard mess, the rest of his mind was being consumed by Joanna. Damn. Damn her, he kept thinking as he tried to remove from his mind what had happened just a few hours ago. Why did this have to happen to him now? Why did he have to feel this way about someone he just thought was a friend? Sleep would not come so easily to him tonight.

Joanna was trying to forget about what had happened in the last few hours. She was trying to believe that all of it had just been some kind of reaction to the dinner, wine, and the warmth of the fireplace.

She found her emotions swinging from the "I don't care—things happen" to the "I hope he is all right. Please let me feel his lips on mine once again." She went to sleep with a glass of wine in her hand and the fireplace flickering the same flames it had been flickering just a few hours ago. She was startled awake by the sound of her glass hitting the floor. After sweeping up the pieces, she walked to her bedroom with more than a few troubling thoughts running through her head. This would be a toss-and-turn night for her, and toss and turn she did.

Jana crawled into bed with the relief of an exhausted person. The sheets felt cool and comforting. She tried to erase from her mind what she had just gone through. She would have to tell her mother about all that was going on in her life. It just didn't have to be tonight, and for that she was grateful; all she wanted to do tonight was sleep a deep and peaceful sleep. The deep and peaceful sleep avoided her.

It had been a very long time since Jill had as an enjoyable time as she had this evening. Clara had hosted a wonderful dinner party, and Jill had been the guest of honor. After the dessert, all of them had gone out on the deck to watch the full moon's light play on the tall pine trees, casting shadows on the meadowland that nestled against the mountain range. The senator and all the problems that surrounded his very name seemed as though they belonged on another planet, certainly not the one she was inhabiting this moment. After all the good-byes had been said, she excused herself to her bedroom; then and only then would she admit to herself how lonely and how worried she was about her friends. She also had to face the feelings she was so desperately wanting to bury. This time she couldn't seem to throw any dirt on their graves. They kept breathing with her every waking moment. Why wouldn't they die? Why, oh, why wouldn't they die? Once again these were her last thoughts before she found the peace of slumber, at least for a few hours.

Mac had stopped by Sharon's apartment after his meeting with Jacob. It was time for him to tell her everything. He had grown to love and trust this woman as he had never loved or trusted anyone in his entire life. He had loved his mother, but he had never trusted anything she told him. She was a pipe dreamer and could never admit to herself, and certainly not to Mac, what poor choices she had made in her life. Sharon was a compassionate, loving woman tempered with clarity and strength. She would understand everything he was about to ask her to do, and he knew that she would carry all of her instructions out to a T. After he related the latest developments, including the fact that Jacob would be making another contact within the next twenty-four hours, she did exactly as he had hoped she would do. She accepted the latest information and request for help with little if any visible reaction to what she had just been told and a simple response of, "Of course I will." After this conversation, they sat on Sharon's couch, cuddling each other as they individually digested the day's events. Neither of them would be getting much sleep this night.

Evelyn awoke at the early hour of 6:00 am. She couldn't remember the last time she had had as good a night's sleep. Things were going according to plan. There were a few more deposits to be made, and that didn't include the money coming from the fashion show. Once that was over, she would make her move. After a long and refreshing shower, she donned one of the most expensive casual garments she owned. After all, it wouldn't do to meet with the Wives of the Senate for breakfast and not look the part. Oh how she enjoyed this part of politics. In a way, she felt sad about missing out on some of the pomp and circumstance of political life. Then again, there was a price to pay for everything. So, she would miss the Senate Wives functions, some of the more exclusive legislative galas, and of course the invitation to the President's Inauguration festivities. She had gone to no less than six of these Inaugurations during her lifetime, and had found each one more exciting than the one before. Again, there was a price to pay for everything, and so be it. Soon. She would be a woman that enjoyed the good life. A life she had worked hard for, and a life due her. She had known the day she walked down the aisle he had not loved her. This hadn't disappointed her as much as perplex her; after all, she was the daughter of Senator Miller, and that alone should have accounted for some kind of emotion, even if it had been contrived. He hadn't even had the decency to pretend he had felt something for her. The honeymoon had been a disaster. In her mind, sex was something a woman did to procreate or use for control. She certainly did not want to procreate, and she felt because of who she was she already had control of this man. When he realized on their wedding night she was not going to have anything to do with him, he began to drink, and that led to the assault. The memory was not so painful as it had been useful. First, she had threatened to tell her father how he had forced himself on her. When she saw his reaction, she knew she had him exactly where she wanted him, and she would keep him there as long as she needed to. All in all, the marriage had worked in her favor and brought her the kind of opportunities that may not have been presented to her otherwise. Opportunities she used to restore the coffers she had counted on her father leaving her after his death. It had come as a shock when her father's will and testament was read. The only thing he had left Evelyn was the monstrosity she now lived in. That, she was told by one of her father's questionable cronies, had been a gift from the boys. Her father had not only enjoyed spending money on his latest paramours, but she soon discovered he had enjoyed a gambling addiction. She had endured years of being at the beck and call of her late father's demands. Most of the time she enjoyed playing the game of dutiful daughter, accompanying him on his campaign trail and learning the art of fund-raising. She had even agreed to marry the young attorney because he thought this would assure her of continued financial success. That afternoon as she listened to the attorney read the will, she felt coldness fill the depths of her soul. It was at that moment she knew no one would get in her way from doing what she was determined to do. Make money. Money bought position and money bought power, and she was going to have them both. As for her husband, he had been useful. When he had the little tryst a few years ago, she had let him know exactly what would happen if he even thought about divorcing her. It helped tremendously to know his little girlfriend had once been a "flower child" and been in the company of the Harrises, who had formed the Liberation Army—among other things, they had kidnapped Patty Hearst. It all ended quickly and quietly, and had given her more of an advantage than she had ever had before. Now. Now. She wouldn't need him. She wouldn't need the Miller or the Howard name, the big cumbersome house, the phony friends. She wouldn't need any of them and just wished she could be around to see the reaction of so many people she genuinely loathed. She didn't realize the coldness she felt that day had turned into ice and eventually had petrified her soul.

Mac waited until he saw her drive through the gate and into the flow of traffic headed for the city. He then waited for the senator's car to appear in the drive; once he watched him leave the grounds, Mac moved with the grace of a cat. He knew he had least three hours to do his work, and he had a lot of work to do. He made his way downstairs to a room that had once been a stable and now housed lawn and snow-removal equipment. Carefully rolling the lawn wagon to the side and pulling the oil-stained burlap from the floor, he opened the trap door and slid silently out of sight, closing the door over himself. His work had begun.

This was not the way Jacob wanted to start his day. He had not slept well. He was going to try and make a sale to his captain he wasn't sure he bought himself, and he knew he was going to catch hell because of Silverfish's request to have all backups dismissed. In spite of all this, his first waking moments were thoughts of the look and feel of a slender, beautiful redhead that had been a good friend for the last twelve years. Now he had desires for her that a good friend should never have.

When he entered the room, he was keenly aware of the man's presence. He was looking very relaxed, almost lounging, in the corner chair of the captain's office. On more than one occasion that same chair had been used for the person that was going to face disciplinary action. The unofficial name for this chair was the "dumbass seat." Anyone that had the heavy hand of the captain come down on him/her while sitting in this chair was there because there had been a "dumbass job" or a "dumb ass" decision made on the part of the agent. Jacob had fully expected to be the one seated in the chair this early morning. Last night he had requested all backups be dismissed, and at one point even argued with the captain of the importance of granting him this request. This morning to find it occupied by an imposing stranger was another reason for him to feel his heart beating faster and louder. The captain seemed unaware of his entry into the room. He was as animated as Jacob had ever seen him. The gestures, smiles, and short bursts of laughter continued while Jacob stood motionless, awaiting his instructions. When he was acknowledged and given the direction to take a seat, he gratefully accepted and sat as still as he had ever remembered sitting. What he heard from these two men in the next hour caused his head to spin. He hoped he had given all the correct responses to the questions thrown at him. As he walked from the office he wasn't sure he was intelligent enough to assimilate this new data. Yet. He must assimilate, plan, and implement a strategy that could help bring this Howard case to a close. He had never felt as inadequate as he felt right after he left the captain's office. Inadequate or not, he was going to have to step up to this job, and step up in a way he had never had to do before.

Sharon had contacted the police department after a rifle had been pawned by a young man who told her his grandfather had left it to him. A few days later, she had read in the local paper that an antique rifle, among other items had been stolen in a break-in. She couldn't believe her eyes when the young police officer walked into the shop. This was the same young officer Mac had told her about the night before. After reviewing the records the owner was required to keep, he closed the book, looked Sharon directly in the eye, and asked if she would like to go out with him. Given another set of circumstances, she would have responded with a polite but firm no. However, he had made a remark while he was studying the pages of the owner's log that gave her reason to consider his offer. In his attempt to impress her, he had let her know he not only was on the police force but he also owned a security agency that provided security for some of the biggest names in town. At the top of the list was Senator Howard. He had spoken the name with pride. He then continued to regal her with all the events he had provided security, how impressed each of his clients had been, and all in all what a perfect male specimen he was, and what a fool she would be if she turned him down for a date. After this last statement, Sharon let out a low chuckle. He responded with a broad smile; if he had realized why she had just chuckled his smile would have instantly disappeared. He did not and would not understand for days why she had agreed to go out with him. When it all came together, it would be too late to correct the mistake he had just made.

Beverly had just turned the coffeepot on when she heard his unmistakable voice. "Anybody home?" came the booming baritone echoing throughout the shop. She rushed from the back office and opened the door. She saw him standing there, looking very out of place among the scarves, purses, "fun" jewelry, and enhanced underwear. As thrilled as she was to see him, she had a mix of joy, concern, and amusement. The emotion of amusement won over all the others as she let out one big laugh while making her way to this man with her arms wide open. They hugged each other as people do when they have shared a grief. Neither of them wanted to let go of the other for fear the acute pain of the grief might return. Finally, Beverly stepped back with tears brimming in her eyes and a large grin on her face as she simply asked, "What in the hell are you doing here?"

Without missing a beat he replied, "Why, my dear, I'm checking up on you." Beverly and Hugh made their way back to her office after the temp arrived. When Jill left for Colorado, Beverly had decided she needed to hire some part-time help to give herself and Jana some breathing room. This was working out nicely, since Beverly continued to devote much of her time to the details of the fashion show. It allowed Jana to work on the books, something Beverly abhorred, and at this very moment, it gave Beverly an opportunity to visit with the brother of her dead husband. After the catching up on family news, how he was doing, and why was he really visiting her, the conversation turned to a subject Beverly was beginning to dread: the senator and his wife, Evelyn. Later she wished that was where the conversation had ended. It had not. She could feel her emotions falling; where they were falling she couldn't tell. She could still hear his voice and she could still make out some of the words he was speaking, but she kept hearing her soul screaming inside. *No. No. This cannot be. This cannot be.* Long after he had left the shop, she could still hear his voice and his words ringing in her head. *You cannot live her life. Beverly. Listen to me. You cannot live her life.*

Steve had called Linda as soon as he and Diane had their first cup of coffee. Linda and Peter would make themselves available for dinner that evening. Steve was going in to the office and was going to confront Sam regarding the meeting or meetings he and Phil had with the senator. It hadn't taken Steve very long into the discussion with Diane as she was laying out the findings Karen had discovered while doing her due diligence for the divorce attorney to realize their business partner may be involved in some type of fraud. What kind of fraud and to what end, none of them were sure. How this all fit with the senator and his wife, none of them knew. The one individual that could help shed some light on all of this was Sam. Steve had noticed a decided change in Sam's behavior in the last few weeks. The once upbeat, self-assured, and sometimes arrogant young man had become a quiet, introverted individual. There had been a few times he acted as though he wanted to talk to Steve, and then backed off. Now was the time for Steve to talk to Sam.

Joanna awoke with the feeling her life had been turned upside down. Why, oh, why did Jacob have to complicate things for her? She had been perfectly happy to have her own little law firm and fight her own little battles and not this … this … complication. Why had he kissed her? No. Why had he made her feel this way? She didn't have the answer; she did, however, have a lot of questions. She was going to call him as soon as she got into the office. He would have to return her phone call if he thought this was a business call. Her first concern was his safety. Was he all right? How did his meeting go with Silverfish? Should she have anything she needed to tell Beverly and Diane? By the time she had showered and applied her makeup, she was sure she and Jacob needed to have an in-depth conversation, and the conversation would have absolutely nothing to do with what had happened last night. She had convinced herself of this fact, and she would hold onto this belief until it was proven to her otherwise.

Jana arrived at the shop shortly after noon. As soon as she entered she saw her mother dealing with a rather high-maintenance customer. This was a woman who considered herself to be one of the elite of the community. This usually amused Jana. Today it did not. The longer she watched this woman demand ridiculous requests—and she was *not* asking, she was demanding—the angrier Jana became. When she heard the woman make a snide remark about how inept Beverly's buying abilities must be, it was all she could take.

"Excuse me. If you are looking for a personal shopper, you have not come to the right shop. My mother has more taste in the style and quality of clothes in her little finger than most people have in their entire bodies. Should you want a personal tailor, I suggest you go to the yellow pages and look under the letter T." With this statement made, Jana stood just two feet away from the customer and her mother. Both women were staring open-mouthed at Jana. It was a few moments before anyone spoke.

It was Beverly who broke the silence. "I would like to introduce you to my darling daughter."

This had been a very long day for Beverly, and it was soon going to be longer. She had just looked at her watch and decided she would be going home early when the phone rang. As soon as she answered, she wished she had not done so. It had been Mildred from the Ladies League, reminding her she had put a foursome together for next Tuesday. Beverly had most certainly not remembered putting the foursome together until she heard Mildred remind her of the fact. How could this woman sound like the only thing in life was a game of golf? Yet, she had promised to get a foursome together, and at the time it seemed like a good thing to do. Now. Everything and everyone around her seemed to be out of control, and the game of golf seemed the most frivolous thing she had ever done in her entire life. Once Beverly became aware of what she was being asked to do, she assured Mildred she would contact all of the three other women and remind them of their foursome. Yes. Jill would be back in town; in fact, she was returning from Colorado this evening. Thank you so much for calling, Beverly had heard herself respond.

Jill was happy to hear the sound of the plane touching down on the tarmac. She looked out of the window as they approached the city.

How insignificant and small everything seemed when you were thirty thousand feet in the air. Yet she knew as soon as the plane parked at the gate, reality would become just that. Reality.

Karen was glad she was taking the steps she had just taken. She was glad she had given Diane copies of the bank statements. She really didn't know all that was going on in her soon-to-be-ex-husband's life, but she knew instinctively she had done the right thing. Little did she know how important those bank statements would become in the investigation of the Howards. Little did she know how important the steps she thought she was taking for herself would be just as important for friends and for strangers.

"You have got to be kidding me! We have a foursome for Tuesday?" Joanna was all but yelling into the telephone. "Beverly, I don't know how in the world I'm going to be able to go out on the golf course and concentrate on the game of golf."

"I know. I know. I thought the very same thing when Mildred called me, but after thinking about it some more, I think it might be a good distraction."

Joanna let out an audible sigh and gave slight acknowledgment to the statement Beverly had just made. "All right. I'll be there. I have no idea what kind of golf I'll be playing, but I'll be there."

The response from Diane had been much the same as it had been from Joanna. It surprised and pleased her when she contacted Jill; not only had Jill remembered that this coming Tuesday was "make your own foursome," but she was looking forward to being able to play with Joanna, Beverly, and Diane. Once Beverly finished making all the calls and put the last touches on the clothes that would be worn for the fashion show, she bid good-bye to Jana and told her to close up shop; she would open the next morning. Nothing was said about Jana's outburst with the customer earlier in the day. Nothing was said about Beverly's visit from Hugh. Nothing needed to be said, because both women knew the issues at hand, and neither wanted to discuss or deal with them at the moment.

Evelyn was a little less than thrilled with the way her day had gone. The Senate Wives breakfast had been okay, nothing extraordinary, but then again, they usually weren't that great. There was something bothering her, and she couldn't quiet put her finger on it. When she had returned home and walked into her bedroom, there was a feeling she didn't like. She had also noticed a difference in Mac. Again, nothing she could put her finger on, but there was this feeling she simply couldn't shake. *Oh, I'm being silly,* she thought to herself. *No one could possibly expect what was about to happen.* She had been very careful to cast the players in this game, and she had been equally careful to keep her dear husband and all of the campaign staff in check. No one. She was absolutely sure no one knew what she had been doing. Yet. There was something that didn't feel the way she wanted it. What was it? Paranoia? Guilt? Fear? Maybe a mix of all three? No. Those emotions didn't belong to Evelyn. She had her act together and she was going to have a life she had worked hard to achieve. Maybe she was just stressed. Yes. That was what it was; she was just stressed.

Mac had worked hard that day. He was sure he had obtained everything that was available. The only thing left to do was to make his contact to Jacob and set the place and time for the delivery of the copies that he had just obtained from Evelyn's bedroom desk. After reviewing some of the names, dates, and amount of money she had amassed, he gave a long, low whistle. He would say one thing for the woman; she had inherited her daddy's ability to know where the wealthiest suckers were and how to get into their pockets. From the looks of the documents, she had not inherited his gambling addiction. Amazing. He had learned several things about his own father while helping with this investigation. Something he had never expected was a newfound respect for the man that had fathered him. The records showed that his father had been a man of integrity. He had crawled inside the bottle, but so had he. What happened between his father and mother was something he would probably never sort out. Now. For the first time in his life he didn't feel ashamed of who he was or who his parents were. This was another reason he would not be revealing the contents of the blue book. Neither of his parents deserved to have this revealed. It had been a hard day's work, but it had been rewarding. He had just enough time to stop by the pawn shop before he checked in with Jacob. He couldn't remember feeling this good in years. He wouldn't reveal all of this to Sharon, but once the papers had been passed to the powers that be, he would ask Sharon for a late-night dinner to celebrate. He had just parked his pickup and had his hand on the door handle when he saw them. They were walking out of the shop. She was smiling up into his face as the man she was with held the door open for her to walk through. He instinctively turned the ignition on and followed the sporty four-wheel-drive vehicle. Why was she risking this? Why hadn't she phoned him? This wasn't the plan they had talked about. If this man laid a hand on her, he would kill him. No. Killing him wouldn't help anything; in fact, it would cost him everything. This was what he wanted to do, but he would not do anything that would cost him to lose Sharon. He knew he would not let them out of his sight. He prayed that the man would not touch her. He was also discovering how frightening it could be to love someone the way he loved her. There was no time to call Jacob. He would take care of that once he knew she was safe and sound and *alone* in her apartment.

Joanna had just gotten home and was toying with the idea of warming up some of the leftover pasta from the night before. Jacob had not returned her call, and she was troubled by this. Before last night, she would have wondered about him not calling, but today she had become obsessed with the sound of ringing phones. She had to ask her paralegal to repeat three different times what she had just told her concerning an upcoming case. Well. This could not go on. She was going to have to get control of herself. These were the words she spoke out loud just seconds before the doorbell rang. When she saw Jacob standing on the other side of her door, she knew control was not going to be something she would be exercising. The exchange between the two was polite bordering on uncomfortable until Joanna asked how the meeting with Silverfish had gone. This launched Jacob into his real concern. "He was supposed to contact me this evening and I haven't heard a word from him. I don't like this at all."

Joanna became concerned when she saw the look on her friend's face. "What do you think might have happened?" She was trying hard to keep her mind on the subject at hand and not his lips.

Jacob was trying hard to feel as concerned as he was claiming to be about Mac but could only wonder if she was as soft and warm as she had been the night before. Both of them knew they were fighting a losing battle, but both were putting up a good fight. After all, they had their jobs to think about, and they didn't have time for some complicated relationship, and why couldn't they just remain friends? Yes. That's what they would do. Remain friends. The night before was just … just something that happened, and they were making a mountain out of a molehill. They both decided they would continue to have their TGIF meetings and would be laughing about last night. It sounded good to both of them until he stood to leave and gave what he intended for a quick hug. Whatever causes chemistry to appear where it had not been before would remain a mystery to both of them for the rest of their lives. These two intelligent, logical, responsible people mixed their chemistries like they had never mixed chemistry before.

Mac had just gotten off the phone with Jacob. He turned to Sharon as he was laying the phone down. *He sounds different.*

Diane was the first of the foursome to arrive. She was sure she was Alice in Wonderland with the rest of the group filling out the roles of Mad Hatter, Tweedle Dee, and Tweedle Dum. She had just checked in when she heard Beverly's voice behind her. "Well, darling, are we ready to hit the links?"

Try as she might to convince herself she should be anywhere but out on the golf course and playing this game with everything around her needing attention, the very instant she heard Beverly's voice she knew this was exactly where she needed to be, and with the people she needed to be with. "Why, yes, my dear. Let the games begin."

LADIES LEAGUE
HOLE NINE
Par Five

The only one in the foursome that seemed glad to be playing in the "make your own foursome" had been Jill. All three women were happy to have her back in town. Beverly had not seen her friend look this rested in years, and told her so. Joanna seemed to have a glow about her, and at different times during the game, all three of the other women had told her as much, to which she responded with a thank-you and a warm smile. Diane confided that she was concerned for Steve. His conversation with Sam had not gone well. In fact, Sam had walked out of the office and would not return phone messages. After two days had elapsed, Steve and Linda went to his house only to find newspapers laying in the driveway, the front porch light on, and empty trash cans sitting at the curb. From the looks of things, Sam and his family had left town the day Sam had walked out of the office. This latest piece of news had been shared with Joanna and Beverly while waiting for Jill to hit her tee shot on hole two. The only other piece of news Diane had to share was the fact that Karen had already told Phil she would not go to China with the Howards.

"How did Phil react to this?" Beverly asked with no small amount of concern in her question.

"Karen told me he took it surprisingly well. In fact, Karen told me she would have been offended by his reaction if she had any feelings for the man."

"Wow," was all the three could say while each was left with their own thoughts about the death of a relationship between two people who had been together for the last twenty-five years.

"When is this trip to China supposed to take place?" Joanna asked as she pulled her driver out to hit her next tee shot.

"From what I understand, they're supposed to leave the Saturday after the fashion show," Diane had responded as she took a practice swing before taking her place on the tee box.

"That's a week from this coming Saturday! I know because a week from tomorrow is the damn fashion show. I'll never be so glad to get something over with as I'll be to be finished with the entire mess." The other three women were looking at Beverly with the same smile on their faces. In the past few weeks the fashion show had come to be known as the "damn fashion show."

"All of you can just wipe those smiles off your faces. If any one of you would have had to put up with some of the shit I've had to put up with from that woman you wouldn't think it was so funny!" With the statement made, Beverly tossed her cigarette on the ground, placed her ball on the tee, and proceeded to hit an outstanding drive.

"We should piss you off more often," Joanna said with her hand held high as she smacked Beverly's on her way back to the cart.

"None of you could piss me off, at least not for very long." With this statement made, they got into their carts and began the search for all of their golf balls. Joanna and Diane were riding in the same cart, which gave Joanna time to ask more questions about Phil Matthews.

"Is Phil still making the trip to China without Karen?"

"As far as I know, the answer to the question is yes. I spoke with Karen the day before yesterday. I am keeping her updated on everything I can keep her updated on. She's concerned about Sam and his family. She feels some responsibility for this latest development and I'm not sure why. She may be holding something back from us as far as the dealings Phil and Sam had with the senator. Again. I don't know what that might be, and I don't know why she would hold anything back. I plan on checking in with her sometime this afternoon. If I get anything further, I'll give you or Beverly a call."

"At this point, Diane, that's all anyone could ask of you. I don't know if I've said this to you before, but I want you know how thankful I am you have helped in all this Howard business."

Diane thanked Joanna for the comment; it meant a lot to her for someone like Joanna to acknowledge her effort.

Beverly and Jill were having an in-depth conversation of their own. Jill was maintaining the calm resolve she had brought to the course earlier that morning. "This trip to Colorado has done you a world of good," Beverly proclaimed as she placed her five-wood back in her golf bag and proceeded to move the cart where Jill's latest shot had landed.

"Beverly. I've had to face some big disappointments in my life. Then, hasn't just about everyone? Do you personally know of anyone our age who has not faced hardships and sometimes tragedy?"

Beverly's reply was a somber, "No one comes to mind." As she spoke the words, the pitiful look on the face of the young state trooper who had told her of her husband's death flashed through her mind.

"Are you all right?" Jill realized all too late that this question had raised a reminder of her own personal tragedy.

"Jill. I'm all right. We're talking about you, remember?"

"Well. It's time we stop talking about me. Let's talk about the damn fashion show! What is there for me to do to help you get through this next week?"

Being on very comfortable ground, Beverly began to outline what Jill could do for the next few days as she prepared to take care of the remaining details in preparation for the show. Jill was most happy to come in the shop for the rest of the week. When she asked Beverly about Jana's role in all of this, Beverly remained uncharacteristically quiet. "Beverly? Beverly? Is there something wrong with Jana?"

"No, my friend. There is nothing wrong with Jana. In fact, the two of us will be having dinner tonight, and I'm very sure after this evening Jana is going to be just fine."

After a long look at Beverly, Jill simply told her she was glad to hear that and walked to the back of her cart to select a club for her next shot.

All four knew the routine after finishing the round. Joanna and Beverly would take the score cards to the pro shop. Jill and Diane would return the carts to the cart barn. The first to arrive in the dining room would hold seats for the rest of the group. Joanna and Beverly had just seated themselves when Mildred came to the table with a frantic look. *Oh, brother,* Diane thought as she watched Mildred's eyes grow bigger when she began to speak. *I wonder what it is now. Someone forgot to turn in their score card?*

The words out of Mildred's mouth caused a mix of reactions around the table. Diane covered her amusement. Beverly frowned. Jill appeared concerned, and Joanna looked horrorstricken.

"I just saw the most terrible news," Mildred announced. "Just minutes ago, we saw Evelyn Howard being interviewed on the News at Noon. It seems she walked in on a robbery at her house. Apparently, she caught their handyman robbing them blind."

There had been very few times in Jacob's professional life that had held a surprise in the development of a case he was working on. This case had held a surprise for him at every turn. First, it was Jill's emotional involvement with the good senator. Then Mac's sudden turn from his demon and his willingness to become a mole for the agency. Of course, Beverly had held one surprise for him after the other. Now, just hours away from getting the needed evidence from Max, Evelyn Howard had him arrested. When he got the call from Sharon telling him of Mac's arrest, and she had just had a date with the arresting officer the night before, his first thought was, *Why not?* He felt a great deal of concern for Mac. The captain didn't waste any time getting in touch with the police chief. The chief was a man of integrity, strength, and intelligence. It didn't hurt that he and the captain had started out as rookie cops in the city nearly twenty years ago. Both men knew a great deal about Evelyn Howard and her family's history as it related to politics, money, and possible criminal activities. There was a long line of people who would like to see justice brought to this woman. At the head of the line would be the captain and the city's chief of police. By the time Jacob and Tim were making their way across town, a plan was already in place on how to proceed with Mac Shaw. The captain and the chief had worked together on some sensitive cases in the past, and the chief understood exactly what he needed to do.

When Sgt. Nelson was told the chief had sent for his prisoner, it came as a surprise. Then again, this was Evelyn Howard, the wife of a state senator, a woman of prominence, so maybe this was going to be an opportunity for the chief to get a little press time. Sgt. Nelson was all but sure this was the angle. He was trying to come up with a good explanation for the prisoner being roughed up. This arrest had been made just a week before his performance evaluation, and he didn't want this scumbag to find a way to throw a bad light on him and screw up a raise and possible promotion. He had to admit, Evelyn Howard was one of the craftiest people he had encountered; she thought of everything. She told him Mac's arrest just might look good for the review board; she knew his was coming up very soon. Oh yes, he would be most happy to take the prisoner to the chief. Apparently, the chief had personally requested he bring the prisoner to his office. Things were looking up for him. It had only been last night when he had taken out one of the nicest-looking women he'd ever dated. He hadn't been home an hour before Evelyn Howard called him to tell him his latest fee for security was ready to pick up. Then she asked him to help her take care of some unfinished business. Mr. Mac Shaw had been sponging off this lady for years because of some partnership between his father and hers. Enough is enough, she had said. He has stolen from me for the last time. They arranged the time he would make the arrest; she would do the rest. She would have enough evidence to keep this man behind bars for a long time. He was pushing Mac into the chief's office with one hand while resting his other on the handle of his service revolver. It was only when both he and the prisoner were well inside, the door closed, the shades to the office were pulled, when he begin to realize his future may not look nearly as rosy as he had just imagined.

Senator Jim Howard was doing everything he knew to keep himself from falling asleep. He had been in a committee meeting for the last two and half hours. Public testimony was being heard on a bill that would come before the Senate during the next session. He invited public testimony; in fact, he encouraged everyone to come before committees when they had a concern about any proposed bill. Today he might have to rethink his stance on the matter. Two of the last individuals had rambled and rambled and as far as he could tell had not made a point. He still wasn't sure if they had been for or against the proposal. When he saw the young page approach his chair, he actually felt relief. His relief lasted for only seconds as he read the message. *Mrs. Evelyn Howard is appearing on the Noon News. An arrest of Mr. Shaw has been made.* He excused himself from the room and made his way to his office through the back hall of the state house. Upon entering the reception area, he saw two men standing at the desk. They both turned as he approached. One of them seemed vaguely familiar; the other was a complete stranger. "Senator. May we speak with you in your office?" This was more of a command than a question. When they both handed him their identification there was no doubt in his mind, it had been a command.

Joanna got out of there and fast. She had to make sure Jacob was all right. She wasn't going to leave any phone messages; she was going straight to his office and beg, plead, threaten anyone who could answer that question. Was he all right?

Diane had watched Joanna's reaction with growing concern. There was a lot more to this story than Evelyn Howard making the noon news. Her first reaction to all of it had been the thought that it couldn't have happened to a better person. However, when she watched Joanna bolt from the room, she felt fear. Beverly and Jill were doing their best to act concerned for Evelyn. They watched the news with all the other League Ladies and made the proper "ohs," and "how frightening," and "what's this world coming to?" Diane knew neither Jill nor Beverly cared a hoot about Evelyn Howard. She watched Beverly's reaction when Sgt. Nelson was being interviewed by the reporter.

"I recognize him," was all she said.

Then Jill gave a startled look to Beverly and said, "I do, too." Diane started to ask both of them why he seemed so familiar and why did it seem to bother them that they had just recognized a police officer. Something in their behavior told her not to ask any more questions, and she did not.

When Joanna got to Jacob's office, she really didn't have a plan of action. She knew she wouldn't leave until someone told her something about Jacob. That is exactly what she told the woman behind the desk. A short time later, a very tall and imposing gentleman came out from one of the offices and introduced himself as Hugh Simpson. "Ms. Barnes? Would you like to come into my office?"

Jacob White and Tim Burke were as anxious as either of them had ever been in the middle of a case. Hugh had given them their orders. First and foremost, they must determine if their informant was working both sides of the street. Jacob felt deep within himself that he most certainly was not. Somehow he chose not to express this feeling. Hugh Simpson was physically and mentally imposing—not to mention the fact he was the regional director of the FBI. Tim assured the director they would thoroughly interrogate the informant. Should either of them have any doubts, they would immediately take action. All of them knew what the action would be. Mr. Shaw would be on his own.

Sgt. Nelson was directed to leave his prisoner with the chief and the two gentlemen who were sitting across from his desk. "Absolutely," came the sergeant's reply. As he turned to leave, he saw the two internal affairs officers waiting outside the doorway for his departure. With a nod from the chief, the sergeant was escorted to an office down the hall.

"Well." Jacob began. "I expected to meet you today but I can honestly tell you I did not expect to meet you like this. By the way, you look like hell."

Mac turned to look at Jacob with his left eye. His right eye was swollen shut. His bottom lip was split and the bruises on his face were just starting to show the deep bluish-purple of a contusion. "Man, I'm just happy to see you under any circumstances."

Joanna was beginning to feel comforted from the knowledge Jacob indeed was all right. In fact, he was in a meeting with the city's police chief and would be reporting his findings surrounding the robbery. She was in the process of collecting her jacket and purse when her eyes fell on a young woman. This young woman was none other than Jana. What in the world was Jana doing in this office? She was talking with a couple of the personnel as though she had known them for some time. Hugh Simpson interrupted her thoughts. "I think you may know my niece."

Jill was driving home with the local radio station reporting the story of Senator Howard's wife discovering her loyal handyman committing a robbery. Her only thoughts were of Jim. Why couldn't she think of anything else other than this man and his stupid mean-spirited wife?

Beverly drove to the boutique with a heavy heart. Indeed. She had a very, very, heavy heart. Not for Jill or Joanna, not even for Jacob, who she was sure had been the contact with Silverfish, and she knew Silverfish was Mac Shaw. The heavy heart was for her daughter. Jana had graduated from the Academy a few months before her stepfather had been killed. The only reason she had remained inactive was because of her. Beverly knew Jana had sacrificed what she wanted to do so she could take care of her for as long as Beverly needed her. Hugh had reminded her of this on his last visit. She knew he had been on target in admonishing her for not letting Jana live her life the way she wanted to live it. Why, oh, why did Jana want to do a job that could cost her very life?! Hadn't Beverly sacrificed enough? Wasn't her dead husband enough sacrifice for the cause? Did she have to put her only daughter on the altar of crime-fighting? Did any of it really matter? There were always going to be people like Evelyn Howard. For whatever reason they saw nothing wrong with lying, stealing, and generally caring for no one but themselves. She saw it every day inside her own little boutique. Women who thought nothing of spending a great deal of money on themselves at the expense of a man who was busting his butt to provide for his family, only to discover at the end of the month he owed much more than he had anticipated and would have to work even harder to keep up with the payments on the credit cards. Women who liked to talk about all they owned, places they traveled, parties they attended, and for what? To impress? Impress who? Her heart was indeed heavy. None of this made any sense.

Diane had a feeling of dread. That was the only word to describe what she felt at the moment. Dread. She wanted to talk to Steve, but she knew his day had been filled with appointments, and she had promised herself years before she would not interrupt her husband's day unless it was urgent. Although the morning's events had been disturbing, they had not been urgent. It came as a surprise when she entered the house to find two messages from Steve, wanting her to call him as soon as possible. She punched in the numbers as fast as her fingers allowed. As soon as she heard his voice, she felt relief mixed with anxiety.

"Let me cut to the chase. Sam called me this morning and wants to meet with all of us this evening at a little cafe north of town."

"All of us? Who is all of us?" Diane hoped she hadn't sounded as squeaky as she just thought she sounded.

"Sam and his wife want to meet with you and me, Linda, and Peter. Linda has already confirmed that both of them will be there. You don't have anything going on this evening, do you?"

"If I did, it would be cancelled. Of course I'm available. Did he give you any indication of what they wanted to talk to us about?"

"No, honey. That's why we're having the meeting."

"Thank you, Mr. Smartass. I'll be ready to go when you get home."

Evelyn had never been more titillated. Cameras were flashing, microphones were being thrust toward her, reporters were asking questions at the same time. How exciting all of this was, and she was at the center of it all. She had been convinced for some time she should have been the state senator and not her insipid husband. In just a few days, none of this was going to matter, but at the present she was in her glory.

Jacob and Tim didn't have to talk to Mac for any length of time before they both knew this man had been truthful with them from the first day he and Sharon had made contact. They had been given the details on what and how he knew Evelyn Howard's most secret banking and financial information. There was absolutely no question about his validity. After a phone call to the captain, Jacob and Tim left the station while Mac awaited Sharon's arrival with the bail money. Sgt. Nelson was still fielding questions from the two officers of Internal Affairs.

It was obvious to both agents that much of what they were telling him was a surprise to the senator. Of course he was aware of their handyman, Mac Shaw. No. He had no idea his wife's father and their handyman's father had been buddies in the USMC. It was quiet in the senator's office for several minutes, aside from the ticking of the old-school clock hanging on the wall, before he responded. "I know neither of you know me. Besides being aware of my political office, I doubt seriously either of you know much about me. So let me fill in some blanks for both of you. First. I am a coward. The very worst sort of coward. I have hidden myself behind the complex workings of government. Hidden myself behind a woman who I let operate my finances, including all of the funds necessary for me to run for public office. I have never held her accountable for anything she does with the funds. For that matter, I have never held her accountable for anything. Secondly. I am a crook. I have aided and abetted Evelyn Howard. My standing still instead of standing up for what was in the best interests of my constituency has turned me into a crook. Lastly. In spite of this I remain a man capable of doing the right thing. I'm not sure I knew that about myself until a few weeks ago. I am ready to help you in any way I am able to help. Please tell me what it is you would like for me to do."

"Are you saying what I think you're saying?! Mac Shaw is out on bail? Who the hell would put money up for that creep?" Evelyn Howard was all but screaming into the telephone.

"Mrs. Howard. I'm as shocked as you are. I have no answer for your question. There are procedures here, and I don't want to raise any red flags. You know we don't want any red flags." Evelyn considered this last statement made by Sgt. Nelson when it occurred to her that if Mac was out on bail, she could be compromised. Her voice had taken on the sound of controlled fear. "Do you have any idea how long he has been free? I mean, he *is* capable of anything. He gets drunk and turns mean. Do you think I should be concerned for my safety?" Sgt. Nelson told her he would be getting as many details as he could get and would report back to her any new findings. "Please keep me informed." Evelyn laid the phone slowly back in its cradle, walked over to the bar in the library, and realized for the first time in her life she was frightened as she poured herself a stiff drink.

"How was that? Did I leave anything out?" Sgt. Nelson asked Jacob after hanging up the phone.

"Perfect. Just perfect," came the reply.

"Sergeant, I think it would be a good idea for you to stay close to home. Report to work. Go home and keep a low profile until all of this is resolved. Understand?" These were the words spoken by the chief.

"Yes, sir. I understand." If there was one thing Sergeant Nelson had always been able to do, it was know which way the wind was blowing the strongest. He knew at this moment there were "gale warnings" coming out of the chief's office, and he was going to strap himself in his seat for the ride.

When Jana walked into the shop, Beverly knew she was there to conduct business for the agency. "Mom. May I see you in the office?" With a nod to Jill, Beverly and Jana made their way to the office in silence.

Once they seated themselves Beverly was the first to speak. "Okay. What is it you want me to do?"

"Get Evelyn Howard to come to the shop on some ruse about the fashion show?" For a few seconds mother and daughter stared at each other.

"Not a problem, my dear. When do you want me to make the call?"

"Is right at the moment to soon?" came Jana's reply as she smiled her special smile for her mother.

"Beverly. Have you been under a rock today? You did hear that I found my handyman robbing me blind. I mean, it was all over the news, and now I've been told he's out on bail, and you want me to come to your shop?" Beverly had to hold the phone away from her ear as Evelyn screamed into it. "I really don't know how I could possibly find the energy or emotional stamina to deal with this fashion show crisis. Really. I thought you knew what you were doing. Now at the eleventh hour you want me to come in to your shop and straighten this mess out? Beverly. I so counted on you." Beverly let Evelyn go on for a few more minutes in her diatribe before using her best pleading tone.

"Oh, my dear. You have every right to be disappointed, dismayed, and whatever else you must be feeling at this moment, but I implore you, please come by this evening. I will have everything ready for you to review, and then neither of us will have to deal with anything until the day of the show." There had been a few times during their conversation Beverly seriously doubted Evelyn would make the trip to her shop that evening. However, after a few more massages to the woman's ego in her best bowing and scraping act, she had finally accomplished the task. "Okay, kiddo. She will be here at seven. Now. It's your turn to get things done. Make sure you call me when it's all clear. I don't want to be with this woman any longer than I have to be."

"You got it, Mom." Jana stood to leave. As her hand fell on the doorknob, she turned to face her mother with tears forming in the corner of her eyes. She simply whispered, "Thank you, Mom. Thank you for everything."

Beverly got up walked to where Jana was standing, pulled her close, and hugged her while she whispered in her daughter's ear. "You be the best damn agent they have ever seen." Stepping back, she took a tissue to Jana's eyes, wiped her tears, turned her around, swatted her on the behind, and then gave her a gentle push through the door. "Guess we'll have to take a rain check on tonight's dinner." Beverly called to Jana's back. Would her daughter ever know how proud she was of her?

The meeting had been set for 7:00 pm. The captain was not taking any chances; there would be a tail on Evelyn Howard the entire time. It had been decided Sharon would be the one to pick Mac up after being released on bail. They were to wait in her apartment for further instructions. Evelyn had been very clever in setting Mac up. She knew he tended to lawn work every Tuesday. He thought it strange she was home this morning, since she usually played in the golf league. He became suspicious when she came out where he was trimming to ask if he would give her a hand with a desk drawer that had become jammed. He had only been working on the desk for a few moments and was about to tell her there didn't seem to be a problem when he heard her tell him he had better not move or she would shoot. She informed him Sgt. Nelson was already on his way. Once the sergeant arrived, Evelyn put her .38 in her purse and proceeded to lead the two men to the carriage house, where she pulled several pieces of her jewelry from various places in Mac's small living space. Only when the sergeant shoved Mac toward the stairs did more trouble ensue. Instinctively, Mac shoved back; this was a mistake Mac wished he had not made. During the scuffle he had a glimpse of Evelyn and realized how much she seemed to be enjoying herself. Mac wasn't sure if he would be taking a trip to the police station or to the morgue. Mac had replayed these events over and over in his mind since his release from jail. Jacob's call telling him he would be picking him up at six-thirty caused Mac to rethink all he needed to do.

Senator Howard had returned some of the calls that had been made to his office expressing concern for Evelyn and the unfortunate news about their handyman. Most of the calls had been political in nature. He wasn't sure anyone really was concerned about Evelyn or, for that matter, about him. Why should they be? Everyone they socialized with were the very same ones they exchanged political favors with. After his meeting with the two agents, he had done a lot of reflecting on his life, and he didn't like the reflection he saw. Why hadn't he walked away from Evelyn? For that matter, why hadn't he walked away from all of it? Was it the deference people paid to him? Good seats at restaurants and at ball games? The neighborhood he lived in? He had no answers. His strongest feeling at the moment was revulsion. He felt this for Evelyn, their way of life, and definitely for himself. Maybe this evening would be his first step on a path that would lead him back to self-respect. The two gentlemen had left him with the understanding they would be in contact with him to give him further instructions. Little did he realize it would only be a matter of hours and not days when the contact would be made. He did exactly as he had been told to do. He had been told Evelyn would not be home. He was to go about his normal routine while waiting for his visitor.

As Hugh Simpson made his way through the evening traffic, he couldn't help but wonder how Beverly was going to make out with Evelyn. As he turned onto the senator's lane, he saw Jacob's Jeep parked in front of the carriage house. Jacob watched the sedan pull up to the manse, and then turned to Mac and Tim and simply nodded. At this, all three made their way to the storage room. Jacob and Tim watched as Mac pulled the oil-stained burlap bag from the trap door. They stood motionless as they saw Mac descend the narrow stairs. Mac looked up at the two men and with a large grin on his face he asked, "Well. What are you two waiting for?" It astonished the agents to see how large the room was, after climbing down such a narrow set of stairs. Mac was giving them a guided tour of a place he had found in the early years of his employment with the Howards. He had first used it as a hideout on the days he had been too hungover to want to be bothered by anyone, especially Evelyn. He happened upon a diary he found in one of the nooks of the room they were now standing in. From what he could determine, the diary had been kept by one of the former owners of the estate. The owner had been a Quaker, and this was one of the stops along the Underground Railroad. There was a hallway leading away from the large room and turning in the direction of the manse. At the end of the hall was another set of narrow stairs, which led to a door. The door was the back of one of the bookcases that sat on either side of the fireplace in Evelyn Howard's bedroom. Mac knew he had found a jewel. He was having a great time spying on his employer. If he saw she was getting ready for bed or dressing for one of their many functions, he would leave. Had Evelyn been twenty-five and well-shaped, this might not have been one of his options. She was not twenty-five and she most certainly was not well-shaped, but his spying had paid off, and tonight might be the best payday a lot of people would have because of it.

"Good evening, Senator," Hugh greeted the senator as he stepped through the doorway and into the large foyer. "I'm Hugh Simpson." With this, the senator was shown his identification. "I'm sorry we're having to meet under these circumstances. My agents have reported their meeting with you earlier today was most beneficial. I want to personally thank you for your cooperation."

Senator Jim Howard flashed a small smile in Hugh's direction and let out an audible sigh. "I'm sorry we're having to meet under these circumstances as well. I'm very glad, however, that I am going to be able to assist you gentlemen in this … this …" The senator gave a small wave of his hand and another audible sigh.

"Investigation, senator. Investigation."

"Oh yes. Of course. Of course." The senator was making his way to the library and was about to ask Hugh if he cared for something to drink when Hugh interrupted his thoughts.

"Senator, would you please show me where Mrs. Howard's bedroom is?"

Somewhat startled by the question, he stopped and turned to make sure he had not misunderstood. "My wife's bedroom?"

"Yes, sir. Could you take me to your wife's bedroom?"

"Yes. Of course. Of course."

Hugh was glad the Senator had not seen the amused look on his face as they made their way up the stairs. The room was very large. On one wall was the fireplace that was still operable although Evelyn forbade anyone to drag wood into this room, leaving a mess on her valuable Oriental. Everything in the room screamed expensive. It was obvious a professional designer had put the room together. The queen-size canopy bed. The antique armoire and the French writing desk were the predominate furnishings. Heavy Damask draperies hung in the bay window with soft silk sheers peeking from behind.

"Well. Here it is," the senator announced.

He had no sooner said this when he heard a familiar voice come from behind him and say, "Here we are." There were times in Jacob's life he knew the moment had been captured and would remain in his memory bank for as long as he lived. The look on the senator's face, the smile on Mac's face, and the next words out of the senator's mouth would be one of those moments.

"I'll be damned. Well, I'll be damned," was all the good man seemed to be able to utter.

"Beverly. You have got to be kidding me. You most certainly have to be kidding!" Beverly watched Evelyn grow from a pale pink to a dark red. She wasn't sure the dark vein on the left side of her neck wasn't going to burst. It seemed to grow larger with each word Evelyn spoke—or yelled, would be a more appropriate description. "Well? Well? What are you suggesting be done?" Apparently by the look on Evelyn's face she was expecting some type of response from her, and for the life of her she didn't know what she was going to say. When she had been asked by Jana to get Evelyn Howard over to the shop that evening she had readily agreed. The only thing she had told Evelyn over the phone was she needed her because they had a real crisis on their hands concerning the fashion show. After Jana left, Beverly knew she needed a crisis, and a big one. While looking through the store room, her eyes fell on a bottle of toilet cleaner. This just might work. A sprinkling of toilet cleaner and a good story might be the exact crisis needed. Well, apparently it worked. Beverly had seen Evelyn Howard at her worst, or so she thought. At this very moment, Beverly decided she had only seen Evelyn Howard warming up for this particular fit!

"Well. I might get some of these dresses with a rush order. Of course that means they have to have the right sizes, colors, and in stock. Shipping wouldn't be a problem. I could always have them shipped overnight. I'm more concerned about sizes and colors being in stock."

"Yes. Yes. I know, Beverly, you've already gone over that with me! How long will it take you to find out if they have these same dresses in the sizes and colors you want?"

"Well. I would call tonight but it would be useless. The people I need to talk to won't be in the office until after nine in the morning. Of course, I could make other selections if they don't have the same garments, but then I'll need the models to come back in for fittings and, you know, jewelry ..." Beverly's voice trailed off as she stood next to the rack of dresses, holding one and then another for inspection. Evelyn's eyes were boring a hole through her the entire time. The more she talked, the more menacing Evelyn's eyes looked. Beverly let the dress she had been holding drop to the floor. She turned and looked Evelyn directly in the eyes. "Evelyn. I know you're disappointed. I know you had counted on me to pull off this fashion show, and I will. I called you tonight so you would see exactly what happened, and I thought you may want some input into the solution. I see now it was a mistake, I have only upset you." Beverly watched Evelyn as she relaxed her stance and began to shift from one foot to the other while lowering her gaze from Beverly's. Beverly stood motionless while staring directly at Evelyn. Nothing else had been said between the two women as each one's body language took control. Evelyn was a bully, not a fighter; just as all bullies do, she chose to back away when her intended target showed signs of confrontation. The next words out of Evelyn's mouth would have softened Beverly if she had not been privy to information regarding this woman's character. *She's good. She's really good*, Beverly kept thinking as she listened to the tone of Evelyn's voice change simultaneously with her downturned mouth and a mournful look coming from those eyes that moments ago had held the look of hate. The next hour was spent on deciding what steps were to be taken to salvage the show. Evelyn had actually contributed some very good ideas, and at one point told Beverly she thought they should have fun with this accident.

"Maybe cracking some jokes about the entire incident during the show will make the audience feel like they're in on the 'almost disaster.'"

"Great idea," Beverly responded as she watched this woman go through another metamorphosis in the matter of minutes. "Well. I think that's about as much as we can do this evening. I'll give you a call in the morning after I've contacted the vendors."

As Evelyn collected her things, she apologized for her outburst and attributed much of her emotional state to the fact she had been betrayed by a man she had felt was a loyal employee, and frankly, she was a little concerned for her very safety. *She's good. She is really, really good,* Beverly kept thinking to herself. Less than ninety minutes ago, she had been ranting and raving and looking as though she was capable of becoming violent, and now this same woman was talking about her safety? The ringing phone startled both women. Beverly answered the phone in a businesslike tone. Other than an "I see. Okay. Talk to you soon," the conversation was at an end. Without looking up from her desk, she simply stated it had been Jana. Evelyn Howard wasn't phased by the call.

Senator Jim Howard was having a difficult time assimilating all the information he had been given in the past twelve hours. It had really come as no surprise to find that his wife had misused campaign funds and was attempting to use a bill that would be voted on in the next legislative session for personal gain. He wasn't even surprised to find out she had no less than six different "pigeons" sending her money each month to assure themselves they would get the state contract once the privatization bill became law. What had shocked him was the records she had kept and how their drunken handyman had managed to copy these records for the last several years. Thank God Mac had found a good woman and AA. Otherwise, none of this would have come to light until it would have been too late. He was deep into these thoughts when he heard her walk into the room. He was holding a glass of wine while twirling the stem when she spoke.

"Your concern for my wellbeing overwhelms me." She sarcastically spit the words out as she made her way to the bar and poured herself a shot of whiskey. He watched silently as she threw the drink down in one gulp and reached for the bottle. "Well? Why didn't you at least go through the motions of acting like you cared? What do you think everyone will say when it's known you didn't even bother to call once the news was out about us being robbed?"

He watched her for a few more moments before giving his response. "Evelyn. I don't think many people give us much thought. Period." As the words left his mouth, he saw the expression on her face change from the hard, haughty look she held in her eyes to a look of shock. That's when he began to laugh. The harder he laughed, the wider her mouth fell open, which caused him to laugh all the more.

Diane had no way of knowing what had occurred on the other side of the city while the six of them were having dinner. It had been uncomfortable for all concerned for the first few minutes. Then, to everyone's surprise, it was Sam's wife who started the discussion. Indeed, Phil had been using Sam to help cover the fact he had been taking significant sums of money from their business each month. The false information had been reported to Linda, Steve, and their controller regarding the cost of supplies, shipping, rise in equipment costs, anywhere and anything that could be used to inflate expenses had been used. The controller had asked repeatedly for invoices, bill of sale, documentation of any kind for the records. Phil and Sam effectively blocked all requests made, first by the controller and lately by the other two owners. The pieces to the puzzle were falling into place with each word spoken by Sam and his wife. When the twenty-four-thousand-dollar question was asked, *Why? Why did Phil want this money?* It was Sam who came up to bat.

"From what I understand, Phil and Senator Jim Howard's wife made a deal almost a year ago. The bill that is coming before the legislative body this current session, which allows the privatization of the cleaning and maintenance of all state-held property, was a job Evelyn Howard assured Phil would be his. She was going to make certain that once bids were accepted, his would be the lowest."

"His bid? Don't you mean our bid?" Linda asked with a look of confusion.

"No. I mean his bid. He has already taken steps to file articles of incorporation for *his* new company."

The silence at the table was broken by Steve's soft, low whistle.

"But why? Why? What have we done to Phil to cause him to take such steps?" Diane's voice had sounded hurt and confused.

Finally, it was Steve that answered the question. "Honey. He knew we wouldn't be part of the scheme, and he knew he could buy what would be left of our company for pennies on the dollar, that is, employees, equipment, chemicals, whatever he felt was worth buying."

"Diane. It's called corporate fraud. It happens all the time. Usually it's simply a matter of greed." This time it was Peter's voice that broke the thoughts of the others sitting at the table.

It was Sam's turn to let the other two couples know why he had helped Phil as long as he had helped. Phil held the mortgage on Sam's house, had made a loan to him and his wife so their daughter could continue the private ice-skating lessons, and in general let Sam know this was the least he could do for someone who had given him the breaks he had enjoyed these last few years. In the beginning, Phil's requests had seemed innocent enough, but lately Phil was requesting larger and larger sums of money be hidden from his partners. The latest request had been for one hundred thousand over the next three months that remained in the year.

"Sure. In light of everything else you've just shared with us, that makes perfect sense. The bill is up for a vote next month. Evelyn needs her last big payoff so she can assure Phil of his winning bid, and the rest of us find out after the deal is done."

"I think you're right on target, my friend," came Peter's reply to Steve's comment.

"I know he's right," Sam remarked as he looked first to Peter and then to Steve.

"Sam." Steve began. "Do you have any proof of what you have just told us? Anything you could point to and show what Phil has been asking you to do? More importantly. Do you have any proof that indeed it is Evelyn Howard he has been dealing with?"

"Proof? Something that would stand up in a court of law? I don't know. I'll be happy to go back through the financials and show where there were inflated expenses. As for proof he was dealing with Evelyn Howard, that's a little more difficult question to answer. There was only one time I overheard a conversation with the two of them that left no doubt about what they were up to. It was during the big cocktail party fund-raiser Phil and Karen held for the senator. As you may remember, Phil had been hitting the sauce pretty hard that night, and he happened to catch Evelyn by herself. Neither of them saw me standing just inside the library door. Phil was very drunk and very angry. Evelyn was trying to get away from him when Phil apparently grabbed her by her arm and told her he had better be the one to get the bid. He had heard some ugly rumors about her dealing with a few other boys that planned on bidding. She assured him he was the only one she had been in communication with, and if he didn't trust her, he could call the deal off. His next response was what confirmed for me what he was doing. He told her the check for the ten thousand would be sent to her that Friday. If you remember, the cocktail party had been on a Wednesday night. The next morning, Phil told me he needed ten thousand by noon Friday."

"Sam. Would you be willing to tell this story to some people we know, who happen to work for the FBI?"

Before Sam could answer the question, his wife said, "We want to do whatever it is you need for us to do."

Jacob had dropped Mac off at Sharon's apartment with instructions to sit tight until given further orders. Mac assured him he had enough excitement going on his life at the moment and he would be most happy to sit tight. As Jacob worked his way through the evening traffic, he realized he hadn't seen Joanna in the last twenty-four hours, and as crazy as it seemed, he missed her. When he rang her doorbell, his pulse quickened as he heard movement coming from inside the condo. Apparently the feeling had been mutual; when she opened the door she pulled him inside and gave him one of the most erotic kisses he had ever experienced. When the two of them separated, he thought about the number of years this woman had been standing right under his nose and he had not given her any more thought than he would have given one of his buddies. Now he stood stupefied at the hold she had miraculously placed on him. Without so much as a glance behind, she had left him standing there while she announced she would have supper on the table in a few minutes. Did he want a glass of wine or was he still on duty?

"I would love a glass of wine, but I think I'd like to take a rain check."

Joanna knew enough about the investigation to know things were coming to a head. Perhaps she had overreacted that afternoon when she went to Jacob's office. The visit with Hugh Simpson had comforted her and concerned her.

"Jacob. I lost it today when I saw Evelyn Howard being interviewed on the news and realized Mac had been arrested. I couldn't help myself, I panicked."

Before another word came out of her mouth, he interrupted her. "I already know, my dear, you talked to my regional director, Hugh Simpson. He told me all about it. By the way, he was impressed with you." He couldn't help but smile as she stared at him with those huge blue eyes.

"Really. He was impressed with me?" She gave him a warm smile that quickly faded as her brow began to furrow, and she asked him in a somber tone, "Are you in danger?"

Jacob tried to make light of the question, but it was of no use. They both knew the job he held was a job that held danger. It was that simple, and it was that complicated. No one in law enforcement could predict when violence would strike. It could be when a state trooper stopped a vehicle for a traffic violation, a sheriff's deputy serving a subpoena, or a city policeman responding to a call of domestic violence . This was part of a warrior's job description. Those who loved the warriors lived with the knowledge their loved one could be the next to fall. So it was with

Joanna this evening. She had joined the ranks of all those who loved a warrior and carried the weighty emotions that come with the package.

The three couples had left the restaurant with assigned tasks. When Diane asked the question about when and if she should speak with Karen, it was unanimously agreed Karen should not be called unless or until the Howard investigation was over. The next steps all of them took needed to be taken carefully. Linda and Peter would pick up the financials on their way home. Linda would call Mary to tell her she was to call in sick and she would be meeting with Sam to go over the last several months of financials. Under no circumstances was she to let anyone know she would be meeting with Sam. None of them felt Mary would be a risk. She was the one who had become concerned months earlier. She had never cared for, and certainly had never fully trusted, Phil. She had let Linda and Steve know this at different times during her employee with the company. They had agreed that Sam would meet with Mary at Linda and Peter's farm. Since Sam was still missing (as far as Phil was concerned), he shouldn't be suspicious of either of his partners knowing anything about his use of Sam or the scheme he and Mrs. Howard were involved in. Steve and Linda would be in the office as usual. Diane was to contact Beverly with the information that had been shared this evening. Once all of these things were in place, all of them would wait. Wait for the documentation Mary and Sam could come up with. Wait for communication to come to Diane. Wait. Wait. Wait.

"Oh, how I hope all of this will come to an end, and soon. I am so tired of dealing with this mess, so tired, so tired." Beverly was saying these things out loud to herself. Several people had remarked about her talking to herself on more than one occasion. Her reply was always the same: "It's one of the few intelligent conversations I have." Tonight she wanted to get into her pajamas, fix a cup of hot chocolate, watch the late news, and crawl into bed. No sooner had these thoughts gone through her head when she heard someone knocking at the door as the phone started ringing. "Oh, for Pete's sake." A quick look at the door told her it was Jana. "Use your key. I have to answer the phone," she yelled as she picked up the receiver. Jana could tell by her mother's voice something significant was happening. She didn't think there had been any new developments with Evelyn. She had been the one to tail her that evening, and the last she saw was the dear woman turning into her driveway. A few more minutes elapsed before her mother hung up the phone and stood staring at her daughter.

"Mom. What is it? What's wrong?"

"Wrong? Did I say there was anything wrong? I just can't believe how fast events are taking place."

"Mom. Will you quit playing with me? Who was that on the phone? And what events are you talking about?"

Beverly couldn't resist her little cat-and-mouse chase with Jana, but once she saw the expression on her face, she decided it was time to drop all games. "It was Diane. They had a meeting with Sam. A lot of new information from that camp. Let me fix us both some hot chocolate and I'll tell you all about it."

Karen was beginning another book. Since her last meeting with Diane and her handing over the bank statements, she had expected to hear something back from her. She wasn't sure what she expected to hear, but it had been several days with no communication. Phil had told her Sam had not been in the office for the last few days, and no one seemed to know where he or, for that matter, his family was. "You would think after all the things I've done for the man he would at least have the decency to call and let me know what's going on." Karen could see Phil was troubled by Sam's sudden disappearance, but not out of any care for Sam. She was trying to get anything she could out of Phil without sounding to interested. She knew Phil could become very guarded when it came to giving information about business matters. His private bank account had been a case in point. The one good thing that seemed to be happening for Karen was the ability to watch the man she had lived with for all of these years not be able to manipulate her. From the day she came out of the attorney's office and up to this very moment, she realized she and Phil had not had one quarrel. He had lost the ability to pull her chain and push her buttons. She was already enjoying freedom. She was going to sit tight until she had some word from Diane or her attorney. In the meantime, she was going to enjoy her new book.

Mac never imagined he could be as deeply in love with someone as he was with Sharon. They had an early dinner, and then she tended his wounds with the dedication of Clara Barton. She had fallen asleep on the living room sofa as the two of them had attempted to watch television. He was mesmerized. He had never known someone so beautiful both inside and out. When all of this Howard mess came to its conclusion, and if he would be allowed to walk away from all of it as a free man, he knew exactly what he was going to do. He would ask Sharon to be his wife, and to become the mother of his children. After this last thought went through his mind, he froze. He had no idea how long he sat there watching her breath. He was very careful as he moved around the room not to make any noise. He closed the door gently and quietly walked down the stairs and into the night air. He had one purpose and one purpose only. He had to retrieve the blue book.

Evelyn and Senator Howard had not had this volatile an argument in their entire married life, unless she counted the honeymoon scene. Evelyn couldn't make any sense of it. First, he had laughed at her when she accused him of not caring about her potential danger in the face of the robbery. At one point, she was sure she saw him sneer at her when she threatened to expose his dalliance, with, of all people, a Democrat! His sneer soon turned to more boisterous laughter. This action disturbed her more than any of the others. What was going on here? Why was he so suddenly unafraid of anything she threw at him? Could he possibly know what she had planned? Impossible. Absolutely impossible. This called for another drink, and another, and another. At what point she decided to turn off the bedroom lights she couldn't recall, but she knew this was the most peaceful she had been in months. Once all of this was over with, she was going to have to enjoy more evenings like this one.

Joanna and Jacob had enjoyed another one of Joanna's culinary masterpieces, as Jacob had come to call her cooking. They were both enjoying the nearness of each other when the phone jarred them.

"It's for you," Joanna said as she held the phone out for Jacob.

"Jacob. We just got a call from Sharon. Mac left her apartment while she was asleep. As you can imagine, she's frantic. Do you have any idea what this is all about or where he might have gone?" Tim sounded close to frantic himself as he fired off the information and questions at Jacob.

In a very matter-of-fact voice, Jacob said, "Yes. I think I might have an idea. I'll meet you at the corner of Elm and Harrison in five minutes." He placed the receiver in the phone cradle and for the next few moments kept his eyes on its resting place. He knew the look he would be receiving from Joanna, and he wanted to avoid it for as long as possible. When he lifted his eyes, he was surprised to see a tenderness coming from her as she moved closer to him. Placing her fingers lightly on his lips to quiet any conversation, she replaced those fingers with her lips and slowly but passionately kissed him.

The only thing she said as she cradled her head in the hollow of his shoulder was, "Please be careful." Jacob had known the night she had fixed pasta for him that he had been a goner. So a goner he would have to be, because he was crazy about this woman.

Mac knew the city buses didn't stop their services until midnight. He had just enough time to take the nine-forty bus to the Howards' and get the ten-thirty bus back to Sharon's. If he and Sharon were going to have the future he wanted them to have, he had to retrieve the blue book. It not only held damning facts about Evelyn's departed father, but it held damning facts about his own. He didn't want Sharon or any offspring they might enjoy together having to face disgrace because of their family name. The only way to be certain this wouldn't take place was for the blue book to be destroyed; so that was his mission this night.

"Okay, man. Are you going to just sit there and stare out of the window, or would you like to give me directions on where we might be going?" Tim was asking this of Jacob as he pulled out of the Walgreen's parking lot and waited for the stoplight to turn.

"I want you to go to the Howards'," was all the response Tim received.

"Oh. All right. I see, I'm to go to the Howards'. That's great. That's cool. Would you like to share with me why you think Mac would go back to a place where his fine upright employer had him arrested earlier today, and oh, I might add, on bogus charges?"

"I can't answer that. I just believe he is going back to a place he has lived for the last twelve years to get something that's important to him. I can't tell you what it is, because I don't know what it is, or if I'm even on the right track, but my gut tells me he has gone back to the Howard estate."

Tim moved the car easily through the dwindling city traffic. Both men were silent for the next several blocks. Tim broke the silence. "You're in love with her, aren't you, man?"

The noise. There had been a scraping noise. Had she dreamed it? No. There it was again. She had not dreamed it. It was coming from the other side of the bookcase. Quietly, she moved from her chair and crept across the room to where she kept the .38 revolver. There was something or someone on the other side of the bookcase, and she was going to find out what or who it was. Holding the revolver in one hand and lightly pushing on the bookcase with the other, she suddenly felt it move. When it began to open, she could make out the silhouette of a man. A man that quickly turned to run until she yelled for him to stop or she would shoot. She was all but certain who this man was going to be, but she didn't want to take any chances. The next voice she heard was that of Mac Shaw. "Evelyn. Put the gun down. Don't make matters worse by shooting me. Just put the gun down."

If she hadn't so much at stake, she would have gladly shot this scumbag. However, she had to think of the big picture, and he had made a good point. Why make matters worse for herself? "Well, well, well. Haven't you become the epitome of reason? Mr. Nose-in-the-Bottle has now found reason. Tell me. Have you found Jesus, too?" She laughed at her own vile joke. Mac stared at her as she laughed her cackling laugh, wanting desperately to do something to stop this current event. There seemed nothing for him to do but stand there and let the scene play out whatever way it was going to play out. "All right, Mr. Mac Shaw. Your day is done. You should have accepted the sentence they would have given you for all the thieving you've done over these past twelve years. It would have at least let you keep your life." "Evelyn. I only stole from you once, and you know it. The rest of those jewels were planted in my apartment, and you planted them. If it hadn't been for your goon security guard, there would never have been any proof that I stole anything from you."

After another bit of laughter she responded. "Oh, my. You're so brilliant. I guess I never knew how brilliant a drunk could be." Mac could see the change come over the woman holding the gun, and he knew she would pull the trigger and make up whatever story she thought she needed to stand as self-defense. He had only one chance, and he was going to take it.

"Evelyn. I think you should know I've been coming into your room for several years and discovered the records you've been keeping of your Cayman and Swiss bank accounts. If something should happen to me, copies of these records will be mailed to the state attorney general's office, the FBI, and of course the *Tribune*." Even in the poorly lighted room, he could see Evelyn Howard blanch. Mac was just about ready to breathe a small sigh of relief when he heard a voice that belonged to Senator Jim Howard.

"Evelyn. What in God's name do you think you're doing? Put that gun down." Evelyn whirled to the sound of her husband's voice; for a second both men thought she was going to do exactly as the senator had instructed. Then a smirk came across the woman's face that signaled the danger both of them faced. As though she had read their thoughts, she smiled as she announced how both of them would be found dead.

"My dear husband. You came to me this evening because I heard a strange noise coming from the other side of this bookcase. Being the brave husband you are, you came to investigate and found this thieving handyman. Once you confronted him, he pulled out this revolver and shot you. He was going to shoot me as well, but I had enough time to throw this candelabra at him. My aim was lucky, and it caught him on his arm. The gun fell, and fearing for my very life, I shot him. So. Senator, I guess you go first."

243 - LADIES LEAGUE FRONT NINE

Without another word from anyone, Evelyn squeezed the trigger of the .38 and watched her husband of twenty-five years drop to the floor. Mac stood motionless, waiting for his fate and waiting for the next sound to be the discharge of his own personal bullet. Instead, he heard Jacob's voice instructing Evelyn Howard to drop the gun. Every movement in the room started in slow motion for Mac. It looked exactly like the instant replays of football games. He could see Jacob walk slowly toward Evelyn; his right hand was closing on her hand that was holding the gun. He heard another explosive sound and at the same instant saw a bullet leave the barrel of the gun and splinter the boards of the floor. Jacob then wrestled the gun away from Evelyn. He watched it fly across the room and land in front of the desk. Evelyn looked like she was going to pull away from Jacob's grip, but then he saw her wince as he watched a contorted look spread across her face. Jacob pulled her arms behind her. He turned to see Tim bending over the senator. He had placed his fingers on the side of the senator's neck. After a few seconds, he gently moved the senator on his back, and Mac could see the ashen gray color of the good man's face and a growing blood stain on the side of his shirt. He saw Tim reach for a piece of cloth from inside his jacket and hold it to the side of the senator's chest. Then, for whatever reason, all the events surrounding him returned to regular speed. He moved further inside the room, asking Jacob what he wanted him to do. Before the question was answered, two other men were standing next to him. Outside he heard the sound of sirens growing louder. Once their sound stopped, there were reflections of red and blue lights coming through the sheers of the bay window.

Beverly had just fixed two large mugs of hot chocolate with marshmallow cream floating on top. She was handing Jana her mug when Jana's beeper sounded. The two looked at each other for several seconds before Jana responded. They both knew this was going to be Jana's existence as long as she worked for the agency. Beverly listened as she heard her daughter respond and knew the hot chocolate would have to wait for another time.

"You might want to check on Joanna," was all Jana said as she flew out the door.

Karen had become so engrossed in her book, she paid no attention to Phil when he began talking to the television set. Usually when he had these outbursts in front of the TV, it was because some ball game wasn't going the way he wanted it to go. When she heard the kitchen door slam, she paused from her reading. In a few more minutes, she heard the loud roar of the Porsche's engine, and then its sound fading into the night. When she glanced at the clock, she saw it was a few minutes after eleven. She then picked up her book and continued to read.

Diane was recounting for Steve all the bits of conversation she and Beverly had concerning Sam's latest revelation. In midsentence, Steve held up his hand and said, "Wait. Wait. Did you just hear what the reporter said?"

Diane turned to focus on the television and watched as the young, excited reporter gave an account of what the late-breaking news story concerned. Diane's mouth flew open as she heard him repeat that Senator Jim Howard had been shot and had been taken to the county hospital. Mrs. Evelyn Howard had been seen taken into custody by the police. *The police spokesman will give no further information. Please stay tuned for further developments.*

Joanna had tried to act as though Jacob's call had nothing to do with the Howard case. She knew there could be all kinds of calls he could get at any time of the day or night. She finished washing the dinner dishes, poured herself a small glass of wine, and turned on the television to catch the late-evening news. She watched in disbelief as she saw the reporter standing in front of the Howard estate, telling his audience the senator had been taken to the county hospital and Evelyn Howard had been taken into custody. As she stared at the television, she heard a sound that kept repeating itself. She was desperately trying to orient herself to her surroundings when she began to realize the sound was her doorbell. Then came that unmistakable voice: "Joanna. Are you in there? Are you all right? Joanna. Answer me!"

It's Beverly, Joanna thought with a slight feeling of irritation and a much greater feeling of relief.

Hugh Simpson stood with Jacob and Tim in the foyer of the Howard estate. It was very clear to Mac that his immediate future was in this man's hands. The conversation between the three men was deliberately hushed. Although there were still police officials going in and out of the manse, none of them disturbed these three. As harrowing an experience as all of this had been for Mac, he couldn't help but think of two things: Sharon and the blue book. He was all but certain he had lost the first, and had not been able to destroy the second. If he had to serve time, it would be just as well for him. Without Sharon in his life, he wouldn't care where he was. Jacob had glanced in Mac's direction a few times during the discussion he was having with the other two. Suddenly, the three of them broke the tight circle. Hugh Simpson turned and walked out of the door without looking back. Tim pitched something to Jacob and hurried to catch up with Hugh. Jacob was walking toward him. "Okay, Mac. We've got some talking to do."

Just a few months ago, Mac had taken his first step in trusting; that trust had been placed in Sharon. For the second time he was placing his trust in another, and it would be Jacob. Then again, what else could he lose? He found himself talking to Jacob like he had never talked to anyone before. He told him of his father's connection with Evelyn Howard's father. The book that had been left to him after his father's death. How he had used this to secure employment with the Howards. When he got to the point of telling Jacob why he came back to the Howards' this night, he hesitated. At long last he would reveal what he had never told another human. What did it matter? What he wanted most in the world could not be his.

"Jacob. My father and Evelyn's had been in service together. They were Marines. You know, 'We'll-all-go-down-together Corp.' Anyway, my old man was impressed with the way Evelyn's dad did business. At least in the beginning. Then there were some problems that developed, shall we say in doing business. Evelyn's dad was keeping company with some characters that were undoubtedly connected with the Mob. Scrap iron was one kind of business, disposing of bodies was another. My dad was never involved in body disposal, but he was convinced the activity had been conducted by Mr. Miller. The illegal gambling wasn't anything my dad thought was horrible, but when he walked in one evening and saw his business partner beating the crap out of a young woman who couldn't have been over fourteen years old and was told it was okay because she was one of the prostitutes who worked for them, my old man lost it. He turned on his partner and beat the crap out of him. He walked away from all of it that night and never looked back. However, he had been keeping a detailed record of the illegal activities he and his partner had been involved in. Evelyn's old man knew about the book and would have had my old man taken out except for the book. My father promised him if anything happened to my mom, me, or himself, the book would land in the hands of law enforcement. Since Mr. Miller wanted to run for public office, he couldn't take any chances. The one time my old man and I had any kind of conversation, he told me the blue book had been his only insurance policy. Jacob. I don't think my old man could ever forgive himself. It's obvious that alcoholism runs in the Shaw family, but I think one of the main reasons he hid in the bottle was his feeling of guilt. I don't know, Jacob. I don't think I know anything anymore."

When Mac looked up he saw Jacob studying him. "Where's the book?" was all Jacob said.

Jill didn't know why she was driving to Joanna's condo. As soon as she heard the first news report, she walked out of her house, got in her car, and drove toward Joanna's as though she were a homing pigeon. Pulling into the parking space, she saw Beverly's car. She was glad. She would need all the emotional support she could get, and these two women were as good as it got for providing that kind of support. When Beverly opened the door, she saw Joanna riveted in front of the television; she was resting her chin on both of her hands that were gripped tightly in front of her. Tears were falling silently down her cheeks; she was making no attempt to brush them away. Beverly motioned her into the room, quietly closed the door, and took a seat next to Joanna. Jill had never seen these two women like this before. As she moved to a chair that faced the television, she wondered who would be getting and who would be giving emotional support this night.

Sharon had never been this frightened before, at least not frightened for fear of losing someone. When she discovered Mac had left the apartment she didn't hesitate to call the agency. It was nearly 1:00 am and still no word from Mac, no word from anyone. She watched closely as the report came over the news about Senator Howard and his wife. She had been unable to see anyone she recognized during the live telecast. Why didn't someone call? What was going on? Was Mac all right? If anything happened to him, she would blame herself for the rest of her life. She had been the one to talk him into coming clean. It was the right thing to do, she told him, you can't go on living a life filled with secrets and you can't go on pretending to be someone you're not. These were all the self-righteous spoutings of a woman who had all the answers. What a complete fool she had been. She would give anything this night to have the man she loved safe and hold him tightly in her arms. She had to wipe the tears from her eyes so she could see the phone to call the beeper number she had been given by Jacob. She was about to punch in the last digit of the number when she heard the knock on her door. Terrified of what or who may be on the other side, she walked slowly to the door and looked through the peephole. She threw the door open and grabbed Mac while pulling both him and Jacob inside the apartment. Nothing was said by any of them while she cried and laughed and hugged the man she loved. Finally, it was Jacob who broke the silence. "You keep tabs on this man until I get back in touch with the two of you. Understand? He is now in your custody." With that, Jacob turned to leave, but before he could exit, Sharon had tugged at his jacket, and when he turned she gave him a quick hug and peck on his cheek.

"Thank you. Oh, thank you," she said through her tears.

Jacob remembered how Joanna had dealt with the lover who had jilted her so many years before. He drove up to the dumpster, soaked the blue book in lighter fluid, and tossed in the match. Once he saw the flames grow into a tall yellow and red light, he called the fire department and drove away.

Karen heard the doorbell. She began to come out of the fog of sleep. A glance at the clock showed it to be 2:00 am. Impossible. Who would be ringing the door bell at 2:00 am? Grabbing her robe and stepping into her slippers, she made her way to the front door. Looking through the glass side panels, she saw a tall, young police officer looking at a piece of paper he was holding. She had wondered how long it would take for Phil to finally be arrested for DUI. With some irritation, she opened the door, fully expecting the young man to tell her she needed to come to the police station with bail money for her husband.

"Mrs. Phil Matthews?"

"Yes. I'm Mrs. Phil Matthews," she answered with slight annoyance in her response. Something about the manner of this young officer suddenly gave Karen a chill. This young man had come to tell her husband was dead.

Who in the world would be calling at his hour? The sound of a ringing phone in the middle of the night was never a good sound to the parents of young men. Diane heard Steve pick it up and listened intently to his side of the conversation. When she heard him ask, "When did this happen?" She sat straight up in bed, switched on the table lamp, and drew the covers up around herself. Which one of the boys was it? She began to pray silently. "Is there anything we can do?" Steve was asking. Diane knew from his question it couldn't be one of their sons. He then placed the receiver back in the cradle, turned to her, and said, "Phil Matthews is dead."

Visits were made to the hospital, and the funeral home. Support and condolences were given and casseroles were made. Each of the four women from the Ladies League found themselves playing roles they never imagined they would have to play. Joanna was going to take Mac's case. She and Jacob had talked about his situation until sunrise that Wednesday morning. Mac understood he was an important witness;

however, he had played a role for Evelyn Howard, and he would stand up to what society decided he had to pay. The irony of a woman he had stalked defending him in court had not gone unnoticed by this man. Each time the two of them met to discuss his charges, Mac would thank her over and over for being so kind to the likes of him. Sharon assured him whatever the outcome, she would be waiting, and she would be more than happy to be his wife. Jacob was falling more deeply in love with Joanna with each passing day. She mesmerized him. He wanted to spend the rest of his life with this woman, but he couldn't believe she would want him for a lifelong partner. She had completely dissolved when he returned from the Howards' that next morning. He didn't think he would ever be able to erase from his mind the look on her face when she saw him walk through the door. He wasn't sure he was brave enough to see that look come from those beautiful eyes again.

Beverly was proud of her daughter for standing up for herself and doing what she loved doing. During a visit to the hospital with Jill, she realized this was the first time she had been able to stand on her own two feet since the death of her husband. She had also found the strength to help hold up a dear friend while she struggled with the pain of watching the man she loved fight for his life.

Diane, Steve, Linda, and Peter did everything they could do for Karen and the children. Karen told Diane the worst part of all was having to watch her children grieve the way they were grieving. Diane listened to Karen but knew Phil had done his wife and children a favor. It was decided by Phil's business partners that nothing would be revealed by any of them as to the dealings Phil and Evelyn Howard may have had. The legal system would have to sort out all the details surrounding Evelyn Howard in the weeks and months ahead. From what Evelyn was already facing, the fact she had been trying to scam Phil Matthews was of little consequence as to what her sentencing was going to be.

Beverly was proud of the women in the community. Once the news was out about the Howards, the fashion show was cancelled, and one of the models came up with the idea of having the money the fashion would have cost be donated to the Horse for Healing program. If anyone wanted a refund, it would be given. There was not one refund made. The country club had also given a sizable donation. The country club's board president told Beverly they had not lost a dime because they had been able to cancel the food order, which would have been their biggest cost, and they believed the Horse for Healing program was one of the best charities the community had seen in years.

Jill was allowed to visit Jim Howard. She would sit at his bedside and talk to him as the machines hummed and beeped. She had been told he was in a medically induced coma, yet she would talk as though he could understand every word she spoke. She had read years before that people in comas could hear what was being said, and so she talked and talked and talked. Beverly would often find her talking to him about their college days, friends the two of them knew, recent community events. Beverly marveled at her friend. She wasn't sure she could do what she watched Jill doing.

The days had stretched into weeks, the weeks into months, and the foursome from the Ladies League stayed in constant communication. "Just checking in," Diane would start her conversation with Beverly.

Beverly would check in with Joanna. "Need to have a little break?" Loosely translated: "Want me to come over with a bottle of wine?" Sometimes Joanna wanted her to come over; sometimes she wanted to be alone.

Jill was called by the other three. "Need a ride to the hospital?" came the offer from Diane.

"Jill. Checking in. You okay?" would be Joanna's voice.

"Okay, Jill. What's going on? Need a ride today?" came the authoritarian voice of Beverly.

Jill began to realize how much these women had come to mean to her. Here they had been joined together by a game called golf, yet there was a bond none of them could have imagined develop as they tried to make sense of the game and the events that had taken place in their lives. Jill continued to make her daily hospital visits. Jim Howard was making progress. Joanna worked as hard as she had ever worked to see that justice was done for the man called Mac Shaw. The more she got to know about Mac and Sharon, the more intent she became in her defense for the man. It was a wonderful day when the jury decided Mac was guilty of misdemeanors but was not guilty of felonies. It became a greater moment when the judge announced Mac Shaw would be on a year's probation for all charges, with a six-month credit for time served on home detention. Sharon had been his home detention officer.

Jacob and Joanna were celebrating with Mac and Sharon the evening after Mac's legal problems had been put to rest. It was no shock to hear Mac announce that he and Sharon were going to be married. What surprised both Joanna and Jacob was they wanted them to stand up with them at the ceremony. Jacob was to be the best man, and Joanna was to be the maid of honor. Joanna wanted to weep. If it hadn't been for the fact they were in a very upscale restaurant, she might have done that very thing. As happy as she was for these dear people, she wanted to be the bride and not the maid of honor. When she looked across the table at Jacob, her heart skipped a beat. When he spoke the next words, she was certain her heart had stopped.

"Joanna. What do you think about making this a double wedding?" She sat motionless. Was she even breathing? The silence around their table had become deafening. Jacob's eyes were wide with expectation as his jaw began to tighten. Had he read all of this wrong? Sharon was gripping Mac's hands until he thought she was going to cut off all circulation to his fingers. Then that incredible smile of hers started to spread across her face as small teardrops began to fall from her eyes.

"I think it would be a wonderful idea."

Jacob reached over grabbed her up and began kissing her tears, her cheeks, her lips. They both began laughing. Mac stood and announced to the room full of diners that she had just accepted his proposal of marriage. Then came the applause. Joanna knew that moment was the happiest moment she had ever experienced in her life.

Beverly was enjoying watching all those she cared for having the time of their lives. She had never seen them as happy as she was seeing them this very minute. Jill was dancing with Tim Burke and having a great laugh at something he had just said. Joanna and Jacob were lost in each other. Joanna was one of the most beautiful brides she had ever seen. It didn't hurt that she had been the one to select the bridesmaids and bridal dresses. She smiled at her own private joke. Joanna insisted the ladies in her foursome be her bridesmaids. Each of them had been honored by the request. Jana was having a wonderful time with a young man Beverly recognized as another one of the agents. The world seemed to be paired off in twos, just like Noah's Ark, yet here she was finding that she could be happy watching those she cared so much about being happy. Jill was going to take the senator to her home until he fully recovered. He would be discharged from the hospital within the next week. It would be a long haul, but caring for others was one of the things Jill did the best. Jana had been assigned to the northern part of the region. Beverly was going to miss seeing her on a daily basis, but this move was healthy for them both. Diane and Steve acted like teenagers; they danced and laughed and held each other as though they couldn't wait to get in the backseat of a sedan. Again, she found herself smiling at her own silly thoughts. A very deep voice interrupted those thoughts. "I hope you don't mind if I join you. You seem to be having a wonderful time." Beverly looked up into the eyes of a tall, distinguished man who was smiling one of the warmest smiles she had seen in a long time.

"How could I refuse anyone who has a smile like that? Please join me."

Hmm, Beverly was thinking to herself. This could be the start of something big.

Breinigsville, PA USA
03 September 2009
223473BV00001B/8/P

9 781438 937113